NUDEY BEACH

For Lynette,

With Best Wishes

NUDEY BEACH

ANGIE ANNETTS

Cockeyed Publishing

This edition first published in 2020

Cockeyed Publishing

ISBN (eBook): 978-1-8380151-1-4
ISBN (Paperback): 978-1-8380151-0-7

Cover design by www.dissectdesigns.com
Typesetting by www.preparetopublish.com

1.

Pebbles and Balls

The day I first visited nudey beach, I'd spent the morning completely unaware I was just hours away from eagerly climbing over a cliff top to reach it. Instead, I'd been happily sat in a static caravan and working like the clappers on my chick lit novel, 'Just Susie' – a truly dreadful piece of shit, but I take encouragement from what seems to sell well these days. Also shit. So I push on. Unfazed by its overall shittiness and in the hope I'll be raising the bar on all things shit.

'Susie' gets on my knockers for the most part and is the ideal candidate for some happy slapping. She has the perfect job – shiny receptionist and sharer of tittle-tattle at a global media company – perfect teeth and friends, and moreover, a perfect boyfriend.

Susie likes shopping with the girlies and guffawing in wine bars with colleagues after a hard day of being super-efficient and popular behind a desk.

She has no idea that her perfect boyfriend (a chinless berk from accounts called Jeremy) will soon be dipping his wick into Clara from the hockey club he attends twice weekly. Which will leave our Susie in a heartbroken pickle and with a tendency to gaze out of windows to wonder if she'll *ever* find true love.

I'd love to stripe her up and pack her off to a brothel in Nairobi. But sadly, a coastal village in the West Country beckons. I'm not quite sure what happens next. Something flowery. And shitty. We'll see.

So, there I'd been. Engrossed in Susie. And her efforts to make sure the office Christmas party went off with a bang. *Well done*, Susie! Look what a lovely couple Susie and Jeremy make! Are we going to be hearing wedding bells soon?

Susie hears them alright; she's already picked her frock.

I looked down at the flashing light on my phone. Email. I'll leave it – I'm on a roll. But stupidly, I didn't. I opened it and read Clarke's words. Within seconds, and using his last wisps of control over me, he achieved what he'd set out to do. Upset me. Hurt me. And put me in a stinking mood.

I suddenly wished everything had been as simple as Clarke dipping his wick into some other daft cow and getting found out. That would have been easy. Get mad. Throw him out. End of. But this? This was messy. In short, he was going back on our deal – to find somewhere else to live while I was away writing for six weeks. I didn't want him. He still wanted me. Messy.

He made sure a reference was thrown in about "wasting my time" – a trademark display of his resentment that I derived so much pleasure from an activity that excluded him. And I am of the firm belief he's always been fearful my shit might one day become successful shit. New wings and all that. Clarke's undermined my writing from day one. Taking any opportunity to sneer or ridicule. Anything to make me give up. But he can fuck off; Susie makes me a better woman.

I re-read the email. His refusal to let go was like a lead cloak hanging from my shoulders, and he knew he was yanking my chain. I went outside, sat on the caravan steps and smoked another cigarette I shouldn't. It was the first Wednesday in June and hotter than average. I stretched my legs, tilted back my head and watched cotton wool clouds slowly move across the perfect blue sky, like a fluffy fleet of silent warships. I let out a sigh; I'd only been at the park since Saturday. Clarke *had* excelled himself – leaving me alone for four days. And for someone who used to stand outside my workplace to make sure I didn't go guffawing in wine bars, the effort must have half-killed him.

I blew out smoke and squinted up at the sun. How did I ever think what he was doing was romantic? How was I so dumb to not see what was coming my way? It took his fully weighted slap across my face, eight days ago, and two years into our relationship, to finally knock some sense into me.

Tossing away the cigarette, I stood, feeling heat on my face and the familiar anger return. I knew I'd be unable to write for a few hours or so. Possibly the rest of the day. I hated myself for allowing Clarke that victory and suddenly wanted to do something to spite him. Ignoring his email would do for starters – a reaction would obviously be expected after stating his refusal to budge. But that didn't feel like enough.

Watching a people carrier slowly drive past made me think of the beach. Fat blotchy parents in the front. Bad sunglasses. A cheap straw hat. Three piglets in the back, all squealing and screeching their heads off. One brandishing a plastic spade. Another, snout pressed to the window, deriving smug pleasure by giving me the finger. I returned the compliment and took obscure comfort as his complaining whines resulted in a twat around the head from mum. The vehicle turned towards the park's exit and disappeared from view. Little shit.

It was a perfect day for the beach. Maybe I should

just get my stuff together and head on down to the front. Give myself a day off from writing and try to chill. I tried to picture myself lying on my towel alongside the blobby family. Or any of the other families who favoured Brightlea as a resort. Term time had no meaning for these people with their shouty, Jeremy Kyle ways, but like me, were quick to take advantage of the caravan parks' cheap deals and late offers.

I suddenly wondered what the naturist beach would be like. Apparently, it was to the right of the main beach, where the cliffs jutted and zigzagged before leading to a long pebbled stretch. I'd heard about it on my first night, when paying a visit to one of the resort's pubs, the aptly named, 'Flabby Mermaid' – or 'Flabby's' as the locals refer to it. A good-looking, but markedly cocky regular, in his late 20's or early 30's had told me about it, adding, if I ever fancied "getting my bits out" to take the tide times into account. High tide apparently meant access around the zigzags was a no-no and a hoof over the cliff top path would be in order.

With a crooked grin he further suggested to let him know if I'd be heading that way – he'd polish up his binoculars and make sure his hands were warm in case I needed any assistance with my suntan cream. I'd laughed him off. 'In your dreams,' I told him.

I'd caused a bit of a stir that night, walking into

Flabby's on my own. It felt like I'd just entered through some swing doors into a Wild West saloon. Full of couples, groups and families, I felt their eyes upon me as I walked up to order my drink. Tall, slim with cropped peroxide blonde hair, black eyebrows and green eyes – I chalk myself down as striking, unconventional-looking, but never beautiful. And at 38, can still attract the attention of a younger man.

The curious oafs at the bar teased and christened me 'JK' when I made the schoolgirl error of telling them I was staying in Brightlea to work on my book. Despite their dogged piss-taking, the cocky one put in a boozy request for an invite back to inspect my caravan, while another, a quieter, shyer one, waited until he was out of earshot of the others to ask if I'd like to meet up the next night. I didn't feel flattered. Or fancy myself. Some people still can't get to grips with a woman wanting to go out on her own for a drink. And just a drink. Whilst others can't bear it if someone has the balls to follow their dream, particularly when they do nothing about chasing their own. Piss-taking comes with the territory for an unpublished writer. But I'd rather take it from tanked-up strangers than a supposed loved one.

When they'd exhausted their jocular comments and suggestive hoots about shaggers, shirt-lifters and rumours of dogging sessions, the cocky one told me some more about nudey beach. Designated by the Council and with its own sign, it was Brightlea's best kept secret. Which everyone knew about. Except me. Despite living just 15 miles away in Exeter. At the time I never imagined I'd contemplate going there. But now, just four days later, it seemed like the most splendid idea on the planet. I was feeling reckless and angry. I had no idea what the beach would be like or if I'd even enjoy it, but the thought of doing something that would make Clarke's bollocks explode felt too delicious to resist.

I went back into the caravan and saw the light flashing on my phone. Clarke. Again. *Already*. Apologising for his earlier email. Wanting to meet up "to talk". The innocent-looking sentiment that "hoped" I was enjoying the night life "*wherever* you are" dripped in unwritten accusations. About to delete his message, I changed my mind and instead settled for putting the phone face down on the table.

Decision made, I went to the bathroom and undressed. I unearthed my wax strips and razor and taking turns with each leg resting on the lowered toilet seat, removed every trace of my faint pubic hair regrowth. Once done, I massaged in some baby oil to soothe the skin and quickly felt aroused. Being completely bald down there always turned me on and I felt further stimulated by the thought of being naked in front of strangers. I pushed my back into the bathroom wall and raised a leg back onto the toilet seat. With my fingers making a 'V' sign, I rubbed up and down, pressing and then pulling apart my lips, as though readying myself for some cock. Dragging up my fingers, I then applied pressure to my already swollen clit.

Making small, urgent circular motions I could feel myself getting wetter. With my free hand I pushed two fingers inside, pressing and rubbing the upper wall to my vagina. I wasn't far away and wished the bathroom mirror was above the toilet so I could watch myself come. Resting my head on the wall, I imagined being pressed up against the cliff on nudey beach by a faceless random guy who was roughly fingering me. He breathes heavily in my ear and tells me in harsh whispers what a filthy whore I am.

His thumb rubs over my clit as his fingers work hard on my throbbing G-spot. As I feel a fresh wave of wet release over my fingers, I hope me and Mister Random are putting on a good show for the other nudey beachers.

My free hand roughly squeezed each breast, and in turn, tugged my stiff nipples as my breath shortened and caught in small gasps.

The orgasm was powerful and lengthy and made the leg I was standing on tremble. I kept going, and after a few moments, came again.

I lowered my leg and stood before the mirror. Flushed and catching my breath, I saw my eyes were clear and sparkling; I looked like a woman who liked adventures.

And one who was ready to get naked on a beach.

After watching myself lazily taste my fingers, I washed my hands and put on a thin-strapped stretchy dress and flip flops. I then packed my bag, including my notebook, a paperback and one cigarette, before grabbing my yoga mat and setting off.

Leaving the caravan park, I hit the road, turned left and walked past the competition, 'Happy Holidays!' and 'Sunshine Boulevard'. Both were larger than my 'Brightlea Sands', and boasted better facilities – making them more expensive – but as I had no need for a bouncy castle, or swimming pool full of inflatable toys (although an alcohol-fuelled, adult only session would doubtless offer up some entertainment), my current digs did me just fine.

Turning left again, I hit the main drag with its lardy cafes, noisy amusement arcades and shops full of seaside tat. Roughly halfway down and on a corner, was Flabby's, whilst further along on the right, and close to the seafront, stood another pub, The Captain's Table. Themed and family-orientated and whose threshold I have no intention of crossing.

At the end of the road, a car park to one side and Big Shot Crazy Golf to the other. I walked between the two and stood for a moment to take stock. The tide was in, covering the sand and leaving just the crunchy pebbles exposed. To the left, the beach swept on for about half a mile, halted only by a stunning, red clay cliff protruding deep into the sea. It was busy enough, with plenty of families dotted around. Buckets, spades, beach balls, smoky barbeques, and squeals of children laughing or being loudly chastised. To the right, the cliff was nearer, a few hundred yards or so. With nudey beach waiting for me on the other side.

I made my way over. Here the beach narrowed and tapered off as it met the cliff, with the pebbles looking more like mini boulders compared to the main stretch. The only people down this end were an elderly couple, enjoying tea from their flask as they sat on a tartan picnic blanket. I imagined them younger and sharing the same blanket on another sunny day. As I passed, we exchanged kind smiles, and I got a sudden sense of peace and other worldliness that seemed detached from the rest of the resort.

Reaching the cliff base, I looked up at the well-trodden pathway which made a distinct stripe through the dry grass, and with a feeling of resolve, began the stiff climb. Stopping halfway for a rest, I wiped sweat from my forehead and began to laugh. It felt good to be doing something crazy – it'd been far too long. Recently (and pre-slap), I'd been getting my kicks from using Clarke's underpants as a duster and putting them back in his drawer. I let out a snort, shifted my yoga mat to the other armpit and continued on my way.

When I reached the top, the view was breathtaking. 'My, oh my,' I said quietly. I scanned the dramatic coastline in both directions and soaked in its beauty. The sea twinkled like a pirate's treasure chest of stolen jewels, whilst above, seagulls lazily swooped and made their sharp cries. I also caught my first glimpse of nudey beach, but from the snapshot on offer, couldn't spot a soul, making me wonder if the crew from Flabby's had been winding me up.

Beginning my descent, I was grateful that the path was gentle in its weaving decline. As I passed a prettily painted large pebble placed by a bend, any thoughts of a wind-up were soon dismissed. Inside the bright scalloped edging bore the inscription, 'BEWARE! Nudists Ahead!' in pink and blue letters. I smiled. It was quite sweet in its naivety and made me feel as if I was about to join some exclusive club.

I wound around another bend, and suddenly found myself on the pebbles of nudey beach and greeted by further confirmation – the local Council's large and imposing sign the cocky one had told me about. Its heading read, 'Brightlea Naturist Beach' and below, 'Clothing Optional Beyond This Point'. I bobbed my head to the side of the sign, scanned the length of the beach and immediately felt disappointed. I hadn't really had time to think what the place would actually be like in reality. Naked bodies aside. But from what I could make out, there was just a sprinkling of grey-haired men stretched out in the sun. Another stood at the water's edge, peering out to the waves and wearing only a sun hat as he absently gave himself a tug.

I even wondered how a few of them had managed the climb; there'd been a marked absence of a chairlift on the way over. Well, at least there weren't any rampant dogging sessions going on. That I could see. Just a lone geriatric wanker. I crunched along the beach and passed the first of the men – saggy arse pointing to the heavens and immersed in his newspaper. When I reached the second, he sat up open-legged and smiled at me. 'Lovely day, isn't it?' he asked with a smile. I glanced down and took in his shrivelled body. His scrotum was resting on a towel and spread like melted ice cream.

'Isn't it just?' I said, squinting through my sunglasses towards the sun,

'Haven't seen you here before.'

I looked back down at him and felt remarkably indifferent about speaking to a naked stranger.

'It's my first time. Thought I'd give it a go.'

'Well, we're all a friendly bunch down here. I see you've come well prepared,' he said, gesturing towards my yoga mat with his head.

'Oh, yes,' I half-laughed. 'I think I've brought the entirety of my life possessions – just to be on the safe side.'

'Well, have fun,' he said, settling back down onto his towel.

'Thanks. Will do.'

I pushed on, picking my way over the pebbles that made for a hard walk in flimsy flip flops. Tough on the ankles and with unstable, sliding conditions underfoot due to the slanted tiers created by the tides, I did remarkably well to not fall arse over tit. There was a sizeable gap coming up before the next batch of ageing sunbathers, and spotting a good-sized level area by the base of the cliff, quickly decided to park myself there. It'd be a relief to finally offload all my stuff. Dropping my yoga mat and bag, I looked along the beach to each side of me. No one seemed to be paying me any attention. Further along, the nearest guy lay on his back, hands resting on his stomach. It was time.

All along, I'd had it in mind to get undressed quickly. To just whip off my dress without any fuss or drawing attention to myself. I unrolled the yoga mat, placing it parallel to the cliff and facing the sun, laid my towel upon it and sat down. I wriggled my dress up past my hips and with criss-crossed arms, smoothly pulled it off. I'd saved myself the bother of taking my pants off by not wearing any – more often my style than not – besides, it seemed in keeping with the theme du jour to go the beach commando style.

So, I was finally naked. No fuss. No hysteria. And

it'd been easy-peasy. I delved into my bag for my sun cream and began to rub it in. First my legs and arms. Then my chest and breasts. I glanced up to see that the bloke further along had rolled onto to his side to watch me. Propped up on one elbow, his sleeping cock gave a twitch to attention. For no particular reason, I massaged myself a little longer than necessary; I knew I had good tits – not as big as the current trend for inflatable melons – but perfectly formed handfuls, nevertheless. Besides, I'd never heard any complaints.

I was still being watched. I moved my attention to my stomach, then to between my legs – which I'd slightly parted, and worked in the sun cream. Then, and in a sudden feeling of teasing empowerment, I abruptly stopped, as though becoming bored. I flung my sunglasses on top of my bag, ruffled my hair, lay down on my back and felt the sun rush down to cover my naked body in heat. And it felt like the most liberating thing I'd ever done in my life. It was exhilarating and relaxing all at once.

Yes, me and nudey beach were going to get along just fine.

Geriatric wankers or not.

And like a vampire crossing a threshold, I was in the groovy gang now. And staying. Or was that the nudey gang? I smiled at my daftness. Maybe I should take a selfie to send to Clarke? And if I angled it correctly I might get Captain Tugwash in the background, ejaculating into the sea. Now that *would* give him something to get a hissy fit over.

I closed my eyes and listened to sea hitting the shore, causing pebbles to shift and tumble. This was heaven. Pure heaven.

Maybe if Clarke hadn't suffocated me for those two years (so *gradually* suffocated me) with his increasing jealousy and possessiveness, I might not have felt the need to do something like stripping off in public. And literally bust free. I thought back to the day he struck me. And for what? Talking to a male customer for more time than seemed fitting? Laughing too loudly at his joke? What a joke.

Not wanting to think about Clarke anymore on such a glorious day, I pushed him out of my mind and turned my thoughts to Susie instead. About how she'd find out about Jeremy's wick-dipping. Maybe, she'd 'surprise' him by turning up at one of his hockey club sessions. Wearing her latest purchases that came with the girls' approval. Maybe, she'd take along some homemade sandwiches and M&S 'nibbles' as an extra gesture. Our Jeremy's a bugger for their Thai Sweet Chilli Crunchy Covered Peanuts. Maybe, she could rip the bag open and individually hurl them at Jeremy when she discovers him giving Clara a hearty knee trembler up against the groundsman's groaning shed.

Poor Susie. Play your cards right, love and I'll sort you out a bit of crumpet down on the West Coast...

I must have nodded off.

I became vaguely aware of voices and feet crunching on the pebbles close to me. For a moment I couldn't place where I was, and when I opened my eyes, momentarily felt a degree of surprise to find myself naked on a beach.

The crunching had come from a couple who had just walked past. From behind, they looked like they were in their forties. The man was carrying a windbreaker under his arm, its sharpened poles pointing towards me like giant toothpicks. The woman was carrying a few extra pounds and her short shorts revealed heavily dimpled legs she evidently didn't give a fuck about. Top girl.

I sat up and reached for my sunglasses. The beach was totally different from earlier. Busier. A lot busier. I'd gained a grinning (50-something?) bloke stretched out a couple of yards from my feet. Christ. He'd probably spent the last however-long-it-was gawping between my legs. I wondered if I should feel annoyed, but when I looked around, saw the tide had come in further and with more people on the beach, there simply wasn't enough space to provide relative privacy. For a naturist beach.

Besides, had I really thought no one would be interested in looking at me? Grow up, Amber. And get real, for fuck's sake.

I hugged up my knees in a belated gesture of modesty and eagerly checked out the new dynamics

– I felt like a keen student attending a really cool class in something. The most obvious change was the smattering of brightly coloured tents; semi-circular domes which housed one or two sets of protruding legs. Dipping my sunglasses, I squinted towards a garish purple-coloured tent – the furthest one away, and close to the lapping waves. I could just about make out one set of legs lying neatly on top of another and the small movements of the top set sliding up and down.

I felt no surprise or shock or disgust – I'm fairly liberal in my views about sex and like to think I'm reasonably unshockable. (Well, aside from the time my ex-husband produced a GIANT black dildo to add to our toy collection. Ta-dah! En garde!) And hadn't really doubted for a second that people wouldn't be getting up to all sorts on the beach. Let them crack on, I say. At least that couple are having a stab at being a bit discreet in their pleasure dome.

Meanwhile, I now had some proper people-watching on offer. Marvellous. A writer can never get enough material. Mind you, I can't quite see Susie teetering about on the pebbles in her high heels before stripping off her frilly blouse and Wednesday knickers.

But never say never.

So, who else did we have? Couples. Quite a few couples. None of them seemed particularly young. About my age and upwards and all shapes and sizes.

Mostly no shape and large in size. And there were more single men. And not all of them coffin-dodgers.

And unless my eyes deceived me, there seemed to be quite a congregation of men down the far end, past a rock formation that made an unsymmetrical 'w' of the beach. Could it possibly be that this was home to the gay contingent of the beach? I could see two men, carefully wading into the sea as they tried to keep their footing on the shifting pebbles. After moments, they began splashing one another. Elsewhere, male solos, couples and groups were dotted about. Chatting or just enjoying the sun.

Oh, happy days, I thought. Brokeback Bay! Love it.

But where had everyone sprung from? Off work early? Staying at Brightlea just to use this beach? Travelling in? It was a whole new world down here, one I knew nothing about. Behind me, the next people along were a late middle-aged couple. Like me, their preference was to sunbathe lengthwise, towards the sun. They had a large colourful brolly shielding them from the slight breeze, its handle pushed deep into the pebbles behind their heads. I cast my eyes over their sparse pubic hair and ageing privates. It was impossible not to. They both had their legs spread open and seemed to be contentedly snoozing with their arms resting on their stomachs. Their brolly blocked my view beyond, but I could see that Captain Tugwash had vacated his spot. God knows how all that panned out. But I silently vowed to knock fresh fish on the head for a while.

How long had I slept for all these people to crunch their way past me, doubtless casting a curious eye over my body? I reached into my bag for my phone. Nearly an hour. That's not like me. I must have been tired after burning the midnight oil with Susie last night. With relief I saw that my phone had no reception, courtesy of the cliffs, I assumed. Fabulous – a Clarke-Free Zone. I opened up my sunglasses case, took out my cigarette and lighter and sparked up.

The guy in front of me abruptly sat up and delved into neatly folded jeans that were beside his towel. Producing a packet of cigarettes, he plucked one out and twirled it between two fingers.

'Can I cadge a light?' he asked, revealing a soft Irish accent.

'Sure,' I replied. Not wanting him to come over, I threw the lighter his way and silently groaned when it fell woefully short.

He smiled, climbed to his feet and gingerly picked his way over the pebbles to pick it up, affording me the opportunity to turn the tables and give him the once over. He was actually quite buff for an older fella, with a smooth, tanned and athletic physique – this was clearly someone who took measures to keep his middle-aged spread at bay. And his cock wasn't displeasing on the eye, either. He lit his cigarette and walked towards me, holding out the lighter. I hurriedly drew my legs up tighter.

'Thanks,' he said, as he handed it back and crouched down beside me. I stifled a laugh – his clean-shaven balls (of which I *thoroughly* approved) hung neatly between his legs, but I couldn't think beyond the fact he looked like he was trying for a shit. He inhaled deeply and blew out smoke, and I was relieved to see it didn't come out his arse. I had to speak to stop myself giggling.

'Lovely day, isn't it?'

He looked towards the sea with small nods. 'It sure is.' He sat down and shifted his body to a straight-legged position and leaned back on one of his hands. Better. His cock rested obediently upon a thigh. I had a brief glance; it was a very good cock, indeed. And was obviously house-trained.

We sat in silence for a while and smoked our cigarettes. I gazed into the distance; a woman was venturing into the sea with a male companion and outstretched arms for balance. Seconds later, she lost her battle with the pebbles and crashed unceremoniously into the sea with shrieks of laughter. I blew out smoke and wondered if I wanted to be hit on. Probably not.

'Are you on holiday? Local?' he asked.

'Yes – kind of. And reasonably,' I replied, turning to face him.

'Ah! A woman of mystery,' he said, stubbing out

his cigarette on a pebble. 'Would you care to elaborate?'

'I'll tell you when you're older,' I replied with a tight-lipped smile.

He examined my face. 'Do you mind me talking to you?'

I put out my cigarette and shrugged. 'I'm not sure,' I replied, truthfully.

'Well, while you're busy being unsure, I'm Luke,' he said, leaning forward and extending a hand. I looked at his hand and then him. His face had an intelligence about it; piercing grey/blue eyes, thick arching eyebrows, a straight slim nose and defined cheekbones. In contrast his mouth had a girly fullness that didn't sit quite right and made me think of someone putting the wrong piece into a photofit. His short salt and pepper hair had a slight wave and was swept off his face. He didn't look a million miles away from the kind of bloke I was going to palm onto Susie when she got to her coastal village – a bit older, granted – but definitely out of the same stable.

I took his hand and lightly shook it. 'Are you posh?' I asked, half-surprising myself by the question.

He gave me a broad smile. 'I'll tell you when you're older.'

'Touché. And by the way, I'm Amber.'

'Well, Amber, just to prove what a posh

gentleman I am, if you're unsure about wanting company, I'm going to leave you in peace. Unless of course, you require any assistance with your suntan cream? Or maybe need escorting into the sea? We're always dropping like flies around here, trying to get in and out.'

I laughed. 'No thanks. I'm good on all counts.'

Luke stood up. His genitals were eye level. I stroked my chin and looked into the distance.

'Maybe catch you down here again?'

I diverted my gaze directly to his face and raised a hand to shield my eyes from the sun's glare. 'Maybe,' I smiled.

'Ah, there's the mystery woman again. Well, it was nice to meet you.'

'And you.'

Luke turned and began to pick his way back to his towel. 'And thanks for the wonderful view!' he called over his shoulder.

I'd wanted to call out something like, 'Oi! Cheeky!' after him – but feared I'd sound like someone off the set of EastEnders. Besides, inside, my ego was purring. Feeling suddenly playful, I applied cream to the parts of my back I could reach and rolled onto my front. I pulled out my paperback and slightly parted my legs. If he wants a wonderful view, I thought, I'll give him one.

It seemed I'd become a voyeur and an exhibitionist in one afternoon.

Which was all rather splendid, I thought.

Later, when tired of my book and stretched out face down on my towel, I heard the now familiar crunch of approaching footsteps. They came to a temporary halt beside me.

'I'm beginning to think that you might be a dreadful woman,' I heard Luke say.

I lifted my head and saw him walking away from me. He was dressed in the jeans I saw earlier, a loose shirt and was heading towards the pathway. Without turning, Luke raised a hand and wriggled his fingers in a goodbye to me.

Raising myself onto my elbows, I watched him go with a smile on my face. Dreadful woman – I quite liked that. And maybe I was, I thought. But on balance, I didn't give a shit. As I settled back down, the smile was still going strong.

About half an hour later I was ready to leave the beach. I wriggled my dress over my head before standing to gather up my towel and belongings and roll up my yoga mat. The mixture of sun and novelty of the beach had been a fabulous tonic. I felt wonderful. People were still arriving. Some were leaving. The couple that had been having sex were now dressed and standing as they folded away their tent. They were an attractive couple. Late twenties/ early thirties, maybe. I briefly wondered what lives everyone had outside of this mini world.

Making my way back to the path, I smiled at the

reverse of the Council sign. 'You are now leaving the Clothing Optional Area. Please Ensure you are Wearing Clothing'. I fought back a daft desire to pat myself down for clothes, and instead, pushed on over the pebbles and slowly climbed over the cliff behind a gay couple who bickered all the way about someone called Steve.

Back at the caravan, I emptied out my bag and checked my phone. Emails. But none from Clarke. Instead, three missed calls. Two voicemails. The first showed whining concern – was I *alright*? The second, back to his old self. Accusing me of going off with someone. Was I busy fucking someone? Was *that* why I wasn't returning his emails or calls? WHAT THE FUCK *WAS* I DOING?

It crossed my mind to email him back.

No, Clarke – I have not been fucking anybody. Not that it is any longer your business. But as you ask, I've just spent the afternoon showing my cunt to the world. I so hope this satisfies your curiosity. Regards, Amber.

I'd half-planned to take a wander down to Flabby's a bit later, for a JK piss-taking session washed down with some vodka. I'd even been feeling chipper enough to give Susie a bit of a bash before going. But now, back to square one. The mood from hell. Just get out of my flat, Clarke.

And out of my life.

2.

Happy Holidays and a Mad Ex

I'm rather in love with my caravan. It's my hidey hole. My writing retreat. And I answer to no one. I had done some research into 'proper' writing retreats, but soon discovered that for what they'd wanted to charge for a fortnight, bought me six weeks in a static caravan in a crappy resort. Besides, these retreats invariably involve 'group' and the horror of communal meal-making and a bit of ging-gang-goolie around the kitchen table before reading aloud from your current efforts. I'd rather put pins in my eyes. Me and 'group' are not as one. So it's just me and Susie and a static caravan. My shit is my private shit.

The caravans are all lined up in rows, as though waiting to go into battle. Parked to the left are our cars, who ride shotgun. My battered old Golf waits patiently, poised for action. We are eight caravans abreast. I am number 56. Directly opposite is 69. The model of my caravan is a 'Sophia Classique' as detailed in scripty writing on a plastique plaque by the door. I'm waiting for the night I get back pissed from a Flabby's session and change 'Sophia' to 'Susie' with a marker pen. I doubt it will be too long.

Upon my arrival at Brightlea Sands, I schmoozed the young receptionist into a free upgrade and came out of it with a shiny Sophia Classique 8-berth. I have the luxury of the two toilets, yet feel a degree of guilt that I am yet to suffer from a bout of the shits to take full advantage of these additional facilities.

Oh, for a rogue bit of fish...

I have a neat open plan lounge and kitchen area, with L-shaped seating and a table, from where I sit and work. Beyond the caravans, trees line the park's boundary. I am one caravan from the end of my row and derive much pleasure from their heavy, waving branches and often gaze towards them for Susie inspiration. I'm extremely partial to a bit of tree action. My bedroom is snug, with little room to manoeuvre around the surprisingly comfortable double bed. A bedside cabinet is home to a small selection of sex toys and bedtime vitamins and supplements. A small built-in wardrobe can hold only half of my clothes – and I travel quite light for a woman.

The bathroom has no bath, but a shower cubicle

– home to a surprisingly strong shower. A real bit of ooh-la-la between the legs come hose-down time. The other two bedrooms are tiny; two single beds almost squashed together and designed for the titchiest of children. God only knows how some of the adult hefties manage when they come down in groups. Anyway, these rooms are dumping grounds for my bags, dirty laundry and house the rest of my clothes.

The lounge has a flat screen telly that stands on a low, shelved cabinet. Alongside it sits the small wireless speaker I brought from home for some downtime music. The L-shaped seating provides comfy berths 7&8, upon which I sometimes stretch out for a break from the computer screen. To read, relax, have a crafty nap or the occasional low-level wank. There's even central heating and a gas fire, in the unlikely event of any early morning or late night chills.

Yes, the caravan has everything I need.

Except, (and to my astonishment) some net curtains. We caravan dwellers are on full view to one another. We peer into each other's lives, with each caravan like a mini soap opera, and offering up a new set of characters come changeover days. Take 69 – directly opposite – a middle-aged couple arrived the same day as me. She – portly and dressed older than her age (I'm imagining) – seemingly does only two things; cook, and tend to her awful hairstyle by means of the gruesome hairbrush and tongs she keeps on the dining table. 'He' has yet to change clothes from the day he arrived; a red-checked shirt and shapeless jeans combo, and is seemingly welded to the L-shaped seating and daytime TV. I am yet to see them venture out during the day. The wife examines her hair in a handheld mirror and tweaks and smoothes and brushes and applies the tongs. Sometimes, dissatisfied, she goes to the sink, to run her fingers beneath the tap before dampening non-compliant strands of hair. Then the whole rigmarole starts all over again.

Sometimes, I'll peer up from my laptop and hoot out, 'Happy Holidays!' when I see them having such a whale of a time.

Aside from eating from his lap and jean-hoisting trips to the bathroom, the only other activity the husband can summon is a half-hearted effort to smoke out of the lounge window. Our caravans here at Brightlea Sands are all non-smoking – Classique or otherwise – and when I venture out to the steps of my van for a cigarette I really shouldn't have, I occasionally see other smokers along the rows, wearing their slops and having their fix. Even the most slovenly looking seem to manage it as far as the doorway and stand there puffing away in their dressing gowns and slippers.

Chummy across the way is a shit. He smokes with the window opened about an inch and exerts himself by giving occasional half-hearted waves of a hand to disperse the smoke. Meanwhile, the wife peels potatoes at the sink or wrestles with that pesky horror hair. I'm not even sure I've seen them speak.

When they have extracted themselves from their caravan – her, still anxiously patting her hair, him tucking that checked shirt into his jeans as they tentatively step into the elements as though from hibernation – it has doubtless been to visit the clubhouse for the grim entertainment on offer. Early evening, it's japes and larks for the kiddies with camp mascots Benny the Bear and Duckface Ducky (staff bundled into cheap costumes – and based on his deformities, I'm thinking Benny may have had a previous life as donkey), followed by a lengthy bingo session, which culminates with 'The Big One'. Then it's the nightly 'entertainment' before the goodnight campers disco.

I caught some of the 'entertainment' after my squiffy return from Flabby's on my first night. Hopeful that the vodka would be favourably priced and fancying a night cap, I ventured in. I didn't last too long. Two songs, in fact. The enthusiastic, yet markedly untalented entertainers, had me in stitches and I had to despatch myself as I was beginning to attract frowning glances as I sat alone at a table, snorting into a cupped hand.

It was 'Dancing in the Street' that finished me off. Two slightly overweight females squeezed into black and white mini-dresses performed an energetic bent-elbowed backstroke centre stage (you could see their sweat through the thick make-up) and were soon joined by two happy chappies, who leapt on stage from behind each curtain (one of the leaps I chalked down as 'over ambitious' as the bloke stumbled forward and nearly off the stage...) before bounding up to the girls where they all partook in a large dose of the V-signs across the eyes malarkey to one another, (*believe me,* Pulp Fiction, it wasn't...).

The guys wore shiny aqua-coloured suits, were fake-tanned into a frenzy and looked as camp as a row of tents. As they all turned to face the audience and shimmied with arms pumping twice to each side, and invited every guy to grab a girl, things were whipped into a heightened level of excitement when some seemingly ancient smoke machine got cranked into life and duly covered the stage and front part of the dance floor in a dense layer of fog.

At this juncture, I couldn't get beyond thinking that a couple of hired help in brown overcoats – like something from an old Two Ronnies sketch – tasked with the responsibility of operating the smoke machine backstage, were in fact playing cards and/or having a crafty fag while the machine continued to rumble and pump more smoke into the clubhouse.

By now, all that was visible of our plucky quartet were their outstretched arms doing small downwards scooping motions, while the dance floor was invaded by small children who squealed as they ran like aeroplanes through the ever increasing fog. Or 'low-tech guff' as I'd mentally christened it through a snort of vodka.

And that was me done for the night. Thank you and goodnight. Marvellous stuff. I could have stayed. Probably should have stayed. But again, I was sticking out like a sore thumb. And whilst others also roared with laughter, it seemed a lone woman reduced to tears amongst the families somehow didn't fit in. No matter. I'd had my fill for the night. Maybe I'll brave the disco another time and watch the Dads busting some moves. Although, probably not.

And to the castrated strains of 'Ain't no Mountain High Enough' I set off back to my Sophia Classique. Number 56.

The family to one side of me (57) have a decoy bowl of fruit on their dining table. I see them munching their way through the packets of crisps, sweets, the doughnuts and nuked meals – Mum, Dad and the two young boys. Slaves to the television as they shovel it all in. But the fruit remains aloof and untouched. I half have it in mind to pop across and ask if it's for display purposes only.

I don't mind this lot actually, as they bugger off during the day and leave me in peace, with only a few curious glances from Mum and Dad as I wrestle with my keyboard or daily kettlebell exercises, while the boys climb up on their L-shaped to steal an occasional wide-eyed peep. Besides, as I spend most of my time with my back to them – either at my table or own L-shaped – 57 and the diagonal 68 are rarely in my eyeline.

To my other side, (55) an elderly couple. Who rather look like they've booked themselves into the wrong place by accident. They don't look happy at all. And sit on their L-shaped peering out the window with downturned mouths as though it's continually raining. I don't think Brightlea Sands is their cup of tea, at all. They stay in quite a bit – but not on the scale of chummy and his missus in 69. I see them tackling the complexities of getting into their car without leaving anything behind. Ooh, those frayed tempers. And bitter looks of wasted years.

'Happy Holidays,' I mutter as they pull away with their loaded scowls.

No. 70, diagonally to my left, doesn't give me too much grief – although in the firing line of my trees, the view inside is often partly obscured by the sun bouncing off its windows. Dependent on the time of day, you sometimes have to work pretty hard to get a proper snoop in there. So, in real terms, prime spectator sport comes from 69, 55 and a whack of 70 if you squint. With 57 and 68 for back-up on a rainy day.

Another great thing about my Sophia Classique (No. 56) is that I feel surprisingly safe there. We snoopers can spot an axe-wielding murderer without shifting from our L-shaped. All that aside, it's a refreshingly different world in caravan land, one totally removed from my life in Exeter with Clarke, the flat and our fledgling business – a small café in the City centre called The Grub Shack.

I've told Clarke he can keep my share of the place. Once he extracts it from the depths of his arse. What started as his great adventure soon developed into a way of keeping an eye on me. And it was always his dream, never mine. He was the foodie out the pair of us, always on red alert for a quick drizzle or sprinkle of something poncy. Or a firm twist of his pepper mill. I was just front of house. Trendy black apron and smiles. That was, until the smiles were graded into acceptable and unacceptable. Dependent on how attractive a male customer might be deemed.

Which swiftly heralded the end of our cutesy gingham table cloth period.

Funnily enough (or not), it was my smile that first attracted Clarke to me. I was working in an art gallery just around the corner from where The Grub Shack now is – selling contemporary paintings and ceramics – some bits of jewellery and other stuff, mostly made by local artists and crafters.

Clarke bowled in one day, looking arty and interesting, tousled hair and a canvas bag. He admired a couple of abstract paintings but preferred my smile. He bought nothing, but asked me out to dinner, and his toothbrush moved into my flat just a few weeks before he did. But I didn't care at the time. I was happy. I'd moved from London for a fresh start, leaving behind my job in an advertising agency as an art buyer and a failed marriage. The gallery position came up and it felt right. Clarke came along, and at the time, he felt right, too.

At the start, the gestures were welcome, 'surprising' me at work with a bunch of flowers, or at the end of day, to whisk me out for a meal or drink. The sex had been energetic and rough. And sorely missed. All was good.

My first inkling of Clarke's jealousy came when a female colleague fell pregnant and resigned from the gallery. Richard replaced her. Good-looking in a delicate way, he was a giggle and a delight. And could spot the browsing tight wads at ten paces. My gaydar – although known to be faulty on occasion – had Richard firmly chalked down as batting for the other team. Clarke, meanwhile, had him chalked down as a threat and would 'just happen' to be passing whichever bar Richard and I had gone to for a quick post-work drink.

Stupidly, I let my ego rule my brain. Clarke was really into me. Couldn't get enough of me. And I thought I was the one in control. Christ. There's no fool like a blind fool. I must have been fancying the tits off myself when I held court, with both of them vying for my attention. I'd laughingly tell Clarke to stop it when he'd ridicule Richard or pick him up over something he'd said. And still I couldn't see.

Clarke scuppered any further pub or wine bar forays with Richard by getting our evenings all busy and booked up. You name it, we did it. Meals, films, gym sessions, walks, plays, comedians, bands, a fleeting introduction to archery (I nearly took someone's eye out, and Clarke disapproved of the instructor's arms around me – our first argument...), or simply an organised night in, complete with a lavishly cooked meal, candles, massage, some agreeable porn and a lengthy sex session. Clarke could do wonders with a candle.

After some months, he spoke of becoming bored with his job as a junior architect. He wanted to put his creativity into his passion – food. Before I knew it, he'd found some premises for a café. He came up with the menu. I came up with the name. He had cash to put in. I gave my support and helped out at weekends. It was buzzy, busy, fun and made money. Before too long, Clarke asked me to give up the gallery and work at The Grub Shack full time –

he'd make me a full partner. We were riding a wave. I said 'yes'.

Although it soon transpired I was also saying 'yes' to us being together 24/7, as any attempted deviation was suddenly made into a 'thing'. Initially, there was the fake concern; surely I was too tired to go and meet up with a friend? Why not let him run me bath instead and cook my favourite dinner? Or the sudden, rare (and doubtless, insincere) encouragement to spend a few hours working on Susie, instead. As time went on, it turned to accusations – did I want to go out just to pick up some bloke to fuck?

I sleep walked into it. So gradual. So clever. I began to not recognise myself. Defending myself over crimes not committed. Where had I gone?

I can't remember what the joke was about – the one that earned me a slap across the face, but the guy had been good-looking – I'll give Clarke that. He'd come into the café on his own, with a broad smile and request for a strong black coffee in the largest receptacle available. He was nursing a gruesome hangover and said he needed saving. I think I said, 'Don't we all?' Maybe that's what we laughed about.

Clarke had popped out the kitchen and witnessed our shared laughter. Back at the flat, and during our row, he slapped me with such head-turning force, I dropped to the floor. The side of my face smarted for over a day.

And when it stopped smarting, I told him it was over.

He slammed me up against the lounge wall, his forearm pressing across my throat. I looked into his snarling face as he hissed threats and did what I should have done months earlier, ramming a knee firmly into his nuts. And suddenly, I was back.

As he folded to the floor and writhed about in pain, I took the opportunity to partake in a little plot explaining to him – kicking off with; lay another finger on me and I'd get him arrested. Then I calmly detailed how I would get some things together and book into a hotel for a few nights. I didn't want to be around him. Or even my tainted flat. Meanwhile, he could find somewhere else to live. Or just fuck off back to his fuckwit parents in Norfolk. Whichever was quicker. While I, would undoubtedly make good use of the hotel's bar and maybe, just maybe, pick up a random guy to fuck. Now, wouldn't that make all his allegations worthwhile?

I left Clarke sitting on the couch and looking bloodhound sorry for himself. 'Don't go,' he said, quietly. I felt nothing but disgust. What on earth had I ever seen in him? When I returned after those two nights – and a tidal wave of apologetic texts and voicemails – he was still there. Not much of a surprise, really – even Machiavellian bastards like Clarke can't magic up rental accommodation and move in within two days.

The flat was spotless and Clarke fussed over me as though I was visiting royalty. It was pathetic. He spoke as though nothing had happened, instead asking if I'd like to go out for a meal that evening. Seemingly, he hadn't been to work while I'd been away.

I took the glass of wine he offered and immediately placed it down. I told him I wasn't staying. That I'd been online and had booked up to go away somewhere to write for six weeks. Six whole weeks. More than enough time for him to find somewhere else to live.

'Of course, I should have thrown you out when you went for me,' I told him. 'But I have to take some responsibility for allowing things to get so bad. Besides, I did have feelings for you. Once.'

Clarke moved forward with an arm outstretched. I recoiled sharply.

'It doesn't need to be the end,' he said, taking another step and resting his hand on my shoulder. His touch was abhorrent and I brushed it away.

'It's the end, Clarke. Deal with it.'

Placing his hands on his hips, he shook his head, as though trying to dislodge something in his ear.

'So let me get this right,' he said, scrunching his face into ugly confusion. 'You're leaving *me* and going God knows *where*, to *write*? For six weeks? You do *know* that you're not any good, don't you?' The snarl was back.

I looked at him for what he was. 'You just can't stop, can you?'

'Stop what? Stop you from wasting your time on your stupid book that no-one will ever want to read?'

'I'm not playing this game anymore, Clarke. I'm done with you and I need to start packing.'

A cupped hand flew to his mouth. 'Oh, God, Amber! I'm sorry. I'm so sorry! I didn't mean any of that. I was just joshing. Look – why don't I book us a table at the Moroccan restaurant on Cathedral Green? We always enjoy it in there.'

As I moved past him to go to the bedroom, I leaned into his face. 'You do know that you're quite mad, don't you?'

When he spoke, I could feel his breath on my cheek. 'Am I?' he asked, softly.

'Six weeks, Clarke. Six weeks, max. Not a minute more. And I want you gone.'

When I left an hour later, he was sitting on the couch looking intently at his tablet. He seemed oddly indifferent to me hoofing my bags towards the front door and had a curiously smug expression on his face.

'You haven't asked where I'm going,' I said, surprised by his lack of interest.

'Why? Would you tell me?' he said, without looking up.

'No.'

'Well, that's why I haven't asked. I'm not an idiot.'

I paused for a moment, before opening the door and lugging my bags into the communal hallway.

'Okay, I'm off now. And despite everything's that happened... take care.' I had no idea why I'd wished him well. Sitting there on the couch, he hadn't looked beaten. Instead, he just appeared smaller, somehow. Insignificant. But the words were out. And it was too late to take them back.

He looked up and gave me a tight-lipped smile before returning his gaze to the screen.

'You too, Amber.'

'Six weeks, right?'

'Yup. Got that. Six weeks. I'll be long gone. Seriously, don't sweat it. I'm already on the case,' he said, gesturing towards his tablet. Then he gave me the charming smile that helped me fall in love in with him.

'And er... make sure you leave the keys behind.'

'Not a problem,' he said with that smile again.

As I closed the flat door behind me, I could just make out Clarke's sarcastic drawl. 'That's right – go to whoever you were fucking last night.'

Six weeks, Amber. Six little weeks.

Then he's history.

I've shoe-horned Susie into Cornwall – which all took a bit of doing. Namely, as she was reluctant to go. The girlies at work rally around once they learn of Jeremy's pronging sessions with Clara. 'You're better off without him!' they cry. 'Show him what he's missing!' as they encourage her into a soft perm and lowlights. Susie isn't sure though, as she fingers her new spaniel look in the wine bar.

She defiantly talks of not letting Jeremy ruin her life or making her feel awkward at work. 'That's the way!' the girlies cheer. Yet none of them see Susie's chin wobble as she presses the lipstick-smudged wine glass to her lips.

Susie tries her best to look chipper and indifferent when Jeremy breezes past reception with his briefcase firmly wedged up his armpit. Sometimes, if she sees him coming, she'll pick up her mobile and guffaw into it while twirling a lock of bolloxed hair. 'Oh! You are *so* funny!' she'll squeal. Other times, she'll loudly make dates with herself. 'So, that's 8'clock at the new TexMex restaurant. Can't wait!'

The effort is killing her.

Poor Susie. She and her chin never knew what hard work it was to be defiant.

She presses on. Our Susie will not be moved.

But the battle is finally lost the day Clara sweeps into reception sporting the huge engagement ring Susie had so dreamed of. She watches on as Jeremy comes down to collect Clara. He puts his arm around her shoulder as he leads her to the door. They rock their heads back and have their own guffawing to do. They are seemingly off to the new TexMex restaurant.

Susie's chin waves the white flag.

'Don't go!' the girlies cry, as Susie outlines her plans for a fresh start. She nearly doesn't. They plead and encourage. They tell her to get a new job instead. Susie is tempted and says, perhaps and maybe. She says she'll think about it.

But when Susie is alone in her bed at night, she can only think about the size of that ring. Such a whopper. And when she cries, she dabs away the tears with a corner of her quilt.

So a fresh start in Cornwall it is. Full of fond childhood holiday memories. She still has some inheritance money from her parents – who both drowned in a freak kayaking accident in Peru some years earlier – to support her with a modest property purchase and until she finds work. With an impressive employment record under her belt, she's hopeful it shouldn't take too long. See? Our Susie's already feeling a bit chirpier.

The girlies buy her polka dot wellies and an indoor plant to remember them by. They all get tipsy in the wine bar and give each other sloppy kisses on the cheeks when they say goodbye.

Good luck, Susie! Stay in touch!

Thanks, girls – I will!

Susie sleeps well that night. Trewithiel, here I come!!

3.

The Flabby Mermaid

I've got into a routine of sorts and I think it's working rather well. I get up early and to the horror that is breakfast television, I do my exercises. And I'm thinking one day, I might just twat that Piers Morgan right in the chops with one of the kettlebells I purchased (along with my trusty yoga mat) on my way out of Exeter. Then it's a quick bit of breakfast and a shower before getting to work on Susie. The occasional tap-dancing seagull on the roof keeps me company and I crack on. I'm loving it.

Once lunch is done, I check my phone. I'm getting quite used to Clarke's voicemails, emails and texts that swing between apologetic, begging me to come back, or just plain abusive. He refers to me as being in 'that place'. God knows where he thinks I am, but I'd readily wager it isn't tucked away in a Sophia Classique a mere twenty minute drive or so from the flat.

Occasionally, when I've been a bit post Flabby's tipsy, I message him back. Stupid, of course – but there you have it. The wonders of vodka. I regret every single one of those messages, and know that with each press of the send button, I'm also sending him a bit of power. And some of his much-loved control. In the main, I just demand to know when he'll be leaving the flat. Other times, I simply tell him to fuck off and leave me alone.

In an adult and mature fashion, of course...

Clarke fluctuates between being on the verge of signing up a tenancy agreement for a new flat and refusing to budge. I have no idea what I'll do if he's still there when I return. But I'm warming to the idea of getting the Police involved. If they'll have me. With that in mind, I never delete any of his stuff. And I'm already toying with taking someone with me when I first go back to my flat. Maybe I'll call upon Spencer, my ex-husband, to help me out. He owes me big time. All things considered.

Meanwhile, the messages come. And for the most part, I just block them out. Block Clarke out. This is my Susie time. And Clarke's going to do what he's going to do. Regardless.

After an early lunch, I might have a little relax on my L-shaped. Maybe masturbate. Or maybe I retire to the bedroom to give myself one with a favoured sex toy du jour. My current fantasy is about getting picked up by a black couple. She is rounded and has beautiful skin. He is solidly built and well-hung. I go to town on licking her out, spreading her pink lips and burying my face right in there. She tastes delicious. Her clit is pert. I suck on it and hear her groan. My probing fingers feel her waves of wetness.

I am on all fours, and from behind, the husband repays the compliment I am giving his wife. We are two very wet women. He teases with his cock. Trailing it between my ass and cunt, which he dips his tip into before withdrawing. He does this again and again. I am gagging for its entry. When he finally pushes in, it makes me gasp and take his wife's clit between my teeth. He pounds away. I am watching the scene as if a porno film.

Before he comes, he pulls out and we women eagerly share the task of licking his cock and balls. And when he ejaculates over his wife's cunt, I hungrily lick it off. My face is glistening with her wetness and his come as I feel her convulse in orgasm. I straddle her face, grinding myself down onto her flickering tongue. It doesn't take long...

Sigh.

Sometimes, I'll have a little nap afterwards.

After my post-lunch ritual, I get my head down with Susie for another hour or so. Then I get my stuff together and head for the beach, where the recent tide pattern has given me the luxury of being able to walk around the zigzags of the cliff's base to access it. Fit I may be, but this sweltering temperature can be mightily energy sapping on that walk over the cliff top. The change in tide has also meant an extension to the beach's width, giving everyone a bit of extra space.

For those who want it.

The old boy who greeted me on my first day was right; they are a friendly bunch down there. And I'm really getting into the swing of things. 'Lovely day, isn't it?' remains the standard greeting. I can hobble and wobble my way along those pebbles and get greeted by that any number of times before I park my arse. Sometimes, I'll just reply my standard response, 'Isn't it just?' and continue on my way. Other times, I might pause and exchange a few niceties with whoever has spoken to me. And if the person in question has his wrinkly dick in his hand at the time of asking, I invariably press on.

The nudity aspect has become so normal to me now, I've begun to question why I hadn't thought of doing this years ago. (Although I don't think Clarke would have been overly supportive...) Aside from giving me an enormous sense of wellbeing, from a vanity point of view, I no longer have to concern myself with any strap marks and the like as when ordinarily sunbathing. I'm guessing – if I looked – there must be other naturist beaches in sunny Devon. And God knows how many nooks and crannies along its beautiful coastline where people could strip off.

The beach is always busier than the first day I ventured down. Maybe the nudey brigade is getting more into its stride as this hit of good weather continues. I've taken to pushing on towards the far end, close to Brokeback Bay. I like it down there and it minimises the chances of sweaty tuggers having a hand shandy whilst looking at me.

I had all that on my third trip – some bloated fuck trying to have a surreptitious yank while using his knapsack as cover for his vile doings. After a lengthy session stretched out on my back, I'd sat up to apply some more cream and found him a) inappropriately close to me b) at it. He was laying on his back and straining to keep his head lifted to alternatively watch what he was doing and glance my way. Knapsack or not, there's not many things a bloke's doing when his arm's jerking around like someone's just put a new battery in it.

To be honest, I'm not sure if I found it more repulsive because *he* was repulsive and have since questioned if I'd have put my clothes back on and moved further down the beach (hence my introduction to the Brokeback vicinity) had the guy been attractive. I don't know, is the answer. I'm normally quite partial to watching my boyfriends or lovers smack away.

Perhaps I am a dreadful woman, after all.

Or maybe this beach is changing me.

I feel like changing.

When he saw I was preparing to move away, and moreover, stand up, he panicked and rolled onto his side, facing away from me. When I crunched past him, I paused briefly.

'Don't even think about following me,' I said.

He'd been pretending to sleep.

'Wha? Wha? Sorry.' Squints and rubbing of piggy eyes. His surprisingly small cock was lowering itself onto his thigh and shrivelling like an exhausted slug. I can say with more than a degree of certainty that I have never more wished to have some salt about my person.

I spat out the words, 'You heard me,' and threw him a glare before crunching off.

Wanker.

When I'm done on the beach, I head back to my Sophia Classique. I make something to eat and then type up any Susie notes I've made on the beach. Then dependent upon how I'm feeling, I either stay in and carry on working, and/or have a chill, or head out for a drink in Flabby's – where, like the beach, they're gradually getting used to me and have even given me a new nickname. I am currently known as 'The Bond Girl'. *Much* more preferable to 'JK'.

The cocky one wormed my surname out of me.

'So, you're Amber *Stone*?' he hooted in disbelief. 'Sounds like the name of a Bond Girl.' And that was that. When I walk into Flabby's now, it's all, 'Here she is, Blondie The Bond Girl. Stone. Amber Stone. Shaking in all the right places and stirring my groin.'

Yup. We go through the lot. Licensed to thrill. Pussy Galore. And so on.

I don't mind. They're harmless enough and have seemingly got it into their heads that I won't be dragging anyone back to my Sophia Classique any time soon. Well, kinda got it. Besides, there's not a whole lot of options when it comes to chatting to someone when I'm out. The couples and families aren't on the cards. So in real terms, it just leaves the local guys, as I'm not seeing a whole heap of other single people out and about. Nudey beach excluded.

In a strange way, with the guys being a bit rough and ready, and not the kind of people I'd normally mix with back in Exeter (or London, for that matter) it just adds to the feeling of distancing myself from my life with Clarke. Different. Opposite. My flat might only be 15 miles away, but it currently feels like two-hundred. Which is what I need at the moment. So I smile at the lewd banter. And sometimes, after a few vodkas have slid down, throw in some of my own.

Yeah. The guys are alright. Diamond geezers.

But I never let on that most afternoons I can be found naked on the beach. Now, *that* really would be a schoolgirl error.

There's a few characters amongst them. First off, is Fucker Frank; stocky and gobby, works in removals, and is so-named due to being a 'right fucker' for shamelessly asking for tips once the unloading has been completed. Irrespective as to whether everything got unloaded in one piece – which invariably, it hasn't. A right fucker, indeed. One of the guys, Wayne, works in the arcade a few doors along. He spends half his time tackling the fruit machine cheats and their indignant threats as they get found out. Wayne has none of it. When he's not necking pints in Flabby's, he's pumping weights at the local gym and happily kicks them up the arse on their way out the door.

Then there's the two Steves. Steve One used to have a local taxi company, of which he was the workforce in its entirety. Struggling to cope with the irregular work, he basically carried on doing what he was doing until the phone rang with a booking. Unfortunately, this also involved going to the pub. Apparently (and according to Fucker Frank – whose account I'll try to faithfully replicate), after a heavy drinking session watching England play in a Euros qualifying game, he ended up slumped in the corner and having a bit of a nap. Not a problem.

Until, that is, some bloke – upon seeing Steve's business card pinned up by the bar – phoned him to get a lift home. Apparently, some kind of comedy sketch unfolded, where Steve was jolted out of his kip by his phone bursting into life and although the guy at the bar was only a few yards away and had seen Steve answering a call, didn't correlate that the pissed-up punter grappling with his phone, was in fact, 'Steve's Taxis'.

It wasn't until they began talking to one another – the guy at the bar enquiring, 'Is this Steve's Taxis?' and then hearing, 'Where to, mate?' both through his mobile and the mouth of Steve as he managed to shift himself into a sitting position – that it became evident all was not as it should be. Bizarrely, they continued talking to one another. With the guy asking, 'Is that you sat in the corner?' And a befuddled Steve responding with, 'Um... er... where are you mate? I can be there in five.' They continued speaking on their phones right up until the point the guy walked up to Steve, took his phone away and said, 'I'm not going anywhere with you. You're pissed.'

A complaint got put in behind the bar. The business card taken down. And Steve's Taxis was no more. And Steve One promptly entered the world of removals with Fucker Frank. He doesn't come out as often as the others and is apparently under doctor's orders to curb his drinking. But when he does, he gives every appearance of being pickled; standing on the periphery of the group and silently gurning like a village idiot, as though sharing a good joke with himself.

The cocky one, who christened me The Bond Girl, is Steve Two, a plasterer and lover of footie. And he really is a proper cocky charmer of a geezer. Good looking and full of cheesy one-liners designed to get a girl's knickers off and their ankles around his neck in record time. His success rate with the tourist girls is quite something to behold. They love him. And by and large seem more than happy to accommodate his quest for a seaside fumble.

He claims to be of Italian descent – which always raises a Stewards Enquiry and jeers from the rest of the guys when mentioned. Maybe his surname of Parker doesn't invoke images of a swarthy, tight-vested Mediterranean type offering up a lick on his Cornetto in a gondola. Mind you, with his black slicked back hair and dark eyes, it might not be outside the realms of possibility.

Either way, when he homes in on a table of girls, he inevitably asks his prey, 'Excuse me – but I've been looking at you and wondering – have you got any Italian in you?' And inevitably, the particular girl he'd been eyeing up would be blonde. So she'd inevitably answer, 'No'. At which point, he'll lean in further and ask, 'Would you like some?' And he'll flash his teeth. Click-click out the side of his mouth. Throw her a wink. And be in.

His good looks, easy manner and awful charm make his company quite agreeable, and when I get Flabby's pissed, I sometimes wonder what it would be like to get him back to my Classique for some uncomplicated filth.

Oh, the wonders of vodka.

And yet, I do wonder.

The quiet one of the group is Matty. He, along with Steve Two, are the ones who asked me out on my first foray into Flabby's. On first inspection, he has one of those personas that could be easily dismissed. But scratch beneath the fringe and sad eyes, the beginnings of a slight stoop for someone still in their early thirties, and you'll discover that prior to Matty's current two-year stint in a fish and chip shop in the next town along, he was someone to be reckoned with in IT. Until the stress made him ill. Sad. And ultimately, give it all up.

Get Matty on your own for a few minutes and you'll soon discover what an articulate, well-read, intelligent and moreover, sensitive guy he is. Give him an interested audience and you'll listen to him talk about a passion for reading crime thrillers or watching historical documentaries and those sad eyes will sparkle into life, his posture straightens and you get a glimpse of the person who once commanded a healthy salary in a job he loved. But will never go back to.

Matty more or less single-handedly wins the weekly Sunday night quiz at Flabby's for the guys, whose token input invariably involves sport or TV. Their team name is 'Kiss My Plums and Call me Brutus' – dreamed up by Steve Two and which never fails to cause hoots of laughter when the broad-accented, Glaswegian quiz master hands out the scores on the doors.

Otherwise, Matty seems content to just stand in their bawdy company, nursing his lager and offering up the occasional comment. And aside from winning the guys a cash prize each Sunday, they seem oblivious as to how much more there is to him beyond presiding over deep fat fryers twice daily.

I like Matty. And I think it took quite a lot for him to ask me out. Shyly, discreetly. For a quiet drink 'somewhere else'. Showing an interest in my writing. I got the feeling it was more for some half-intelligent company more than anything else. As opposed to Steve Two's, 'How about it, Blondie? You and me?' With his trademark, click-click out the side of his mouth and that dazzling smile. Matty's rejection came kindly, as I had no wish to mislead – I was just coming out of a long-term relationship. Etc. To Steve Two, I informed that this would only be of interest come the day I fancied a STD to call my very own. But thanks for the offer. It was a good one. Etc.

'One day, Blondie,' he replied, laughing. 'One day.'

One day, indeed. This hot weather and nudity is making me randy. And I'm beginning to wonder if I'm giving out sex signals; someone's written 'DIRTY' on the boot of my old battered Golf in large letters.

They don't know the half of it.

4.

My Beautiful Spencer

Susie's rallied. And the girl's done good. She's entered Trewithiel with a new granite jaw and a pot plant, and secured a two-bedroom stone cottage to rent while she finds something within budget to buy. Her budget is modest, so takes on the cottage for just a few months. There is urgency to find both a property and a job, but our Susie is full of new resolve these days. She wants people to know that she is someone to be reckoned with. And displays this by growing out the bastard perm. Well *done*, Susie.

Susie is served well by her non-bolloxed nut and previous NHS experience, as she responds to an advert for a medical secretary at the local doctors' surgery and fights off all-comers to get the job. Back in the cottage, she toasts her success with a cheeky glass of Prosecco and marks the moment by posting a triumphant selfie on Facebook to let the girls know (who will doubtless let chinless Jeremy know) that life is moving on. And in the right direction.

But once the 'Go You!' comments on Facebook begin to fade and finally rumble to a halt, Susie takes a moment to reflect that maybe, just maybe, she should have let the old gang know that in the sleepy village of Trewithiel, she was, in fact, the only applicant.

Tsk, tsk, Susie.

But, no matter! Susie starts in a few days and has a million things to do. Where to put that pesky pot plant, for starters? And surely, some new blouses are in order? Before she knows it, Susie polishes off the bottle. And that night, and for the first time, when she lies in bed, her mind doesn't wander to Jeremy and the japes they used to have. Instead, she thinks about the surgery and promotion to office manager. With her hair piled high upon her head and a clipboard to call her own.

And when she sleeps, she dreams she is a mermaid. In the blue Cornish sea. Trailing her hand over the soft, white sand as she dives deep to the sea's floor. And when she emerges, hair slicked back and glistening, she waves to a little boy on the beach before flipping her tail and diving back down to the depths. She hears the boy's whoops of pleasure and excited cries to his nearby Mother, telling her about the mermaid with polka dot wellies on her fins.

As Susie nestles into her pillow, and the

beginnings of a smile creeps across her lips, she also hears the unmistakable thwack of the little boy being clapped around the head for telling lies.

... I think I'll take that last bit out.

Plus I really need to try and curb my dislike for children.

Couldn't eat a whole one.

Etc.

I just thank God that Spencer and I both saw eye-to-eye on the subject of children.

I met him back in London, when I worked in advertising. As an art buyer, one of my responsibilities included booking photographers. Spencer was up-and-coming, his portfolio impressive and growing. His fees were more favourable than the better known photographers, so it was a no-brainer to give him a go. Charge him out at an extortionate rate to the client. Spencer gets paid and adds to his portfolio. We get a job well done and make a huge mark-up. Trebles all round.

He asked me out at the end of a testing shoot for a well-known fashion designer. The studio was booked. Everything was in place. The clothes, the props, the lighting, the make-up artist, the assistants and the digi operator. Everything was good to go. Except the model didn't show up. Frantic phone calls to her agency revealed she'd come down with glandular fever, and not wanting to lose our business, quickly dispatched not one, but two, vacuous brunette airheads over to the studio. The pair of them were a nightmare and had seemingly never taken direction before.

Both looked stiff and clumsy in their expensive outfits, and struck predictable model poses which couldn't be further away from screaming high-end luxury if they'd tried – in fact, they more shouted bargain basement catalogue.

We were all getting a bit fraught and studio time was running out to get some good shots.

Frustrated, Spencer produced his phone and hooked it up to the studio sound system. Then in turn, he asked each of the models to dance to the music. He wanted some attitude from them. He wanted to see some power in their faces. And with that, he blared out some unfamiliar, but catchy, heavy dance music with a grinding beat. At first the girls giggled, blushed and looked awkward and shy as they self-consciously shuffled about on the spot.

Spencer halted the music and told them to shake out their limbs and get dancing.

'Imagine you're in a nightclub and wanting to attract the attention of some buff guy you've just spotted,' he told them. 'But *you're* the one deciding whether you want them or not. You're the one with the power and control. And *that's* what I want to see. Okay?' Then he restarted the music. And instructed the rest of us to get dancing, too. We looked at each other, shrugged, laughed, and aside from the digi operator, got on with it. The atmosphere in the studio changed in an instant. Amongst the laughter, arse shaking, grinding moves and dancing, Spencer pulled it off. With the girls losing all inhibitions, he got any number of strong shots from model one as she swirled and moved, revealing perfectly toned legs from the slits in her flowing dress whilst delivering a piercing gaze down the barrel of the lens.

Whilst model two's best shots showed her hands on hips, back to camera, legs apart, torso twisted to towards the camera and with a look that said, 'I am going to eat you for breakfast'. The halter neck dress she had on looked amazing. Her back, graceful and sexy. Our client was going to be thrilled. And we finished just in time.

The mood was buoyant. The dancing had been good fun. And Spencer's energy and enthusiasm, contagious.

I went over to thank and congratulate him.

'You do know that was all a bit cheesy?' I tagged on with a smile.

He stopped packing his equipment away and laughed. 'Of course,' he said. 'But it worked, didn't it?'

'It certainly seems that way,' I replied.

'Mind you, it all would have been a lot easier if you'd been my model,' he said with a grin. 'I sneaked a peek at you; you're quite some mover. And as for those green eyes. I really need to photograph you one of these days.'

'Are you being cheesy again?'

'No. Just serious.'

Handsome Spencer. Perfect in almost every way. Charming. Talented. Intelligent. Good humoured. We went for drinks that night. We laughed. We flirted. We went back to his place. He tied me up and stripped me naked. And gave me the best oral sex I've ever had. I orgasmed into his mouth. Then he untied me, turned me over, and fingered my ass before feeding his sizeable cock into it. He talked filth as he fucked me, and when he come, it was all over my ass cheeks, which I duly rubbed in with both hands. Making sure some of it went into each hole. It was sex heaven for me. And as I lay, sweaty and (very) satisfied on his bed, he reached for a camera and took photos of me.

Spencer ended up taking lots of naked photos of me during our years together. Sometimes, I'd be masturbating or touching my breasts. Or both. Sometimes, there'd be the toys. The dildos. The rabbits. The plugs. The beads. The balls. Other times, he had a camera set up on timer for shots of us having sex. Or playfully swiping at one another with pillows.

Spencer would develop some of the photos in the privacy of his small converted dark room in the flat, and we'd buy frames and dot them around the bedroom. Black and white, mostly. One of my favourites is a post-sex shot of me kneeling and smearing Spencer's glistening come over my breasts and cunt. I'm peering up at him. My hair damp with sweat. Watching Spencer watching me. And I look like I'm ready to do it all over again. Yeah. Spencer's been a hard act to follow.

Initially, we kept our relationship quiet. I was putting more work his way and didn't want to be accused of favouritism or being unprofessional. But along with the deep love and friendship that was forming, the attraction and chemistry were impossible to hide: the electricity between us could have lit up the National Grid. It didn't take long for the game to be well and truly up. And I was relieved when it was. Particularly as no-one gave a damn – instead, they were pleased for us. What a good match, they all said. We'd guessed, they all said.

After a few months, I rented out my Islington flat and moved into Spencer's more spacious one in Camden. We spent our free time visiting art galleries or photographic exhibitions. Took in West End shows. Trawled the Soho and Covent Garden bars and eateries. Browsed through Camden Market and had walks and picnics in Primrose Hill Park.

And of course, there was the wonderfully rough, but exquisite sex. Sometimes fuelled with poppers.

Everything was nigh on perfect.

When Spencer proposed, I wasn't entirely surprised. It just seemed the most natural next step. We'd gone for a meal at the OXO Tower and were outside, admiring the view of the Thames with its evening pleasure cruises slowly passing by and booming out music. Sometimes we gave the boozy revellers a boozy wave. Sometimes we got a boozy one back. One of them gave us a boozy finger. Spencer and I looked at one another and laughed.

At one point, Spencer rummaged in his jacket pocket and pulled out an envelope with my name on it.

'Before I forget,' he said, 'there's a couple of my expenses that need signing off.'

'*Now*? You *are* kidding me, right? Whatever happened to email?' I asked, turning the envelope over in my hand. 'Jeez. You do know how to spoil a girl on a date.'

'Sorry, Amber – one of my suppliers still operates from an ark, but if you could just give them a quick once over – you know how rubbish I am with admin. And if you don't do it now, I'll probably forget and end up losing them.'

I gave Spencer a mock reprimanding look. 'Hmmm. Just this once,' I said as I opened the envelope. 'Whoever said the art of romance was dead?'

I pulled out the envelope's contents. It was a photograph that Spencer had taken of our feet a few weeks earlier; post-sex, side-by-side and our big toes touching. Across the top of the photograph he'd written, 'Marry Me?' with a silver marker pen and in his elaborate and feminine handwriting. I looked at Spencer with a broad smile and saw that he'd sunk to one knee and held open a small box containing a solitaire diamond engagement ring.

We married eight weeks later in Camden Town Hall with just a handful of colleagues and friends present. After a meal (and rather a lot of drink) with our guests, we spent our first night of marriage at home before a wonderful honeymoon in Corsica. We giggled, whooped and cheered as Spencer drunkenly staggered when carrying me over the threshold, snagging the hem to my green skirt suit on the door handle.

'Ssssssh,' he'd said to it, juggling my body to press a finger to his lips.

That night, with the bedroom candlelit and filled champagne glasses sitting on the bedside tables, I produced the strap-on dildo Spencer had expressed a keen interest in trying out. I emerged from the bathroom wearing white hold-up stockings, a white cupless bra, white stilettos and a beast of a dick between my legs. I don't think we've ever laughed so much.

Swaying slightly, I instructed Spencer to get on his knees and suck my dick. I stood with my legs apart and watched him do just that and took some photos. Then he clambered on to the bed on all fours, took a swig of champagne and told me to fuck him.

I knelt behind and bent to lick his arse, whilst massaging his balls and stroking his cock. Then I leaned forward to fill my mouth with champagne before spitting it over his arse cheeks which I'd pulled apart.

'Ooh! You dirty bitch!' Spencer laughed.

'That's me, alright!' I replied. And with more awkwardness than I've ever seen in a porn film, I adjusted my position, Spencer's hips and my harness, and eased the tip of the dildo into his arse.

'You okay – or do you want the lube?' I called out.

Spencer's breathing was deep and sharp.

'No – I'm fine. Keep going.'

'I'll put some on anyway. Poppers?'

'Yeah,' he replied, huskily. Spencer reached out an arm and fumbled in a bedside drawer. Finding the lube first, he passed it behind and I squeezed some over my cock. Then came the poppers. He unscrewed the lid, took a long, noisy snort up each nostril and handed me the bottle. I took a couple of hefty whacks and as I got hit by the rush, I pushed in and began to slowly grind deeper in my husband while my hands held his hips and melted into him.

We snorted poppers three times. And Spencer wanked all the while I fucked him. He told me to pull out when he was about to come. I sat back on my heels and Spencer turned over and ejaculated over my tits and cock with a loud and lengthy groan. Which was all rather splendid.

I had to wait until the morning to get my first married sex. At the time, it didn't matter – I'd made do with a clumsy, drunken wank – as all I'd wanted to do that night was give my wonderful husband what he'd wanted.

For all the boyfriends, lovers and one-night stands I've had before or since Spencer, for all the agreeable or regrettable sex I've had – no one's quite had his special magic. And in many ways. And even today, I still regard Spencer as my best and dearest friend.

Naturally, we'd talked about children. And it was a brief discussion. We were happy. Careers going well. We were both ambitious. And living our lives with no ties. Our freedom was important to us. We wouldn't even consider a pet.

In my early twenties, I'd fallen pregnant. An accident. My boyfriend at the time was casual, with neither of us in it for the long haul. When the pregnancy was confirmed and it hit home how much my life would change, I felt horrified. I'd always felt some kind of disconnect from my old school friends who had happily resigned their young lives to being a parent.

When I horribly miscarried a few weeks later, any decision had been taken away from me. And the relief I felt was immense. To most women, having children is their dream. To me, it just equated to 'burden'. I guess I'll never know. I've had a lot of spontaneous sex in my life, and to my eternal shame, not always protected. I've never fallen pregnant since and harbour a strong feeling that I can't. It's just an intuitive thing. But I bet I'm right.

Anyway, it seemed there'd be less and less chance of me having any accidents with Spencer as the vaginal sex gradually became more infrequent and was replaced by anal penetration. We both explored new things. More anal toys were purchased. The beads grew in size. The butt plugs got busy. And the pegging sessions roared on. It was all great fun. It was filthy. It was pleasurable. God knows how many photos were taken.

After a session we'd sit up in bed and go through them.

'Check you with a dildo in each hole,' Spencer would say.

'That's nothing,' I'd reply. 'Will ya look at that knobbly thing going into your sweet ass? Dear Lord – lost forever.'

And we'd sit there giggling, as we admired or deleted photos. Yeah, they were good times. We laughed a lot. We talked a lot. We loved a lot. And we fucked a lot.

Then suddenly we didn't.

Spencer became distant and moody. And

sometimes, uncharacteristically short-tempered. Our sex life dwindled. We argued over nothing. I tried to get to the bottom of what was going wrong. Spencer cited work pressure – he was in demand and working a lot of hours. I probed further – he'd always worked hard – what had changed?

And finally, one evening, as we sat exhausted after another pointless argument, he took my hand, let his tears fall and told me the truth. That these days, his preference was to photograph naked men. Post-sex.

We had nowhere to go. And no one to blame.

And just a heavy sadness in our hearts.

I tried to explore the possibility of an open marriage to cope with his bisexuality. But Spencer just bit his lip, dropped his beautiful head and shook it side-to-side as fresh tears rolled down his cheeks.

It was over. Freedom has always been so very important to us. And is the greatest gift a person can give.

I carried my married name of Stone with me when I moved to Exeter. And will carry it with me for as long as my ex-husband remains so firmly embedded in my heart.

I don't think I'll be changing it anytime soon.

Poor Amber.

5.

The Sights I See and Storm Bollockchops

There's been a few odd sights on the beach recently and I half wonder if I should ditch Susie and start writing about there instead.

Just kidding, Susie! (Kinda...)

The first occurred late one afternoon, when our nudey peace was shattered by repeated, loud bellows of, 'Oi! Perverts!' coming from the direction of the sea. Poking our heads up like an army of nudey meerkats, we were greeted by the sight of a trio of bare backsides pointing our way as three lads bent over and precariously balanced on one of the mackerel fishing boats the tourists hired out.

Some of my fellow nudeys were markedly unimpressed, and glared and tut-tutted, but I roared with laughter. One of the regular older gay guys (who I've nicknamed 'Penguin Man' – due to his tentative waddling across the pebbles to the sea; feet pointing out; rigid arms with flexed hands) was sunbathing within shouting distance.

'Isn't that hysterical?' I asked. 'Mooning at naked people? We've all got our arses poking up to the heavens most of the day, so I think we all know what one looks like.'

'Amen to that,' Penguin Man shouted back. 'I guess that makes them the perverts, then?'

'Perhaps we all are,' I replied with a laugh. Sitting up, I put on my sunglasses, lit a cigarette and gave the lads a cheery wave, a wide smile and a jiggle of my tits.

'Let's see if the boys are man enough to do anything about that,' I called over to Penguin Man.

We both squinted into the sun.

'Doesn't look like it, love – they're leaving,' Penguin Man shouted in reply.

We watched on as they carefully hoisted up their shorts and got the rocking boat chugging into action without incident.

'Ha! Never send a boy to do a man's work, eh?'

'Amen to that.'

Pervert? Moi?

How *rude!*

The next sight was probably more disturbing than odd, and happened a few days later when a young, slim woman, dressed in a white blouse and black skirt made her way along the beach carrying a small handbag and a plastic bag. She abruptly stopped. Peeled her clothes off. Went into the sea. Came out. Dried off on a small towel she pulled from her plastic bag. Put her bra, blouse and pants back on. Delved back into the plastic bag to produce a pair of black trousers. She put them on. Then her shoes. Picked her bags up and promptly left. Leaving us meerkats gawping at one another with shrugs.

I'm yet to see her again and wonder what makes a young woman wash in the sea before a shift as a waitress or barmaid or whatever. She had the sharp facial features that are sometimes associated with Eastern Europeans, and I've since wondered about her story. I hope she's okay.

I probably should have asked. And still feel a tug of guilt that I didn't.

The third odd sight came courtesy of some guy who tried to hit on me. I was nursing a bit of a Flabby's hangover at the time, so when I rolled over and saw this guy emerging from the sea and striding towards me with a mass of unruly horror pubes – like some fucked up, trippy version of a Bond film – I briefly wondered if I was still pissed and seeing things.

Without a hello, goodbye or a kiss my arse (let alone, 'lovely day, isn't it?') he plonked himself down, propped himself up on an elbow and stretched out before me, which resulted in the offending pubes being positioned directly in my line of vision. I'd never seen anything like it in my life; like some form of Kevin Keegan wig (and we're talking 'the perm' here) with a post-salt slug protruding from it.

If I'd not been so caught on the hop (and hung over), I should have whipped out my Zippo and done both of us a favour by torching the bloody lot.

Having had the temerity to confront me with such an unsavoury sight, he then proceeded to fire off a series of questions into my unresponsive face without pausing for breath. Did I get to the beach often? Did I live nearby? Etc. Etc.

When he eventually ground to a halt and looked at me expectantly for some answers, I just squinted up and asked if he'd do me the favour of 'fucking off'. And el pronto.

Which thankfully, he did, without complaint, delay or further comment. Aside from a surprised, 'Oh!'

'Ta-ta, Kevin,' my hangover mumbled, as I watched him dejectedly walk his soggy, jumbo wad of horror pubes across the pebbles. And doubtless onto his next unsuspecting victim.

I'm telling you, spend enough time on that beach and you'll see more than you've bargained for.

Dear, oh dear.

I've had a rather unsettling email from Clarke. One of his ranting efforts and calling me a "DIRTY

WHORE" a number of times (amongst a vast array of other things) – he's never used that particular expression before and I feel suddenly curious as to who wrote 'DIRTY' on the back of my battered old Golf.

And with his voicemails, texts and emails all flip-flopping between abuse and grovelling apology, I also wonder how Clarke managed to disguise his true self for so long. Or how I was unable to spot it.

Did that make him dangerous?

I didn't know, was the simple answer, and expected I was just being ridiculous – he had no idea where I was. He hadn't followed me here. Last I saw of him he was sitting on the couch, and showing no signs of readying himself to leap out the front door and trail me once I'd left.

Besides, as things stood, Clarke wasn't my biggest problem. Susie was. She's playing up something rotten and digging those pesky sensible heels into the ground and come to a halt. She simply won't budge and I've no idea what to do with her next. Especially as joining a troupe of dancing girls working their way around the Baltic States doesn't seem on the cards.

I looked up from my laptop and across at number 69. Temporary home to a spectacled guy sitting on his L-shaped. He arrived yesterday, so was probably doing the Monday to Friday shift and appeared to be on his own. Mind you, it's not always possible to tell – there's a lot of flopping around that goes on in these caravans. He also appeared to be devoting all his attention to his laptop.

'Well, you're not looking at porn,' I said aloud. 'I've tried that, matey, and the camp's wifi won't let you on. Bastards.'

As a sudden realisation hit me, I got to my feet. 'Dear Lord!' I continued, 'You're not writing a shitty chick lit, as well, are you?'

Sensing movement, Mister 69 glanced up and gave me a small awkward smile before returning his eyes to the screen.

'Ha! I knew it! I'm in a race to get out the next best-selling Susie Chronicles. Well, in that case, matey – let battle commence!"

I sat back down, opened my notebook and scanned through it for inspiration. But there was none to be found. I sighed heavily. I never knew that writing could be so darn tough. I mean, I never thought it'd be a doddle, and relished the times I hit a sweet spot and everything just flowed. That's when you understood why you loved doing it so much. But when it sucked, it truly sucked. And I'm a woman who knows a lot about sucking.

And why on earth had I chosen chick lit as a genre? It's as far removed from me as Jupiter or my marriage. Writing about some drippy mare and her corduroy gusset, I mean, *really?*

I flipped though it again, but my notebook still

refused to offer up any ideas. I looked across at Mister 69 as he hunched over his laptop.

'What's your excuse?' I asked. 'Me? I'm chick litting because I thought it would be easier. And a quicker route to the bucks. But what do I know?'

No answer.

Maybe he's just online gambling. Or bulk-buying on Amazon. Or maybe just ignoring me. Even though he can't hear me.

I glanced at my phone. Nothing else from Clarke and not too long until nudey beach time.

Come on, Amber. Get a grip. Let's do this.

I picked up my pen and pored through my notes once more.

It'll come to me. I'm not giving up on Susie – that much is for sure. I had to give up Spencer, so I'm not letting her go as well. Besides, she's all I've got at the moment and I daftly like her company.

The drippy mare.

Later on, as I worked my way over the cliff top, hazy ideas swooped down from nowhere and began to take form. Feeling impatient to get settled and jot them down before they disappeared, I picked up speed. When I reached the beach I was quite out of breath and distractedly answered the usual greetings as I walked and slid as quickly as possible over the pebbles. Yes, it *was* a lovely day, I told them. I pushed on down towards Brokeback Bay, found a good spot and hastily laid out my yoga mat and towel, undressed, pulled my notebook from my bag and got to work.

The afternoon turned out to be satisfyingly productive. So when I finally put my notebook to one side and stretched out to relax, I felt a real sense of achievement at getting Susie firmly back on track. Stretching out my arms, I inspected my tan; it was deepening to a lovely golden colour. I squinted up at a seagull circling against its perfect blue backdrop and hoped the forecasters were right – we were in for a long heatwave summer.

I wondered if I'd ever return to nudey beach, once I was back to whatever constituted normal, post-Clarke life. My initial plan was to pick up some office temp work, just to tide me over and pay the bills. Then I'd tackle finding something permanent with a creative angle which, in theory, I'd find more fulfilling and rewarding. Exeter seemed to be awash with temp roles, so I wasn't overly worried about that side, but recognised the long term role might take a bit more time to unearth, and moreover, land.

But yeah, now I knew about nudey beach, I could easily return at weekends or even post-work in the summer. I mean, what wasn't there to like for a woman like me? As I rolled onto my front and watched a distant pleasure boat ferrying tourists along the coastline, I became aware of sharp pressure on my bladder and grimly acknowledged the urgent need for a toilet.

I wondered about the sea. I'd not been in yet. Not with those killer pebbles. Part of the comedy value down here was watching fellow nudeys slipping and sliding as they tried to get out of sea with a shifting platform beneath them. Some days, they'd almost be lined up like beached whales, flapping around and helpless. Boof! There goes another one! I might be happy to take all my clothes off in public, but I drew the line at frantically trying to scramble out the sea on all fours. And very possibly without success.

I looked at my bottle of water. Empty. That was a first. Normally I rationed myself because of this very reason – Susie must have distracted me, the saucy minx. I rolled back over and reached for my clothes. Seemed I'd be going back over that cliff top as quickly I came. Maybe I'd find a bush I could squat behind; I *really* needed to go.

As it turned out, there were a number of sparse-looking bushes that could have offered a degree of privacy, but the heavy flow of nudey traffic going either way gave me no choice but to push on.

Finally reaching the base of the cliff, I scanned ahead of me for some public toilets. Surely there must be some by the main drag, car park or seafront. As I quickly walked on, I spotted The Captain's Table, the family theme pub. Bingo! A wee *and* a cold drink. Victory shall be mine! I jerked up the yoga mat tighter under my armpit and broke in to a semi jog.

It didn't take long to get there, and as I dashed through the busy beer garden, I heard someone speak to me. 'Hello, stranger.'

I glanced down to a guy wearing sunglasses, with a half-filled pint glass and opened magazine on the table front of him. It took me moment to place who he was.

'Not now!' I cried, as I twirled back around in a circle and dumped my yoga mat on his table. 'Look after this – I need the loo!'

Luke raised his glass and toasted me with a laugh.

I returned several minutes later and sat down at his table with a glass of wine. Luke looked at me with a broad grin. 'All better?' he enquired, as I took a much needed sip.

'Very much better, thanks,' I replied with a relieved sigh. 'Blimey. This pub's as grim as I thought it would be. Have you ever seen so many ship wheels, lanterns, tatty old bits of knotted rope or deformed mermaid mastheads in your life?'

'I expect not, but I don't come here for the decoration,' Luke replied, lifting his glass. 'Anyway, I haven't seen you around lately on the beach. Mind you, I've not been getting down as often as I'd like.'

I took another sip. 'Well, I'm there.'

Luke leaned forward, took off his sunglasses and rested them on the table. 'You're not getting all mysterious with me again, are you?' His grey/blue eyes were as piercing as I remembered.

'I've begun going down to the far end. Or Brokeback Bay, as I call it.'

'Brokeback Bay?' Luke laughed. 'Now there's a thing. And is it good down there?'

'Depends what you mean by good,' I replied. 'But I don't get pestered so much.'

'Ah. And you don't want to be pestered?'

His words hung in the air. His eyes gazed steadily into mine. With the slight hit from the wine, I suddenly wondered what it would be like to have sex with him. And not for the first time.

'What's that you're reading?'

Luke let out a small laugh. 'It's just one of the Sunday supplements. There's a feature about contemporary landscape painting I wanted to have a look at.'

'Oh! You like art?'

'You want to be pestered?'

I raised my glass to my lips. 'Maybe that depends on who's doing the pestering,' I replied, taking a mouthful of wine.

'I guess it does.'

We appeared to be flirting, and to be honest, since first meeting Luke, and despite giving him the brush-off, I'd always felt a small twinge of regret when not spotting him (and his shaved balls) on the beach again. I guess he must have been arriving after me and leaving before – like the last time.

I must also confess to a crafty and rather delicious L-shaped wank about an indistinct, random guy, who morphed into Luke as I got towards the business end of matters.

And very nice, too.

In fact, so nice, I pushed on for a second helping.

Greedy bitch.

Yeah, warm weather and nudity were no good (or very good) for a woman like me. But someone like chummy with the Brillo Pad pubes wasn't going to whet my sexual appetite or get me turning a few tricks in the sack.

God. It really had been a while.

'Another?' asked Luke, draining his glass and pointing to mine. I took a moment or two to decide. I looked at the scant remains of my wine. Then, Luke. He seemed like he could be an interesting guy. Hmm. Then I thought of all my hard work with Susie that afternoon – which all needed typing up and fiddling with.

'When are you down next?' I asked.

'Does that mean 'no' to a drink?' He replied.

I laughed. 'We don't seem to be very good at answering questions.'

Luke cocked his head to one side, as though deciding something.

'Okay. Let's try something different,' he said. 'I'm

Luke Martin, struggling local artist. Originally from West Cork in sunny Ireland. Forty nine and a half years old. Twice divorced. Once my fault. Once hers. I'm over both of them. Currently single and living the high life is sunny Shaldon. Known to get naked on the beach.'

Luke Martin. I knew him. Or rather, I knew his work – we used to sell it at the gallery I worked at in Exeter. He was an abstract painter. Stunning land and seascapes with his trademark broad and sweeping strokes in bold colours that breathed life and energy into the subject. His larger pieces of work could command thousands.

'I know you,' I replied rather smugly.

Luke arched an eyebrow and leaned towards me. 'You do?'

'I used to work at The Stokes Gallery on Cathedral Green. And you might be pleased to learn that I've even sold one of your Dartmoor paintings – the one of Haytor in the autumn.'

'Good Lord! Now, isn't that something?' Luke sat back and looked at me with small nods. 'Well, that's me, then. And you?'

I fleetingly toyed with lying. But then, couldn't see the point.

'Amber Stone. Wannabe writer. 38-years old. Once divorced – from husband who suddenly turned gay on me. *Very* not over it – but hey ho. Currently residing in a static caravan park close by whilst working on an awful novel and waiting for psycho ex-boyfriend to vacate my Exeter flat. Very much over it. I'm also resting between jobs between getting naked on the beach.'

Luke smiled at me. 'Is that so?'

'That's about the strength of it,' I replied with a shrug and downing the last of my wine.

'The gay ex-husband – Brokebay Bay doesn't evoke any bad memories?'

I'd never thought about it, to be honest.

'No. Not really. It's not the fault of anyone down there.'

'Well, it seems we've learned a little about each other today. So how about that drink?'

It was tempting. The wine had given me the taste for more. And more wine would lead to more wine. And possibly sex.

'I can't,' I announced, with genuine regret. 'I've got these notes to type up. Bad novels don't write themselves, you know.'

'I do know,' Luke replied with a light laugh. 'And on that note, I've got a commission that needs finishing. Should get it done in the next day or so. See you on the beach Friday?'

I thought about it for a few seconds. 'Yeah, why not? You gonna come find me down Brokeback?'

Luke flicked a finger off his temple. 'That I will,' he said. 'Would you like a lift anywhere?'

I stood and began to gather my things. 'I'm good, thanks. It's not far.'

'So, Friday, then?'

I gave him a smile. 'Friday. It's a date.'

'Oh, is it, now?'

'We'll see.'

When I got back to my Sophia Classique, 69 was still bent over his laptop, his face etched in concentration. Pulling my notebook from my beach bag, I waved it in the air. 'Suck on this, Mister!' I cried out. 'Now we'll get to see who types, "The End" first!'

He looked up, squinted his face into a frown of recognition and let the beginnings of a smile emerge that never quite reached the finishing line. My notebook was still held aloft and I suddenly felt ridiculous. With a laugh I gave him a thumbs up. He took off his glasses, stood, and from the slight movement in his arm, I fleetingly thought he was shaping up to return the gesture or give a small wave. But then he seemed to think better of it, promptly sat back down, put his glasses on and returned his attention to his laptop.

'Ha!' I said. 'Lagging behind, are we, Mister 69?'

I put my notebook down on the table, cranked up my laptop and as I waited for it to kick into life, went outside and lazily smoked a cigarette in the late afternoon sunshine. I was feeling pretty good about things. Back on track with Susie, *and* I hadn't wee'd myself in public; something that should always be chalked down as a success. Plus I had a whole range of 'no strings attached' Luke scenarios to play around with before Friday. All good. And nothing that lurked in my inbox from Clarke was going to upset me. Besides, his bizarre emails were so much the norm, they were losing their impact. Whatever. Let him crack on with it.

The next two days were good Susie days; I gave her a bit of what for and let her know who was boss. Wednesday saw me scribbling away on the beach, only glancing up occasionally to disinterestedly cast my eye over a young Oriental woman wank off her markedly older male companion. And it appeared she was having a bit of a time with it all. The stubborn old fool looked like he was going to resist coming forever, and for brief periods both of them seemed slightly bored and put out by proceedings. Oh, such yanking and tugging! The frantic, twanged stretching!

He seemingly rallied when she lowered her mouth (with a degree of reluctance, I felt) over his jerking knob. Her long hair obscured all head-dipping activity, but before too long, the old fellow hastily pushed her away by means of a pressed palm to her forehead, and promptly come. Half over his stomach, and half over the side of her face and hair. Which she seemed to take in her stride.

As did us nudeys, who'd been privy to such a lacklustre performance. And rather than titillate, it was just something that held our attention for a short while before we were back to our sunbathing ways and wondering what we'd be having for our tea.

Although a smattering of polite applause all around may have been in order for the woman's heroic efforts...

Thursday was odd, as out of the blue, it rained. Heavily and persistently. Apparently, it was the tail end of Storm Bollockchops (or whatever the latest offering was called) – which, according to our weather forecast, was meant to run out of puff somewhere over the Atlantic and not hit UK shores. I was quite taken aback by the unrelenting and sharp hammering on the caravan roof as I sat at my table, glumly watching 69 buried in his laptop as he tapped away, seemingly oblivious to the darkened skies and roof rattling rain. A real sense of confinement hung over me at the thought of being trapped in my caravan for the day and not getting out to the beach.

To each side of me, families happily flopped on their L-shapes, with a conveyor belt of snacks entering their mouths as they gawped towards their tellys. But all I could think about was being stretched out naked and feeling the sun on my body.

As I sat, eyeing the rain stream down the windows, my thoughts turned to Luke, and how I'd be stretched out naked beside him the next day, feeling his body against mine.

As the families chomped their way through daytime telly, and 69 remained engrossed, I retired to my bedroom and cheered myself up with a consolation wank. I brought my jelly dildo into play, and as I slid it inside me, imagined Luke's cock doing the same. Him using me roughly from behind.

Maybe a cheeky slap or bite of my arse.

Sigh...

When I was done – and feeling a whole heap perkier about life, I had a shower, washed my hair, dressed in a vest and some jog pants, then sat at the table and tackled Susie head-on. What else to do in such weather? Besides, she was the whole reason I was in my Sophia Classique in the first place. Clarke aside.

I looked across to Mister 69. 'Once more unto the breach!' I cried out to his oblivion, as I punched a fist into the air. 'Chaaarrge!!' And into battle I jolly well went – and what a belter of a Susie writeathon I had. I was dead proud of her. And slightly proud of me. It was my best writing session yet. I worked for 9 hours straight, more or less – stopping only for an occasional hoot at 69, a hurried snack, or a huddle in the doorway to stretch my legs and peer up at the incessant rain whilst smoking a cigarette I really shouldn't.

When I ground to a halt, my eyes suddenly tired, the seating beginning to give me arse and back ache, I got up to inspect the fridge. Not much. I needed to do a supermarket shop – but didn't have the energy. I thought of the food on offer in Brightlea. Not ideal, but it'd have to do – one night of something in batter wouldn't kill me.

Feeling the need for some exercise, I unearthed one of the few pairs of socks I'd brought with me, put on my trainers, a hooded top, a light dusting of make-up, stuffed some cash into a zipped pocket on my jog pants and set off.

I was in luck; the rain was beginning to ease and the earlier strong winds that had rattled my caravan seemed to be on their way to London to give it a bit of grief. I pulled up my hood and broke into a light jog. It seemed odd seeing the streets so deserted, with no signs of the usual happy campers milling about. Even when I passed 'Happy Holidays!' they all appeared to be tucked up in their caravans or the club house.

Reaching the main drag, it appeared more depressing than usual in the drizzle and I got an idea of how grim Brightlea might look in the winter months. I scanned ahead of me at the blinking neon signs. The offers of burger meals, kebabs, the best fish and chips in town. One of these would have to do.

Feeling a sudden sense of nostalgia for something I couldn't quite place, I darted into the nearby, 'Cod Almighty' and settled into a seat by the window. Aside from an elderly couple, I was the only other customer there. I scanned the laminate menu, and when a chirpy young waitress came over, ordered my meal.

As I waited for my food to arrive, I peered out the window as rain drops made their jinking journey down. And the memory hit me. A rainy childhood day in North Devon with my parents. Sat in a cafe in Croyde and waiting for the rain to stop, so we could get back out on the path and continue our coastal walk. It gave me a warm feeling to think back to that time as I recalled us all doing big colourful drawings on napkins whilst we dragged out the remains of our drinks.

Both of my parents were very 'outdoorsy' in their pagan, hippyish ways. Mother dropped her Christian name of Sheila a year or so after I was born and reinvented herself as 'Cassandra'. She never wore trousers, whatever the weather – even if it meant going out in wellies and layers of long skirts. She loved nature, the freedom of being outside and despised any cruelty to animals. My father felt the same, and I suspect my feelings about freedom stem from my somewhat unconventional upbringing.

Neither wanted me to refer to them as 'Mum' and 'Dad' (and got angry when I did), instead, they were always Cassandra and Michael. When their friends paid a visit to our house in Streatham, joints were openly smoked in front of me, and at the age of fourteen, when I chanced my luck and asked for a drag, no one told me, 'no'. Sometimes I'd sit in our chaotic lounge while everyone got high, invariably with a few of them dancing to whatever music was being played. Sometimes there'd be a couple who'd play and sing along to the guitars they'd brought with them – and sometimes, Mother would go over to one of the men present, pull him up from his seat or cushion on the floor to get him to dance with her. Without a care as to who was watching, she'd allow his hands to wander all over her body – and hers, his – as Dad and I watched on in a stupefied state.

Even at that age, it didn't take a genius to work out what was going on when Dad unsteadily rose to his feet to follow Mum as she led her man de jour upstairs to the marital bedroom. And I'd be left with drink and fags and joint to amuse myself, while a stoned semi-orgy took place in the lounge. No small wonder then, that a lot of what I witness on nudey beach doesn't bother me.

My parents didn't believe in restrictions or rules. They spoke openly in front of me about sex, and often of their love for one another. A deep love that allowed them to sleep with other people, saying, they only gave their bodies away – not their hearts or minds.

They're still together. And happy. Or so I last heard.

I haven't seen 'Michael' and 'Cassandra' for years. The drugs finally caught up with them and fucked up their minds. They live in Lewes now, not far from Brighton. In semi-squalor in a basement flat. Not quite at retirement age, they live off the state; not wanting to work – or capable of doing so – they happily spend their days stoned. Pity I can't share my marital surname with them.

Over the years, they became increasingly hostile towards me, ever since it became evident I had no desire to live their kind of non-conformist life. It's just something we don't see eye-to-eye about, probably never will, and they whole-heartedly resent me for it. And as their only child, I guess their focus of disappointment and failure has nowhere else to go.

Yet despite it all, they did give me a wonderful early childhood, full of adventures, laughter and love. They opened up my mind to a lot of things – including my creativity – for which I am eternally grateful. As I am for my name. Amber. Which in Ancient Greek translates to Elektron, meaning sun or shining light. I can live with that.

'One regular Cod Almighty,' a voice said, shaking me out of my thoughts. I turned my gaze from the window to the waitress standing beside me. Placing my meal in front of me, I gawped down in disbelief.

'That's a regular?' I asked, incredulously. 'Are you *sure?*'

'That's right,' she replied with a smile. 'Regular.'

'But it's the size of Jaws!' I said with dismay.

The waitress let out a tinkly laugh. 'Well in that case, you should see what our large ones look like! They're our best sellers.'

'Good grief,' I said, poking my fork into the plump flesh. 'No wonder there's an obesity problem.'

She let out another laugh. 'That's right tho', isn't it? Have you got enough sachets of ketchup?'

'Yes. Enough to sink a ship, thank you.'

'You are funny,' she said with a smile. 'Let me know if you need anything else.'

'Just liposuction after all this.'

'Ha!' And then she was gone.

I managed about a third of my meal and it was delicious. And as the drizzle did its stuff on the window, I let my mind drift back to childhood days of sandcastles, pebble art, paddling and eating fish and chips on the beach. With hugs and laughter.

Funny how things turn out.

6.

The Horror Family from Hell

Friday. The good weather returned with force, as though indignant yesterday's poor performance had slurred its reputation. And it was one helluva scorcher. Looking out my front window, I saw Mister 69 packing his stuff into his car, unaware that I sat watching him.

As a last defiant attempt at writing one-upmanship, I began to tap away on my keyboard at turbo speed. Nothing. I began to say aloud the words I typed in an unfamiliar and undulating voice, and wished I could spirit up a pair of intellectual-looking reading glasses to put on. Still nothing. It looked like his car-loading was nearly finished. I could bear it no longer. This called for dramatic action. I stood up, plucked a naughty cigarette from its packet, grabbed my lighter and went outside.

Noticing me descend the caravan steps, 69 finally looked over.

'Oh, hi there!' I said, trying to look surprised to see him.

As he slammed down the boot of his car, I tagged on, 'Off home today?' and immediately cringed at the stupidity of my question.

The briefest of smiles passed over his lips. 'That's right,' he replied curtly as he walked towards the driver door, car keys jingling in a hand.

'I see you've spent a lot of time on your laptop,' I half-blurted. 'Are you a writer by any chance?'

He stopped in his tracks and wore an expression of strained patience. I moved a bit closer to him.

'Sorry,' I said, waving my unlit cigarette in the air. 'I guess it sounds nosey, but I've come here to finish the novel I'm writing and just wondered...' I trailed off. This suddenly felt like a bad idea. And I felt like an idiot; of course novels were *written*.

'No. It's fine,' he said. But sounded like it wasn't. He looked at my cigarette and regarded me with a lofty expression. 'As you seem interested, I've come here to work on my distance course in Physics.' He waved a hand around dismissively, 'I've got a team of builders in at the moment – so just needed somewhere to stay and work while they finish up.'

'Ah.'

I toyed with probing further, but decided against it. We stood in awkward silence for a moment or two.

'And you?' he asked, sounding decidedly bored. 'Your novel – what's it's about?' He drawled out the word 'novel' with a small smile on his face.

I looked down for a moment and twirled the cigarette between my fingers.

I cleared my throat. 'It's a saga,' I began. 'Spanning three generations in Dickensian times. Charting disease, destitution, hardship, sibling rivalry and love. That kind of thing.' I chanced a look; he'd arched one of his eyebrows, either in interest or disbelief. 'Obviously, I can't give you all the ins and outs,' I tagged on.

'No. *Obviously*.' His eyebrow remained arched. It seemed like an interested eyebrow.

'You know how it is,' I said with a small shrug.

We had another mini silence and I wondered if he'd seen through me. He gently bit down on his lip and nodded his head a few times, as though trying to weigh something up.

'You must tell me your name,' he said, suddenly. 'So I can keep my eye out for it in the bookshops.'

I answered in a beat. 'Cassandra Michaels. It won't be out for a while yet, I'm still on the first draft. But I'm hoping next year, sometime.'

'Well, Cassandra, I wish you all the best with it.'

'Thank you. And you with your course,' I replied, sweetly.

'Thanks. And what's the name of your novel?'

My smile froze as I blinked at him dumbly for a few seconds. 'No title yet. I'm still kicking some around.' I managed a pathetic laugh, 'It's daft, but sometimes I think the title's harder to come up with than the rest of it.'

His eyes narrowed. He didn't seem convinced.

'I see,' he said, looking me up and down. 'Well, I must get going...'

'Yes. Safe journey.'

'Thanks.'

A moment later he was in his car and driving away.

I waved him off with my cigarette.

'Repeat after me, Amber, "I am a tit, I am a tit",' I muttered as I waved.

As I walked back to my caravan, I shook my head and asked out loud, 'Why the *hell* did I just do that?'

Inside my Sophia Classique, I put the cigarette back in its packet; it was far too early for one of those. Which I shouldn't have anyway. Thanks Mum and Dad. I might be indifferent to the joint these days, but those pesky critters just keep hanging onto my ankle like a dry-humping terrier.

I sat down at my table, looked across at the empty 69, then down at my laptop.

'Susie girl, forgive me. I was ashamed of you.'

And do you know what that Susie did? She tut-tutted and wagged a finger at me.

'But 69 did turn out to be a bit of prick, didn't he?'

And Susie nodded in agreement.

'Sorry, Susie. I won't do it again. Me and you against the world, right?'

Susie folded her arms. 'And don't you forget it,' she told me.

Susie knows best. I won't forget it.

About an hour later, a cleaner went into 69. They're a right bunch, these cleaners. A real mixed bag. And I think I've sussed out the wheat from the chaff when it comes to duster waving and Domestos duties.

Take the one who went in to clear up Mister 69's shit and toe nail clippings (the snotty bastard) – he's a good 'un. Young lad – looks like he's in his early twenties – he rocks up with his headphones firmly in place and cracks on. Some of them (the very worst being the young females) are in and out in five minutes. They get in. Put the telly on. Whip their phones out to see if the world's coped without them since they last looked. Then aimlessly shake out the cushions to the L-shaped whilst watching whatever daytime bollocks is on. Then it's a quick damp cloth over the sink and surfaces. A disappear off to change the sheets and probably a quick swill of a tap in the bathroom, a flush of the loo, a squirt of bleach, then a couple of more minutes staring at the telly between picking up any bits on the floor, or a lacklustre sweep with the resident soft broom. One last phone check. And they're off.

Laddo across the way takes pride in his work, minimum wage or not. And he's got a bit of energy to him. He gives the windows a quick buff, the floor a going over with the Henry hoover he's brought with him, checks the cupboards to see they're still fully stocked and tidy, before cleaning around the sink, cupboard doors, surfaces, oven top and the dining table. He does all this with the windows wide open to get some fresh air in.

He then disappears off to the bedrooms and bathroom with his carrier of cleaning products, re-emerging about ten minutes later with the dirty sheets all bundled up. I reckon he must have been the one to clean my Sophia Classique – it was spotless when I arrived.

On balance, I'd say, based on what I've seen to date, the male cleaners piss over the women here and do a much more thorough job. And by some distance.

It sure is a cocking mad world out there.

I think Susie's having a sulk because of my low quality behaviour, as she's showing me her pearly white arse cheeks and has put the brakes on. Again. At times like this, I'd love to bung her a fiver to continue, but alas, writing doesn't work like that. How remiss that no bugger's bothered to explain this to me.

I stared at my screen. It wasn't budging. I looked around. Laddo was now in number 70, going about his business. It seemed as though all the caravans around me had bailed out today. Give it a few hours and there'd be a load of fresh blood arriving later for their happy holidays. Good luck to them, I say; I'm sure Cod Almighty will be on red alert.

I spent another ten minutes starting sentences that didn't work, then began to get frustrated. It was no good.

'You are one pest of a woman,' I said loudly, before saving my work and shutting down my laptop. 'I said "sorry" didn't I? Pah!'

What to do now if writing was on hold until Susie saw fit to come out of her trailer? I looked across to the trees and let my thoughts wander to my meeting with Luke that afternoon. Immediately, I felt the familiar strong throb between my legs; seemed I was feeling frustrated in more ways than one. I thought about retiring to the bedroom to give myself some relief, but decided against it; staying in a prolonged state of sexual arousal could be highly enjoyable. And bring out the animal in me.

Naughty Amber.

I looked around and tried to ignore my pulsating clit. Okay. Some tidying and washing up could be in order. And then a drive in the battered old Golf for some much needed shopping. Yeah, that sounded a plan.

When I returned and parked up, I was eager to get inside; Susie had made a surprise and ill-timed return as I'd wandered the fruit and veg aisle, filling my head with ideas that urgently needed transferring to my notebook. As I got out of the Golf, I discovered numbers 69, 70 and 55 had all seemingly been invaded by the horror mob from hell. There were screeching and squealing children running around, kicking balls, each other or whacking the bejesus out of one another with plastic swords. Or in some instances, their fists. Parents shouted at them. And one other.

What looked like a set of grandparents, sat on fold-up chairs, contentedly munching crumbling sausage rolls, impervious to the unfolding mayhem around them. And from what I could see, all the adults had either a can of lager or glass of wine in their hands.

As I got out of the car and began to wrestle a couple of hefty shopping bags from the boot, two children ran past hollering at the top of their voices. One of them bumped into me. Or rather, bounced off me. 'Careful!' I called out. I looked over my shoulder to some of the adults for support – but they were oblivious. Fresh foaming cans were being opened, wine poured, and cigarettes sparked up. (God, I *really* must stop – it looks just awful.) It was evident they were all together.

I let myself in, dumped the bags and closed the door. The noise from outside easily penetrated the sanctuary of my Classique. I stood by the window, hands on hips, and watched them with a growing feeling of resignation. It would be impossible to work with this racket going on. A woman stood drinking in number 70's doorway spotted me in the window and raised her can towards me in a mock toast. 'Alright, love?' she bellowed. I dipped back from view. This was going to be horrendous.

Thankfully, my fears were short-lived. As I unpacked my groceries – unable to do nothing but listen to their coarse voices ringing out – details about their stay quickly emerged; they were down for a wedding. (I think some of the brats were going to be bridesmaids and page boys.) Whose wedding? No idea. But the reception was being held in the upstairs function room at The Captain's Table (as I could probably have wagered) – where they were all going tonight. Amongst all the talk of getting, "shit-faced" and "wankered", there was a glorious mention of, '... when we get back on Monday...'. Oh, joy! They were only here for the weekend! And they'd be out for all, or most of Saturday. Probably hung over on Sunday and L-shaped flopping. Then on Monday morning, gone.

Gone.

Goodbye.

Ta-ta.

My dipped mood soared and I almost felt euphoric. I went back to the window to survey the chaos.

'Go on, do your worst,' I half-laughed as I looked out at them.

Disposable barbeques were being produced (a serious Brightlea Sands no-no). People huddled around them, arguing about how best to light them. A bare-chested man stood belching and drinking whilst holding a packet of frozen burgers. Paper plates were being taken out of cellophane wrapping. And next to 69, a little girl was squatting and urinating on the grass. She caught me watching and eyed me with a scowl as she emptied her bladder.

'Charming,' I said, out loud, 'how totally charming,' and in the instant before I averted my eyes, she scrunched her face into a hard expression and poked her tongue out at me.

But I didn't care. They'd be gone soon enough. Back to their swamps. Then, bring on the next batch, I say.

I made a sandwich and took it, along with my notebook, to my bedroom at the back of the caravan and closed the door. The racket outside became marginally more bearable.

After I'd eaten, I opened my notebook and

between managing to ignore my continual throbbing and brief thoughts of Luke, jotted down everything Susie had whispered to me in the supermarket. I wasn't letting those knuckle-dragging fuckers get in the way of me and literary stardom. Or a good afternoon of potential filth.

Ooh!

Keep writing, Amber... stay focused, girl.

The barbeque was in full burnt-burger-flow when I stepped out of the caravan with my yoga mat and beach bag.

'Hello, love!' the bare-chested oaf called over. 'Fancy a sausage?'

I threw him a withering look as one of the women dished out a hard slap to his shoulder and a sharply barked, 'Stop it!'

I turned around and briskly began to walk away, not wanting to spend a moment more than necessary in the immediate vicinity of these people.

A child's voice rang out after me. 'Stuck up cow!' I didn't need to look to know it belonged to the young girl I'd seen using the grass as a toilet earlier.

'Happy holidays,' I muttered to myself with a small laugh. 'Roll on Monday.'

I quickly dismissed all thoughts of static-based hill billies and their food poisoning extravaganza and quickly pushed on. I had bigger Cod Almighty's to fry.

Before too long, I had to slow down and take a drink of water – it really was a humdinger of a hot one. By the time I hit the main drag, beads of perspiration ran freely from my forehead. I squinted up at the sky through my sunglasses – I was going to be as brown as a berry before the day was out. Thankfully, I'd bought a fresh bottle of suntan lotion earlier, along with extra drinking water – which I was sure I'd be sweating out without any problems.

As I reached the Captain's Table, I let out a small snort; they had no idea what was coming their way, with the wedding group from hell due for touchdown.

'Unlucky,' I murmured.

When I hit the front and saw that the tide was coming in, I groaned in disappointment. I had been hoping to avoid a cliff climb in the oppressive heat. With a heavy sigh, I eyed the step pathway and unconvincingly told myself to think of the exercise. But as I began my ascent, soon knew it was going to be one killer of a hoof.

I passed gasping stragglers on the way; some who were making their way to the beach, and those who'd had enough sunbathing for the day and were waving the white flag. When I finally stepped onto the pebbles, sweaty and breathless, it was with no small amount of relief. Taking a moment to catch my breath, I looked at the shimmering heat haze ahead of me, and man, oh man, I'd never seen the place so busy. Once I'd sufficiently recovered, I picked my way through the nudeys, spotting a few who already looked like lobsters. (Ouch! Watch out for those sunburnt bits, guys!) It immediately became apparent the vast majority of beachgoers seemed unwilling to walk any further than necessary in the scorching heat, as they were nigh on lying on top of one another down the near end.

I scanned around for Luke – not really believing I'd see him (particularly this early) anywhere close to the beach's access point – so felt no surprise when not spotting his shaved balls soaking up the sunshine amongst the other sardines. Crazy really, but I was surprisingly keen to see him again. And as for the rest...

As I pushed on further, the nudey congregation became markedly more spread out and sparse. I passed the occasional lone old boy, stretched out and wrinkling in the heat. A few middle-aged couples dotted here and there. The rare sight of another solo female; my age(ish), Amazonian in stature and virtually spread-eagled on her towel. (Good luck with that...) And an extremely fat young bloke with badly sunburnt shoulders, sitting at the water's edge as gentle waves lapped over his feet and legs. Brokeback Bay was further along yet. I shielded my eyes and peered ahead. It seemed pretty busy down there, but in my favoured spot, a little way before Brokeback, there was plenty of space. Perfect.

Despite the temperature and steady trickle of sweat running down my spine, I picked up pace and almost immediately stumbled as I slid heavily on the uneven pebbles.

'Steady, Amber,' I muttered aloud. 'Someone's keen to get laid today.'

I righted myself and continued in my usual cautious fashion.

When I reached a good, level patch against the cliff edge, I looked again for Luke. Not here. Yet. I gratefully dropped my bag, unrolled my yoga mat and had a drink of water before quickly stripping off and laying down. Since the novelty factor of my first day, I'd taken to applying my first round of suntan lotion back in my Classique, to give it a chance to soak in before my 'exposure' to the sun. Plus, (and as I've learned here) the decrepit pervs were clued up enough to know fresh arrivals were more prone to giving themselves a rub down with the lotions and oils once they've disrobed. Therefore, affording them some very welcome tug fodder on the house.

Oh, those dirty old meerkats.

I stretched out and felt the sun swoop down and flood over my body. The sea lazily rolled back and forth over the pebbles, making a soothing sound that wiped away any lingering thoughts of yobs and urinating children. Instead, I let my thoughts drift to Luke. Had I already decided I was going to have sex with him? Probably. I could sure do with some no strings action and was very definitely on heat in the heat.

'Maybe I'll just use him for sex,' I said out loud, feeling playful and naughty in the sunshine. I let out a small laugh.

Knowing that no one was within reasonable distance, I reached down and cupped a hand tight between my legs, and with the ball of my palm kneaded my aching clitoris. I then crooked a finger and pushed its tip into my vagina. Wet. Very.

Withdrawing my hand, I tasted my finger.

Beautiful.

I was primed and ready to go.

Rolling onto my front, I opened my legs slightly, thought delicious rude thoughts, and dropped off into a contented doze.

7.

A Quick Dip in Brokeback Bay

Luke never showed up. He was a frustrating (in every sense of the word) no-show and my feelings flip-flopped between anger and indignation – he'd snubbed me, *particularly* when I'd decided to have sex with him. Ouch! Was that my ego wincing in pain? I think it was. Then there was concern – was he okay? Unwell? Or just tied up finishing his commission?

I'd been on the beach for the best part of three hours, with hopes of Luke's arrival fading with each passing half hour. I tossed aside the book I'd been reading, sat up and looked around. Plenty of people still seemed to be enjoying the sun down the far end, while in the other direction, Brokeback, the faintest strains of music could be heard and it looked as though some kind of beach party was taking place.

They were certainly going to have the perfect evening for it.

I reached into my sunglasses case and plucked out my cigarette. Once lit, I blew out a lengthy plume of smoke and had a think. I wasn't used to being stood up. Particularly if I was naked at the time. That Luke had some explaining to do. And apologising.

Suddenly, the music from Brokeback seemed a little louder, which in turn, made me briefly wonder what barbecue bedlam had unfolded back at the caravan park while I'd been waiting like an idiot for the invisible man to rock up. Maybe the entire place had been burned down by now. Or maybe a robust family brawl had been enjoyed by one and all. I thought about going back, but the idea of seeing them gargle cans of lager, or hear them let rip with thunderous farts and belches, unsurprisingly, held zero-minus appeal. Maybe they were already deeply entrenched at The Captain's Table, but there was no way I wanted to risk going back so soon.

Yes, that music was definitely louder. I looked across to Brokeback and saw a few of the guys standing and chatting. One of them – who I'd often 'lovely day' with – gave me a wave and enthusiastically flagged for me to join them.

I gave him a smile, wave backed and let out a small laugh.

'Well, not quite what I planned for today,' I said as

I waved. 'But this looks like the best offer I'm going to get.'

I turned my wave into a thumbs up, stubbed out my cigarette and reached for my dress: I might be going to a nudey gay beach party, but no way was I trotting over there starkers with the risk of falling over and literally going tits up on these pesky pebbles.

One *does* has standards after all.

To be honest, I don't recall a lot of the finer detail about that evening. I got really quite squiffy and really quite quickly. After I'd been welcomed and said some hellos, I was invited to 'plonk myself down' and 'have a drink, love'. On offer was the choice of wine or lager from the cooler bags scattered around. Requesting some wine, I gratefully took a generously filled plastic glass from a deeply bronzed old man dressed only in a red and white neckerchief, and placed my yoga mat and towel close to Penguin Man – him being the most familiar of the group.

After I sat down and began to tug my dress up over my head, I suddenly felt hesitant and self-conscious – I wasn't used to being in such close proximity to anyone when undressing, let alone a group. Pausing to take a bravado-inducing large mouthful of wine, I reminded myself that these guys had no interest in my body – aside from the usual passing beach curiosity. Plus, as I recognised most of them, they'd seen it all before when walking past me to reach Brokeback. Without losing a beat in my chat with Penguin Man about the blistering heat, I whipped off my dress, remained sitting up and continued our exchange between sips of wine. It felt like another notch in my nudey liberation. And in imitation of some of the guys, I treated myself to the unprecedented luxury of sitting cross-legged on the beach.

As the drinks slid down, cigarettes and roll-ups were passed around, and agreeable summer tunes filled the air as the soft, early evening breeze blew a perfect warmth over my face and body. I chatted to this one and that. Nothing too taxing. It was all very pleasant, friendly and easy going. From memory, amongst some of the guys I spoke to, were a young couple down from London for the weekend, who visited Brightlea every summer. They seemed smitten and finished each other's sentences. Then there was another guy (I don't recall any of their names), who used to own an antique shop in Exeter and knew about The Grub Shack, having eaten there occasionally. He was pretty interesting. Although I think I may have bored him with my squiffy waffling.

Our nudity seemed totally incidental. And despite the wine increasingly fuelling my day-long feeling of randiness, and harbouring the feeling I'd gatecrashed a boys' camping trip, I felt mellow and relaxed. And when The Beach Boys', 'God Only Knows,' filled the air of a perfect summer's evening, a feeling of contentment consumed us, as we sat quietly singing or humming along, each caught up in our thoughts.

I remember thinking about Spencer.

The disposable barbeques had been lit prior to my arrival, and sat within makeshift, circular walls of pebbles. Butcher's bangers, burgers and marinated chicken were on standby, and an extremely tall and skinny guy (with an extremely long and skinny cock) announced he also had large bowls of salad and rice waiting for us in his cooler bags.

'Looks like a few of us will have to eat with our hands,' someone said. 'I don't think there's enough cutlery to go around.' But I couldn't care less about having a plastic knife and fork; I was getting hungry and *really* needed some food to soak up all the wine.

'Fancy a swim before dinner?' I heard from above me.

I squinted up to see a dark haired guy with a great smile and smooth olive skin. Early thirties? I'd spotted him earlier, what with his good looks and seemingly easy manner as he chatted and laughed with the couple from London. Then there'd been his small wave when he saw me glancing his way. He now stood in front of me. My eyes passed over him. Fit. Very. What a shame.

Same old, same old...

I remember joking about not being able to get in/ out of the sea in one piece, and being left stranded on the shore, to hopelessly flap about for all eternity. He held out a hand, 'Come on,' he laughed. 'I'll take care of you.'

Despite losing some of its strength, the sun still beat down with intent and I dabbed at the beads of perspiration on my forehead (although I don't think the wine overly helped matters...). I looked across to the sea; the water seemed highly appealing and was being enjoyed by some of the other guys as they splashed around, swam or simply waded to cool down. It really did look enticing. Besides, when else would I get the opportunity to go in the sea with assistance?

'Yeah, why not?' I said, taking his hand and letting him pull me to my feet. It took me a blurry second or two to realise that I'd never stood up naked before, let alone walked on the beach with no clothes on. But hey ho. I was a bit drunk. The guys were gay. And before I knew it, I was being led over the uncomfortable pebbles as though I were a toddler.

I recall having a few unstylish moments of sliding and nearly falling over. Embarrassed snorty laughs. Grabbing onto Olive Man's arm. Him saying, 'Steady, now'. Or something like that. And I do recall the sea being warmer than I'd expected. And that we gingerly edged our way forward, still hand-in-hand, until the pebbles suddenly turned to soft sand underfoot and the water reached past our waists. We let go of hands. And I began to swim away from the shore.

But the sun and its reflection off the water dazzled my eyes. I abruptly stood and rubbed them, briefly feeling disorientated and unsteady. I felt hands on my waist. Olive Man behind me, his head against mine, whispering, 'Are you okay?' Or something similar. A slight squeeze or stroke of my back? Maybe both? His chest pressed up against me.

I know I pulled away and childishly splashed him. I think I might have tried to dunk his head under the water, then attempted to swim away to avoid getting the same treatment back, but soon felt a firm hand around an ankle pulling me backwards. I must have twisted onto my back in a futile attempt to free myself, because when he let go and I placed my feet on the sand, we stood facing one another and laughingly catching our breaths.

He pulled me towards him. Flesh on flesh. My erect nipples on his chest. Him erect. Pressing against me.

'Shall we?' he said, with a smile and both hands on my arse cheeks.

I remember I laughed at that point.

'Oh, how would that work?' I think I asked him. Or maybe I just pointed out that he was gay. Or perhaps I asked if he was bi. Or straight. Or the man on the moon. Whatever. Who cared?

We ended up fucking in the sea. Deep, probing kisses. Two strangers on heat. His fingers between my legs. Then, inside. His free hand kneading my tits and squeezing nipples in turn. I stroked his solid cock. And reached to massage his balls. Everything was spinning around and bobbing away in the waves and the heat and with the numbness of the wine. I have no precise recollection of the exact order everything went, but at the point I had my legs wrapped around Olive Man's waist and he pushed his cock into me with no messing, I knew it was what I'd been craving all day.

All awareness of the guys on the beach or in the sea was lost. I was somewhere else completely. In a blurry mini bubble of pleasure. But I do know, when I arched my back, and as the back of my head dipped into the water, Olive Man pushed deeper into me and bent his head to roughly suck and bite my nipples, making me explode in waves of melting gold. And I very much remember feeling Olive Man's pulsating cock send his come hurtling deep inside me. Yeah, I think I'll be remembering that for some time yet – a huge advocate of the visuals of come I may be, but to feel a guy pumping his load into you, rates as a closely run second.

We hugged and laughed afterwards. And I think he said, 'Well, that was rather nice.' Or maybe it was me. And Olive Man got me out of the sea and we hobbled back safely to my yoga mat. I know someone passed me a cigarette and said something like, 'Looks like you'll be needing this, love.' But that aside, I don't recall anyone making any comment about what had just happened. Which, in any instance, would have been a bit harsh, as during the rest of my time there, at least two couples – London boys included, got it on in the small recesses that seemed purpose built for the occasion.

I watched on in idle curiosity as the couple with the least privacy, lay spooning and having sex. It was the first time I'd seen gay guys fucking that wasn't in a porn film, and felt a degree of surprise to find it quite erotic.

Olive Man stayed and sat beside me as we enjoyed the food kindly provided by Mister Tall & Skinny. I happily devoured a hefty burger and a few pieces of chicken, sobered up a bit, then drank more wine.

At some point, Olive Man returned to his original spot, while I stayed put. I talked to some of the guys. Laughed. Smoked. Drank. Enjoyed the music. And enjoyed a total feeling of liberation. Luke really had missed out. In more ways than one.

It was only when a few people began to dress and gather their stuff to leave, did it cross my mind to do the same. Although not overly late, it was getting on. Besides, I didn't fancy the walk back to my

Sophia Classique any more drunk than I already was. Number 56 already seemed so very far away.

After saying my goodbyes and offering my thanks and gratitude for the food, drink, cigarettes and roll-ups (oh Christ, *how many* did I smoke?), I ended up walking back to the main drag with the young London couple, another couple and Olive Man, and along the way we chatted about... whatever. The earlier high tide had long since receded, and in my squiffy condition, felt grateful for the easy option of making tracks back around the cliff base.

Before I knew it, I was saying my goodbyes to the guys with hugs and pecks on the cheeks before they drifted away. Leaving myself and Olive Man waving them off like a set of parents.

'Well, then...' Olive Man said with a smile, once we'd stopped waving.

'Well, then...' I replied with a laugh.

Olive Man put out his hand and spoke in a clipped upper class mock military voice, 'Well, I must say, it was splendid meeting you and I'd like to thank you for such a memorable afternoon. Very good, indeed. Well done.'

I took his hand, shook it briskly and tried to mimic his voice. 'Very glad you enjoyed it, old chap. Yes, it was all rather tremendous, wasn't it? See you on the battleground again, sometime?'

'Not sure, Carruthers. Depends if old wifey ever lets me out again.'

For an instant I felt like I wanted to ask Olive Man a lot of questions. But in the next, realised I didn't need to know. None of it mattered.

I reverted to my normal voice. 'Well, you take care,' I said, giving him a hug and quick kiss on the lips.

'And you take care, too,' Olive Man said, before returning the kiss and giving one of my arse cheeks a firm squeeze.

He gave me a smile, turned, and walked towards the car park. Olive Man was gone. The dream random fuck. I blew a kiss his way. 'Adios, Olive Man!' I called after him, as I flicked a salute off my temple. Then with a hoof of my yoga mat, I began the walk back and soon reached The Captain's Table, where from inside, the most appalling racket was booming out. I glanced at the street blackboard which informed me, 'Friday Nite is House Doubles & Karaoke Nite' – The Horror Family from Hell would doubtless be in seventh heaven. I laughed out loud at the image of some hapless staff trying to control them. Good luck with that, I thought, and continued on my way.

When I neared Flabby's, some of the lads were sitting outside on the decked area.

'Come on in, Blondie Bondie!' shouted Steve Two when he saw me. Beside him sat a glum Fucker Frank, bare-chested and displaying the sorest looking vest-shaped sunburn I'd seen for years. I suppressed a snort and paused to think about going in. I was still squiffy enough to be stupid enough to fancy a nightcap. *And* felt in a highly flirtatious and invincible mood. Had I not, after all, just enjoyed the ultimate no strings sex? Was I not a temptress of the seas? The Goddess of Sea Shagging? Albeit, a slightly pissed one?

'You're breaking my heart, here, Double O Stone!' Steve added, as he cupped his hands over his chest. I smiled at his nonsense, hoisted up my mat and feeling playful (and in dire need of the loo), went in.

I had a good night on the lash with the lads. To round off my great afternoon and early evening with the guys. I was drunk enough to fancy myself a bit and flirted with Steve Two, teased Fucker Frank about his sunburn and gave Matty a big smacker on his cheek when he arrived after his shift at the chippie. He went bright red and dipped his head, so I waffled on at length about how much I'd enjoyed his fish and chips, which forced him to interrupt and point out he didn't work at Cod Almighty – it was The Fryer's Delight. In the next town. As he'd already told me. More than once.

Ah. That darned wine/vodka combo strikes again...

And almost went for the double – as I very nearly, accidentally fessed up about nudey beach, when Jen, top Flabby's barmaid, admired and commented on my deepening tan when I approached the bar with Steve Two to get a round in. She asked whereabouts I went sunbathing on the beach, as she'd never seen me around when getting the occasional opportunity to go there between shifts.

'Oh, I don't use *that* beach!' I exclaimed, without thinking. Jen and Steve Two exchanged glances and replied in unison, 'Oh, really?' with surprised expressions.

'Ooh,' said Steve Two, edging closer to me. 'Tell me more.'

I don't know if my expression gave anything away, but I had to swiftly back pedal. I looked at them blankly for a beat or two, and somehow dragged out a semi-plausible lie. 'No, no!' I began, waving a theatrical hand in the air, 'I go down the far left to where I call, 'Susie's Beach' – she's the character in my novel. You know? So I kinda christened the place I sunbathe, 'Susie's Beach'. It's where I get most of my work done.'

I examined their faces, which seemingly looked satisfied.

But Jen probed further. 'So, do you go topless down there or something – you haven't got any strap marks?' I inwardly sighed; only a woman could pick up on that. And my sundress that day had a revealing racer back. I summoned a functioning brain cell. 'Ha! As if! Nope – just a halter neck bikini, which I untie when I'm lying on my front. I just hate those strap marks, don't you?'

That seemed to do the trick. 'Oh yeah,' Jen agreed. 'Sometimes, I'd rather get a spray tan than have those marks.'

'Exactly,' I replied.

Eager to close down the subject, I began to pick up some of the drinks, and looked to Steve Two, who was yet to lift any of the pints in front of him and instead stood deep in thought.

'Coming?' I asked him, with a nod towards the drinks.

Steve threw me his pulling smile, 'All night long, Blondie, all night long.' And as he began to put his hands around the glasses, gave me a sideways glance that I couldn't read.

I'm hoping I got away with it. Dumb ass pissy pants I can be, sometimes.

We carried the drinks outside and continued in the time-honoured pub tradition of talking bollocks and cracking bad jokes. Wayne made an appearance and regaled us with how he'd just bundled a protesting fruit machine scammer through the door. After bundling him into it a few times. And there was even a rare show from Steve One, who sat in his normal mute state of drunkenness with that idiot's grin on his face.

I managed another half of a cigarette before waving the smoking white flag – I'd *really* had enough for one day – and suddenly, like the flick of a switch, everything became a blurry haze; one minute I was sat on Steve Two's lap, drinking vodka and imitating his click-clicks out the side of his mouth and the next, delivering another smacker onto Matty's reddening face, before waving my goodbyes from the pavement, doing a twirl, taking a bow, and making wobbly tracks back to my Classique using my yoga mat as a steadying walking stick.

I made it back in one piece. Just. I drunkenly leant against the outside of my caravan, gazed up at the blurry, clear sky with its jazzy pattern of stars and took some deep breaths in a futile attempt to clear my head. Aside from the distant sounds of a Friday night late TV show coming from someone's van, it was peaceful. It seemed like the Horror Family from Hell were still entrenched in their shots and karaoke evening. Marvellous. Perhaps they'll push on through until the wedding.

With a last deep intake of night air, I let myself in, unceremoniously dumped everything on the L-shaped, before entering the bedroom to half-heartedly pull the curtain across and land heavily and gratefully onto my bed.

The following morning I squinted myself awake to my first real hangover at Brightlea and man, oh man, it was a real stinker. I woke with a dry mouth, a full bladder and the cringing memory outline of wandering around Flabby's like some ageing Lolita. I groaned myself up into a sitting position and saw that the dress I was still wearing, had ridden above my waist. I edged forward on my arse cheeks, pushed myself up and made a very welcome trip to the toilet. As I sat, I pulled my dress over my head, and took in its stale smell of tobacco on the way. And as more snippets of the previous day swept through my mind and brutally challenged me about their accuracy, I let out a small groan and put my head in my heads. I felt truly terrible.

There was nothing else to do but take some headache pills, drink a lot of water and go back to bed. I was not fit for purpose. And the whole world could just fuck right off. Susie included. After finishing in the bathroom, I wandered naked into my kitchen area, pulled a 2-litre bottle of water out of the fridge, some pills from my handbag on the counter and shuffled back to the bedroom. On the edge of the bed, I gulped down nearly a third of the bottle and popped three pills before gratefully flopping back down and pulling the thin quilt over me. As I began to drift off to a faraway place that didn't feature me making a drunken arse of myself, I became vaguely aware of The Horror Family from Hell shouting and screaming themselves into the organisation it took to get to a wedding on time. I jolted slightly out of my slide into unconsciousness before rolling over and crashing into a deep sleep.

I woke a couple of hours later and didn't feel quite so sickly grim, but a post-booze downer had me firmly by the throat. After drinking more water, I got up, unearthed some shorts and a vest from my wardrobe, and with a degree of difficulty, put them on. I shuffled into the lounge/kitchen area and surveyed the dumped beach bag, the yoga mat that had rolled onto the floor and the kicked off sandals, one of which sat upside down on the L-shaped. Vowing to deal with them later, I set about sorting out some breakfast. Or lunch. Or just food in any form – as long as it was simple, and after a brief inspection of the fridge, settled on tea and buttered wholemeal toast. The tentative nibbles soon became mouthfuls and within minutes I could feel the bread's beneficial sponge-like effect on the dreaded wine/vodka combo. When *will* I learn? Stupid, *stupid* Amber.

I sat at the dining table for a while and took my time over the mug of tea. My low mood hadn't improved and as my mind drifted back to my escapade with Olive Man, I could derive no pleasure, while my antics at Flabby's just had me cringing. I got up, stretched and carried my tea over to the L-shaped, where I sat down and rummaged through my beach bag. Extracting my phone, I scanned through my emails and felt no surprise to find an offering from Clarke, telling me I thought I was clever – but was really, so very, very stupid.

A dunce, in fact. A stupid, stupid dunce. A stupid, fucking dunce. And so on.

It was the icing on my Horror Hangover cake. I didn't feel clever at all. In fact, I felt decidedly un-clever. I gazed over to the nearby caravans and with a feeling of resigned sadness, took in the strewn litter and areas of burnt grass around the disposable barbeques that still had remnants of charred meat caked to them. Then I glared bitterly at my laptop and told myself I had no writing talent. Or talent of any kind. Clarke was right. I was a stupid fucking dunce.

'*Never* fancy yourself, Amber,' I faintly muttered.

God, I was feeling I was like a huge, clammy, headachy ball of self-pitying crap.

Feeling an urgent need to go outside for some fresh air – but very definitely not a cigarette – I got up, walked over and opened the caravan door. About to take a step down, I noticed I was about to put my foot on something. Quickly retracting, I stood in the caravan's doorway and looked down in numbed disbelief at a doll on the top step. It looked like a Barbie doll, but its head had been removed and placed about an inch from the body. What would have originally been longer blonde hair had been hacked off into a crude crop and a slash of bright red lipstick stretched beyond the doll's mouth to each side of its face. The undressed body lay on its back with the legs apart and knees bent.

Childlike handwriting just about managed to squeeze the word 'SLUT' lengthways along the body in the same red lipstick.

I glanced over to number 70 – where I believed the young girl was staying. And then the other caravans. Nothing. No one, that I could see. I looked back down at the doll – it seemed grotesque and sinister in equal measure. Why would a child do something like that? Was it even the child? I stood for a while, alternating my gaze between the trees and the doll, trying to make some sense of it, and through the cloud of hangover, I remembered walking naked into the kitchen area that morning to get the water and headache tablets. I might have managed the bedroom curtains (of sorts) the night before – but the lounge/kitchen ones had been an ask too far, given the state I was in, and obviously hadn't even featured on my pissed radar of things to do before passing out.

And now, it seemed evident that I'd 'let myself down' in front of the Horror Family from Hell. During the hangover that just kept giving. Could anything get more *low calibre* than that?

I wanted the doll gone. Away. And gone. And back to its rightful owner. The satanic pissing little shit. Crouching down, I picked up the head and body, and as though nipping through the car park of a bullion warehouse on a midnight heist, looked this way and that, before darting across with my hangover and placing the two parts on 70's doorstep, checking around again and dashing back inside my Classique and swiftly closing the door behind me.

Leaning against it, a burst of adrenalin momentarily elevated my mood, and I even managed a brief outburst of crazed laughter.

'That is nuts!' I told myself. 'Seriously, nuts!'

But within seconds, the downer had me back in its grip again as the heavy hangover cloud swallowed me up, with the image of the ruined doll leaving an increasingly bad taste. I thought about the word on its torso, but my groggy and depressed brain was incapable of processing anything further.

'Oh fuck,' I groaned. I just didn't know what to do to make myself feel better.

I achieved the sum total of zero that day, and spent most of it flopped on the L-shaped, flicking TV channels and unable to concentrate on anything. I wanted the day to be over and was full of self-hatred for wasting valuable writing time.

At ten o'clock, I finally put myself out of my misery and went to bed.

I was stirred from my sleep at about 1.30am. The Horror Family from Hell were evidently returning from the wedding reception. Hollers and hoots and foul language filled the air, and as I groggily rolled over and pulled the quilt up over my head, I clearly heard a male voice bellow out, 'What the fuck is this?' and could only assume he was referring to the decapitated doll on the step. I couldn't hear a clear response – there was just a lot of squawking and screeching from several females in the party, followed by the obvious chastising of (I assumed) the antichrist child, as I did manage to make out a girl's screamed denial of, "not doing nothing wrong". Feeling too tired to concern myself, I buried myself deeper under the quilt and entered a fitful sleep as the al fresco nightcap got into full swing. I have no idea what time it finished, but at some point the racket came to a close and I finally dropped back into heavy and undisturbed sleep.

And suddenly it was Sunday proper. A whole new day. When I tentatively opened my eyes and dared to think about it, I discovered that I actually felt alright. I was human again. And it felt beyond great. I swished myself out of bed, had some breakfast, tidied up, sang a few tunes during a lengthy shower, put on clean clothes and cranked up the laptop. Oh, the joy of being hangover-free! Thank you, Lord!

Never again – I promise!

Lightly humming to myself, I flicked through my notebook between glancing out the windows. Just as I thought. More crap all over the place and still unconscious. It was impossible to see if the doll was amongst the carnage, but as I felt no urge to re-visit anything from the day before, quickly pushed it to the back of my mind. Instead, I set about Susie with a renewed energy and optimism, and worked all day to atone for my sins. No beach. No cigarettes – well, just the one. And no alcohol. I worked, drank water, had a break to do some exercises, and when a bleary-eyed Horror Family from Hell finally emerged from their caravans, they seemed too done in to fight, squabble or screech – even the children – and did me the honour of fucking off to the clubhouse for the discount roast on offer. Marvellous.

I worked hard. My mood was chipper. My hangover all but a distant memory. At one point, I let my mind wander back to my shenanigans in the sea, but quickly dismissed any idea of retreating to the bedroom to replay it in full – Susie needed me. In fact, she'd been crying out for me.

At throwing out time, The Horrors finally returned from the clubhouse (or whichever unfortunate licensed premises they'd deemed worthy of their presence), where they'd obviously been indulging in more than a few hair of the dogs. But in comparison, their noise level was quite tame. By that time, I'd put Susie to bed and was stretched out on the L-shaped listening to some music. Some cans got opened. Some belching ensued. A few shouts, some swearing, a half-hearted attempt at an argument and then they were gone for the night.

And the next day they were gone, gone. Leaving well after the 10am check-out time, they finally got the wagons rolling closer to eleven. A final scowl from the Satan Child as she rummaged a finger deep inside a nostril; some hard-faced looks from others; and a female voice loudly saying something about, 'that fucking bitch thinking she's better than us.'

And they were gone.

The cleaner looked distraught when he came to clean their caravans. And around them. The burnt grass, the litter, the food waste. As I watched him tread about carefully, putting rubbish into a black bin bag, I saw him reach under the steps of number 70 and pull out both parts of the doll and look at them incredulously with a slow shake of his head before dropping them into his bag.

Yep. I guess all of Brightlea sighed a huge sigh of relief that morning.

Happy Holidays, indeed.

Note to self: Leave a generous tip for whoever cleans my Sophia Classique when I leave – most of these guys and gals deserve a medal.

8.

A Dirty Habit

It turns out, that while I'd been otherwise engaged – by getting drunk, shagging in the sea and dealing with a monstrous hangover – our Susie's been going a bit apeshit crazy...

Having quickly established herself as an office dynamo, she's also been giving her colleagues a bit of what for by letting them know what a broad selection of crisply ironed blouses look like.

Take that, Motherfuckers! Boof!

Thursday nights sees Susie joining the gang from the surgery to attend a weekly quiz night at The Old Wreck, Trewithiel's one and only pub, where their team name of Doctor's Orders never fails to raise a titter amongst fellow quizzers. On occasion, the young and dashing Doctor Rogers will join them, which leaves our Susie a bit hot and bothered under her carefully laundered collar. Such looks, such charm, such *manners* this bobby-dazzler of a GP possesses. Sometimes, she thinks of surreptitiously undoing her top button to afford Doctor Rogers a tantalising snapshot of her porcelain white décolletage. But invariably Susie shies away from such sluttish behaviour and pats her button as firm confirmation of her decision to abstain. If she is to win over Doctor Rogers, Susie believes it will not be by behaving like some shameless Jezebel.

Friday afternoons see head receptionist – the motherly Maureen, produce a feast of homemade treats for the staff to enjoy with their 4 o'clock cuppa. No one ever knows what Maureen will produce from that holdall from week to week. Out they come, the cupcakes, the brownies, the heavenly carrot cake. Doctor Rogers politely resists all temptations laid out in the back office, claiming a need to watch his perfectly trim waistline. But Susie wonders if he hankers for something superior to Maureen's offerings, maybe something a little more exotic and sophisticated to entice him out of his resisting ways. With that in mind, Susie silently vows to blow the dust off the cook books she'd last used when cooking for the chinless Jeremy, and to produce something no man in his right mind could refuse. Then we'll see who's the real Queen of Friday Afternoon Munchies. And furthermore, who gives Doctor Rogers' taste buds a little slice of heaven. Yes, next week, Maureen would unwittingly find herself in a bake off to sort out the flan from the gateaux.

Back in her cottage, Susie finally decides upon a dark and white chocolate cardamom swirl, but deviates from her recipe book by recklessly throwing in some crushed pistachios to add some extra va-va voom. She feels this mixture of timeless classic with a bit of the unexpected will speak a thousand words to her hunky doctor. Feeling rather chuffed with her efforts, Susie lightly hums as she applies the final touches to the marbled topping, and envisages Doctor Rogers not only licking his lips and politely asking if a second helping would be in order, but also seeing her in a new light – seeing beyond the office persona that efficiently belts out letters and referrals like the clappers, and files hospital reports in such an orderly fashion. No, he would recognise that she possessed other, more homely, qualities. And as such, had girlfriend potential.

Thursday night sees Susie snuggling beneath her duvet with a smile on her face. She is excited about showing off her home-making skills to her colleagues and simply *cannot* wait for Doctor Rogers to get his lips around her produce. And as Susie rolls over and nestles deep into her pillow, she allows herself to think her first fruity thoughts in months.

Well *done*, Susie.

Friday sees Susie up and out of bed bright and early, as excited as a child on Christmas Day. She takes an extra long shower, while running a few favourable cardamom swirl outcomes through her mind. Then deliberates at length over her blouse selection. Susie finally opts for a rather racy pink and black creation she'd been saving for Doctor Webb's retirement party in a few weeks' time. She'd have to find something else for that particular social function – as today was all about pulling out her big guns.

With an impulsive last minute douse of flowery perfume, Susie sets off to the surgery with her blouse and swirl in good order. She walks with a slight bounce and feels her non-bolloxed hair swish about in the glorious morning sunshine. Yes, today was going to be a good day. The day she got re-evaluated by her peers and more importantly, Doctor Rogers – who would doubtless wonder what other talents (and secrets) lived within the cool machine of efficiency and dedication.

Once at work, Susie tells an aghast Maureen that she's taken the liberty of making something for the Friday afternoon scoff up. Maureen is visibly shaken and has a look that tells Susie she's taken a faaaarking liberty, although her mouth tells her, that'll be lovely – there'll be more for everyone.

As 4 o'clock draws ever closer, the two ladies fuss and cluck over the back office table, with each vying for prime spot in the centre of the table. And each moves the other's offerings to a less favourable position under the thinly veiled guise of re-jigging the napkins and plates to a more convenient position. To Susie's horror, Maureen has pulled out two of her own big guns; firm office favourites – homemade scones and lemon cheesecake.

Chow-down time is almost upon them, and the ladies resort to a light jostling and elbowing session at the table. But they are interrupted by the arrival of the troops. Swinging her head around, Susie is delighted to see the handsome – but decidedly, tired looking – Doctor Rogers milling about at the back with his tea mug. With no time to lose, and with Maureen distracted by a teacup shortage crisis, Susie swiftly switches the cheesecake with her swirl to claim pole position victory.

As the others descend upon the table, Susie boldly beckons Doctor Rogers over – she wants him to see her swirl still intact and in all its glory. He gives a polite smile and briefly hesitates before making his way forward with his mug cupped to his chest. Susie throws all caution to the wind and brazenly asks Doctor Rogers if she can tempt him with her swirl and lists the main ingredients for his approval. But what's this? Doctor Rogers is shaking his head. He tries to interject, but in Susie's excitement, she just gabs on about her swirling technique and even launches into an impromptu demonstration with her hands. Doctor Rogers has to raise his voice to interrupt her mid-marbling flow. Sorry? Allergic to nuts? Are you sure? Yes, of course you're sure – you are a Doctor after all...

Behind Susie, her swirl sits untouched as Maureen's scones and cheesecake are eagerly devoured. Only deaf Barry, the part-time cleaner, stands hesitantly holding a raised knife, as he debates whether to take the plunge. Susie fills with embarrassment, her face reddens, and just as she feels things couldn't possibly get any worse, Nurse Simmons appears at Doctor Roger's side with a slice of lemon cheesecake. She tells Doctor Rogers that she saved a piece especially for him as she *knows* it's just about the only thing that will make him forget his waistline for a few minutes. Nurse Simmons' ample bosom heaves as she presses the plate upon a smiling Doctor Rogers before dishing out a smug and *knowing* look to Susie.

Citing a need to make use of the indoor plumbing facilities, Susie excuses herself and makes a dart to the loos. Doctor Rogers calls out after her, 'Thanks anyway, Susie!' – but his words offer Susie no comfort. In the privacy of a trap, Susie pummels her fists upon the walls. 'What a fool I am!' she cries out loud. 'What a fool!'

That night, when Susie is deep beneath her duvet she has a horrible dream. Everyone from work is gathered in the back office. In unison they cry,

'Thanks anyway, Susie!' over and over again – their mouths smeared with cream, jam and crumbs.

'Thanks anyway, Susie!'

And there's Doctor Rogers and Nurse Simmons. 'Three cheers for Susie!' cries Doctor Rogers. Up the cheers go! And there goes Nurse Simmons, using her hand to wipe cream off her face and bosom before seductively rubbing it over and into Doctor Rogers mouth. Boof! There go her fingers between his hungrily sucking lips. And all the while they are watching Susie with a smile.

'Thanks anyway, Susie!'

'Thanks anyway, Susie!'

And resting on the table behind, sits her untouched swirl.

Poor Susie.

I sat back and smiled at the screen. Chick lit? Chick shit, more like. But hey, I'd seen worse. And what's more, they do alright. And if Susie did more than alright, I could leave Clarke to fester in my flat – or maybe throw in a family of hyperactive Romanian acrobats to keep him company and help out with the obscenely high rent I'd set. Ah yes, come the day of the Susie revolution, things will be a bloody sight different.

Picking up my phone, I re-read Clarke's latest offering. He was going through another of his indifferent stages – not bothered that things were over. Blah blah. Probably for the best. Blah blah. More flat viewings scheduled, with one of them looking particularly promising. Yeah, yeah, I'll believe it when I see it. But again I wondered, what *would* I do if he was still there when I returned, given that Clarke had proven to have an unstable, and moreover, violent side to him?

Without giving it a second thought, I phoned Spencer.

'Hi gorgeous! Long time, no hear!' he greeted me.

'Hi Spence, yeah – it's been a while. How are you?'

'I'm good, good, good, thanks. Same old. Have-camera-will-travel and sinning by night. You?'

For a beat, I thought back to a different time with a heavy stab of sadness, but quickly replaced it with a feeling of pleasure that Spencer was in a good (good, good) place.

'I broke up with Clarke,' I said, simply.

Spencer's voice came low and measured. 'I'm glad. He was wrong for you. Are you okay, Amber?'

I told him all about it. The lot. The possessiveness (of which he already knew a little), the violence (of which he knew nothing) and the subsequent bust-up. Resulting in a six week caravan writing stint – interspersed by abusive/docile messages from Clarke; trips to a nudist beach; sex in the sea with a random, and Flabby quaffing sessions with the lads.

In his usual way, Spencer let me talk

uninterrupted, and when I finished, there was silence for a few moments before he spoke.

'Right. That's a lot to take in, Amber – even by your standards. Right. Let's take things from the top. Are you *okay*? And are you sure this creep is going to budge?'

I told him I was. And that, no, I wasn't sure. I thought so. Or, at least, I hoped so.

'Do you want me to come with you when you go back to the flat? It's no problem at all.'

I smiled at his offer. Despite everything that had gone on, I could always depend on Spencer.

'I don't know,' I answered. 'Why don't we see what unfolds over the coming weeks. You never know, he might surprise us and just fuck off.'

'Do you think that's likely?'

'Not sure. He's off his nut, that much is clear, but I'm hoping he'll just get bored with his games and go.'

'Well, let's just leave it open for now. But if you need me there, I'll make sure I'm on the next train to Exeter – no two ways about it. Okay?'

'Okay,' I said. 'And thank you.'

I heard Spencer breathe out loudly. 'Amber, it's absolutely no problem at all. You know that I'm always here for you. You need some muscle when you go back – you've got it. Not saying my muscles are enough muscles – but we'll give it a go – but as you say, hopefully it won't come to that.'

'Thank you,' I said again.

'Right then... as for the rest of it... details please!'

I laughed out loud. I felt in a warm and familiar place, and happily spent another twenty minutes or so chatting to Spencer about my recent shenanigans. At one point he asked, 'So, this Luke bloke stood you up? Ouch. What are you going to do when you see him again? He sounds pretty interesting, mind.'

I thought about it for a moment, then realised I had no idea.

'Guess I need to find out why he was a no-show,' I told Spencer. 'Besides, no harm done, I still managed to have me a fine ol' time.'

Spencer laughed loudly. 'That you did, alright! Seems like that beach could be my kind of place.'

'Oh! You'd *love* it!' I said, excitedly. 'It's right up your street, well, *our* street to be precise. Besides, you must visit in any instance. Bring down your flame du jour for a trip.'

'Maybe a solo visit, Amber. There's no current flame du jour, but that doesn't stop a man having some fun. Or by the sounds of it, a woman having some fun. What *are* you like?'

And we both laughed at that.

We said our goodbyes soon after, with Spencer wishing me luck with my writing.

'I look forward to reading it!' he added.

'No,' I said, in fake seriousness. 'You shouldn't. You really, *really* shouldn't.'

Moments later, and after a repeat round of goodbyes, he was suddenly gone.

And as with every Spencer phone call, I spent a few minutes in quiet reflection after it ended.

What a shame. What a bloody, bloody shame.

My lovely Spencer Stone.

Monday. Changeover day. And I have a new whole batch of shiny neighbours. Oh yes, I so very do! And they look house-trained – the lot of them. I am surrounded by a sea of couples with not a sprog in sight. By my reckoning, it's some form of divine reward for enduring the Horror Family from Hell and coming out the other side. And besides giving them a cursory once over upon their arrival, I've not really paid them any mind, nor them me. Although I did avert my gaze from the laptop long enough to see if the fifty-something couple entering 70 would dash out moments later, holding handkerchiefs to their noses and dry heaving. But to the cleaner's credit, they happily continued ferrying in their stuff, in blissful oblivion to the pigsty habits of the previous occupants.

A flicker went through my mind about who might have been lurking in my Sophia Classique prior to my arrival, but I swiftly pushed it away. Thoughts of grunting unsavouries having a sweaty bunk up on my bed would serve no purpose, except make me think unkind thoughts about my lovely van.

Be gone, vile thoughts! Be gone!

I looked at my watch; nearly beach time. Somehow it felt as though I hadn't been for ages and I was eager to get back in the sun and stretch out for a few hours. But a sudden wave of delicious flashbacks to Olive Man delayed proceedings as I felt compelled to retire to my L-shaped for some urgent masturbatory relief. And as I lay down out of sight, edged down my shorts and got to sweet work, I couldn't help but be amused to hear the comings and goings of my new neighbours still going about the business of unloading their cars and settling in.

If *only* they knew.

Bad Amber.

Yet another glorious day, with the added bonus of the tide being out just enough to avoid the dreaded climb. I felt in good spirits, with all memories of hangovers, Clarke messages, broken dolls, Horror families, Flabby's shame and tides of self-pity seeming a distant memory. I was back on track. And whizzing along with Susie.

I must have whizzed myself to the beach as well, as in what seemed like no time at all, I was back on those pebbles and dishing out, 'Lovely day, isn't it?' like a returning hero. It was a lot quieter than Saturday so there was no need to go as far as my usual spot close to Brokeback Bay – there were plenty of decent spaces nearer. And although I felt no embarrassment about my 'dip' in the sea with Olive Man, I felt happy to just let things settle with the gay guys for a while; besides I'd rather be writing notes or reading, than chatting or fending off gossipy questions about my nautical knobbing.

Finding a reasonably level spot beside the cliff, I quickly sorted myself out and was soon basking in the sun's warmth. The sea made a relaxingly calm noise as it rhythmically lapped against the pebbles. I entwined my hands and stretched them over my head. 'I fucking love this place,' I sighed.

After a good half hour or so of aura-enhancing sunbathing, I rolled onto my front and took my notebook from my bag. But no matter how I tried, or for whatever reason, I just couldn't concentrate on my writing, and likewise my paperback. Perhaps it all just felt too perfect there. Lots of space. No weirdos. And no wankers giving it the Fist of Fury. I allowed myself to succumb to the simple pleasure of sunbathing and relaxing without any Susie guilt tapping at my temple. Time flew by. And at the point I sat up, reached for a cigarette I shouldn't have and checked my phone, I was surprised to see it had already gone half past five. I'd be doing about another 30 minutes or so before setting off. As it was quiet, I seized the opportunity to swing my legs towards the sea and hug them up as I smoked.

I gazed at the waves, mesmerised by their miniscule nearing with every roll.

'That's a dirty habit you've got there. Mind if I join you?'

I jerked my head around in surprise. Luke stood a few feet away from me, dressed in jeans and a blue t-shirt. My daydreaming into the sea must have made me oblivious to his crunching approach. I looked up, unsure what to say.

'Am I late?' he joked, with a broad grin.

I broke into a smile – the day was far too glorious to be spoiled by anyone or anything. 'Dirty habit? Just one of many, I'm afraid. As for being late? Only by a day or so. *And* you missed *all* the fun. Where were you – I thought we had a date?'

Luke gestured with a hand if it would be alright to join me. I nodded my consent and he sat down beside me, adopting the same hugged knees position.

'Ah, our date,' he said, pulling out a cigarette and lighting it. He exhaled into the soft breeze. 'I'm sorry about that.'

I turned and looked at him. 'So what happened to you? Abducted by aliens?'

Luke laughed and swept his hair from his forehead. 'Nothing as glamorous as that, I'm afraid. No, it was just work. Remember that commission I told you about? Well, it proved to be a bit trickier to finish than I'd first envisaged.'

'What happened? Did your wax crayons snap in half?' I threw him a smile.

'Oi! You cheeky mare!' Luke replied with a grin. '*No*. My wax crayons did not snap in half, for your information.' Adopting a posh accent, he added, 'I *am* a highly trained and respected artist, you know. So. Am I forgiven?'

He was forgiven; his excuse was totally plausible and one I'd half-guessed. Besides, he had no way of letting me know. I punched him lightly on the arm, 'I'll forgive you just this once, okay?' The punch had taken a moment, but in doing so, temporarily exposed one of my breasts. Amused, I saw Luke's eyes dart down for the briefest of glances.

'Well, that's pretty decent of you. I accept your forgiveness,' he replied, returning the compliment of a light punch to my arm. His soft Irish accent was delicious and as his fist made contact with my skin, he lightly kneaded it into my flesh for a second or two. It was the first time he'd touched me and felt oddly erotic, somehow exacerbated by the fact he was dressed and I was naked. I felt my nipples further stiffen.

'Anyway, tell me about "all the fun" I missed out on,' he asked, raising an eyebrow in question.

I looked towards the sea, wondering how much to tell him.

'Oh, it was just a beach party in Brokeback,' I said

lightly as I returned my gaze to Luke. 'Got a bit lively and interesting. You know.'

Luke looked at me, his eyes examining my face. 'I see. And what kind of lively might that have been?'

I smiled at him. 'Oh, the usual. Everyone drank too much booze. I *definitely* smoked too many cigarettes. And ate too much. Good music. Good chatting. It was fun.' I gave a small shrug, 'Yeah, it was good fun.'

'I see,' said Luke. His blue and grey eyes twinkled as if I'd just told him a good joke. 'Sounds like I did miss out.' He looked both ways along the quiet beach then leaned into me.

'Listen,' he said, nudging his shoulder against mine, 'how do you fancy getting dressed and we can go for a beer some place and you can tell me some more about this fun? How does that grab you?'

I hadn't been expecting that. Men didn't normally suggest my getting dressed.

'Oh!' I said, showing clear surprise, 'Didn't you come here to sunbathe?'

Luke stubbed out his cigarette, carefully placed the butt beneath a large pebble, then shifted his body towards me. 'I came here to find you,' he said, 'to explain my no-show, and seek your forgiveness. Which I now have. So how about that beer?'

I suddenly felt a new level of nakedness – of total and overwhelming exposure. My ego stung with rejection from the fact Luke showed no interest in sunbathing naked alongside me, and all I wanted to do was put on my clothes and feel on a level playing field to him.

'Sure, why not?' I said, trying to sound breezy and agreeable to his suggestion. I reached behind for my bag while trying to keep myself as modest as possible. Pulling out my sundress, I swiftly pulled it over my head, knowing that Luke would take the opportunity to check out my body again. I tugged the dress down as quickly as I could, unable to look Luke's way, then busied myself, putting things into my bag. I had the strongest of feelings he was watching me with a smile on his face.

When I got to my feet and tugged down my dress further, Luke also stood and brushed some pebble dust from his jeans. I folded my towel, put it in my bag, rolled up my yoga mat, dropped my sunglasses into position and gave Luke a broad smile.

'Ready!' I boomed with a false confidence, hoping to disguise that I somehow felt like a fool.

'Here, give those to me,' said Luke, gesturing towards my bag and yoga mat. 'You just concentrate on getting off this beach in one piece. I need you intact.' I smiled at his gentlemanly offer and handed them across.

'Thanks, I guess a visit to a pub beats a trip to A&E with a sprained ankle any day of the week.'

Luke turned and gave me a broad grin. 'My thoughts exactly, Amber. Okay? Ready? Beer time?'

And with a laugh that dismissed any feelings of foolishness, I threw Luke a salute.

'Aye, aye Captain!' And as we began making our way over the pebbles side-by-side, I added, 'Talking of Captains, I wish it to be known that I simply refuse to go to The Captain's Table for our beer.'

'Don't worry, that's not where I have in mind.'

'Ooh! How very mysterious and exciting! Just where *are* you taking me?'

'Wait and see, Amber. Wait and see.'

9.

Blondie Goes to Exeter

The next morning I woke to a bad stomach ache and an email from Clarke.

"Who were you fucking last night, you fucking fucked up dumb slag?'

There was more. More of the same, basically. I stood in my kitchen, still half-asleep, and read through his message with a feeling of shock. Had he seen me with Luke? Did he know where I was? But as I gradually came round and thought it through, it was just a message like so many others. Accusing. Insulting. Just Clarke. Besides, if he was somehow stalking me, surely Olive Man would have got a mention – after all, if not on the beach, then he would have seen us coming off it and saying our goodbyes.

No. Clarke threw so much crap at me, the odds were stacked that, sooner or later, they'd actually coincide with me being in male company. It was just his usual bollocks. And my fault for breaking the rules and checking my phone in the morning, before I felt okay with the world and able to deal with his relentless shit.

Without thinking it through, I tapped out a reply and pressed send. 'Just fuck off and find a flat – you're boring me.' Taking my coffee over to the L-shaped, I sat and peered out the window. Nothing unusual. The couple in 69 were watching breakfast television, while 70 were having breakfast. No sign of anyone else rattling around. Yet for an instant, I felt as though Clarke was out there. Circling. Watching.

'Don't let him get to you, Amber,' I said out loud. 'Don't let him win.'

Of course, the greatest irony was that I didn't fuck anyone the night before. And if Clarke really had been spying on me, he would have known that. Instead, Luke had driven me, in his rather lovely old sports car, to the dinky coastal village of Shaldon, where he lives in a Susie-type, white-walled cottage. We parked up and went straight to a cute pub with a beer garden that overlooked both the estuary and the sea. I talked about my writing, my London life, my interest in art, some more about Spencer and very briefly touched on Clarke. He spoke of his earlier life on the West coast of Ireland, his passion for painting and nature, and some more about his ex-wives. It was lovely out there in the early evening sunshine. We drank beer and shared a platter of seafood. Luke was charming. I was me. No smoke or mirrors. Just me.

He apologised again for letting me down. I said, don't worry about it – the beach party wasn't really all that. He told me how he'd looked forward to spending the afternoon with me. I told him, he had *no* idea how much I had. We held each other's gaze as traces of smiles slowly grew and spread across our lips. And the flirting began from there. It all seemed very much on the cards that I'd be going back to his cottage, until a trip to the pub toilet revealed the early onset of a heavy period. And there was never going to be any coming back from that. He gave me some change. I used the machine in the toilet to buy some tampons.

Which all rather killed the moment.

We stayed a while longer and carried on talking. Luke made a jokey reference about dark forces conspiring against us. I laughed and told him I was quite lucky; my periods normally only lasted for a few days. He told me that was too much information, but nevertheless, useful information. Then we clinked glasses and looked at each other with knowing smiles.

Nature's bad timing aside, it had been a lovely date. We exchanged phone numbers and agreed to text soon. He drove me back to my Sophia Classique, fetched in my bag and yoga mat, took a quick tour, laughed at my extravagance at being a two-toilet abode, turned down my offer of coffee, gave me a peck on the cheek, promised to be in touch, and left.

I watched as he walked over to his car, refusing to show the disappointment I felt at such a cursory goodbye. As he reached the driver's door, Luke began to rummage through his pockets and pat down his jeans. 'Jesus Christ,' he muttered. 'What am I like? Don't tell me I've forgotten...'

Assuming he was looking for his car keys, I turned to look on the counters and table. Within seconds, Luke had stepped back inside the caravan, wrapped an arm tight around my waist, pulled me towards him and gave me a heady cocktail of tender and filthy kisses as his free hand cupped the back of my head.

'*That's* what I'd forgotten,' he said, before giving me a final kiss goodbye.

I waved him off from my steps, then stayed there for a while, smoking a cigarette and thinking about the evening. In some ways, it had actually been better than sex. The sex with Luke would come, of that I was sure – but the conversation, the setting with those fabulous views, the food, the flirting – had all been perfect. And in some ways, the onset of my period – which I (rightly or wrongly) believed had put the brakes on an offer back to Luke's – in real terms, probably did us both a favour.

For his part, I had the impression Luke was eyeing me up more as a long-term prospect, and wanting to get to know me a bit better. I'd always been so used to guys just wanting to get into my pants (and me, theirs, for that matter...) more or less from the word 'go' – but the evening had just felt more like the old-fashioned courting ritual. Yeah, it had been lovely. I recognised that I'd been stupid to feel any form of rejection when Luke wanted me to dress and go for a drink with him. If anything, it was compliment; he saw me as more than a naked body on the beach. And that was pretty cool.

As for me, and my desperate track record of picking the wrong men – with a gay husband and psychopathic boyfriend topping a long list – it certainly wouldn't do any harm to decide first if I even wanted to get into another relationship. And if I did, to find out if they were likely to turn into a male bunny boiler down the line. Plus, there was always the matter of trust. A highly sexed creature, I might be – but once I'm properly with someone, the shutters go down on anyone else, and I expect the same from a partner. Well, unless it's consensual... then that really is a different story.

Was I ready for a relationship with Luke? I wasn't sure. Probably. Possibly. He did tick a lot of boxes. I didn't know. I just wanted the cloud of Clarke that hung over me, to go. Which it would. The instant he left my flat and life.

I wondered what might have happened if Luke had shown up at the beach last week. Maybe both of us would have gone over to Brokeback for drinks and a swim in the sea? Hmm. Maybe a cheeky threesome in the sea with Olive Man? Is Luke even into that kind of thing? Hmm... I wonder... would that be good? Or would that be bad? Hmm...

With a last look at the star-filled sky, I went back into my caravan. It took me a second or two to realise that I'd started to softly sing the first few lines of, 'Getting to know you' from the musical, The King and I, which annoyingly stuck with me during a much needed shower and a couple of vodka nightcaps on my L-shaped. Over and over I sang those cheesy lines with a little smile on my face.

Silly mare, Amber.

Don't be such a wanker.

Oops! Too late!

I had a light breakfast, took pain killers for my stomach cramps and half-heartedly set about Susie. It was slow progress. And painful, in more ways than one. After an hour or so, I threw in the towel – I just wasn't feeling up to it. I went and flopped on my L-shaped and peered out the window for any interesting goldfish bowl action. Nada. They were either out, getting ready to go out or behaving like normal human beings.

Naturally, my period meant the beach was a

serious no-no. Liberal I might be, but the thought of lying there with a tampon string hanging out of me, just didn't float my boat. And very possibly the boat of anyone taking a curious glance at me. Luke was away, teaching a group of have-a-go artists in Plymouth for a few days, so in many ways, nature's timing had got it bang on. But the thought of missing out on the beach and feeling cooped up in the caravan all day held no appeal. And I certainly wasn't achieving much in it.

The painkillers were going about their business, and although not feeling great, had taken the edge of my customary first day cramps. I'd live. I got up and shuffled to the bathroom. As I washed my hands, I inspected myself in the mirror; my black roots had become more prominent, giving me the look of an ageing punk rocker. What with all the Clarke hoo-hah, I'd cancelled my last hair appointment, but it was now clear I was in dire need of getting my hair re-coloured and cut. Which could give me something non-beach or Susie-related to do whilst not feeling in the best of shapes.

I went back to my L-shaped and put in a call to my hairdresser in the hope she'd be able to squeeze me in.

'Hi Elena – it's Amber. You okay?'

'Well, hello stranger! Yeah, I'm good. I've been wondering what'd happened – you just went off the radar – haven't got another hairdresser, have you?'

I laughed at that, Elena was a fabulous stylist. 'As if!' I told her. 'No, I've just had a bit of drama to deal with and now I'm in desperate need of some urgent emergency repairs.'

'I bet you are. You must be looking like some creepy doll from a horror film,' Elena teased. 'Hang on, I'll check the bookings.'

I was in luck. 'Well, if you were thinking about today, and seeing as it's you – and seeing as I've had a cancellation, and can't have you walking around with an embarrassing head with my good name attached to it – how does 3 o'clock sound?'

I smiled into my phone. 'It sounds perfect – I'll see you, then.'

'Great. And then you can tell me all about your drama.'

'Ha! How much time do you have?'

'I'm a trained listener, remember?'

'Deal. 3 o'clock. Bye!'

'Bye!'

I felt daftly excited to be seeing a familiar face. Even though it would be odd going back into Exeter. But seeing Elena was like seeing a friend. I'd never been out with her socially, but from my very first appointment, we just kind of clicked and got on. There were never any inane questions about where I'd be holidaying or girly nonsense about celebrities or designer handbags – no, she was straight down the line. Elena was bloody good at what she did, ran a successful salon and she *was* a good listener; never pulling any punches when handing out large doses of common sense and advice. In fact, she'd been telling me for yonks that Clarke was a wrong 'un. Yeah, it'd be good to see her.

Of course, going into Exeter meant running the risk of seeing Clarke. Particularly as The Grub Shack and Elena's salon were only six or seven shops apart in the trendy Gandy Street. But I wasn't feeling up to thinking through anything on that front. I simply wanted my hair done and knew it would make me feel a bit better – both the hair and spending some time in Elena's company.

With a jolt, it occurred to me that this was the first time I'd be doing something in Exeter (post bust-up stay at the hotel aside) without having to run it past Clarke. *That's* how bad it'd got in the end. And for what seemed like the millionth time, I mentally beat myself up for being so bloody stupid.

I thought about it again later, when I got in the battered old Golf and set off to Exeter. Not only did it seem incomprehensible I'd become that unfamiliar person, but now, and after a matter of only weeks, I was answering to no-one and back to doing what I wanted. And with whom I wanted. I allowed myself a broad grin as I thought about Olive Man, Luke and my drinking sessions with the lads in Flabby's. Clarke really would have a head explosion if he knew what I'd been up to in Brightlea. I let out a laugh as I turned on the radio, cranked up the volume and picked up speed.

Fighting off a late challenge from a Range Rover, I secured a rare parking spot in one of Exeter's city centre streets, and before long, I was on the cobbles of Gandy Street, where I paused and took stock. As I looked down the small pedestrian street, with its fashionable shops, bars and eateries, my eyes were immediately drawn to The Grub Shack, which had once seemed like the answer to all my prayers.

A sense of apprehension flooded through me. Suppose Clarke saw me walking past? By rights he should be slaving over his latest creation in the kitchen. But then again, it wasn't outside the realms of possibility that he'd pop front of house for something or other – like the time that earned me a hefty slap across the face for joking with a male customer.

I still hadn't thought through what I'd do if I bumped into Clarke, and although a second dose of painkillers had all but dismissed any stomach pain, I was still experiencing some of the usual brain fogging associated with the start of my menstrual cycle. But as I replayed that slap, and moreover, the force of it and my subsequent crash to the floor, I reminded myself I was no longer the victim. I was done with all that. Done. So I pushed my shoulders back, held my head high and walked on.

When I passed the cafe, two of its four outside tables were occupied by customers enjoying coffees and slices of cake. The main lunchtime rush was over and although I didn't properly look into The Grub Shack, was aware of a few people dotted about. I had a sense of someone standing at a table near the window – it could have been a customer, a new waiter or waitress (heaven help them) – or possibly Clarke. But within seconds the place was behind me and I was being greeted by a smiling and open-armed Elena in her smart salon.

'Well, look at you with your shameful roots!' she said, once we'd hugged and exchanged pleasantries.

'Well, I guess I'm in the right place, then,' I replied with a smile.

Elena helped me into a gown and guided me to a seat in front of her work station. I looked at her in the mirror. She looked as great as ever, and was the polar opposite of me – for my peroxide cropped hair, Elena's was jet black and shoulder length with a heavy fringe that framed large brown eyes.

She rested her hands on my shoulders, leaned in and spoke to my reflection.

'I see you're not at the cafe anymore. Would I be right in assuming that's all part of the drama you were telling me about?'

Of course she would have known: Elena, or one of her team, often popped in for takeaway lunches.

It was how I first got to know her and began using the salon.

I rolled my eyes upwards. 'It's a bit of a long story. Start slapping some gunk on my head and I'll tell you all about it.'

She gave my shoulders a squeeze. 'Sounds like a plan.'

And as Elena got to work, I gave her the rundown on Clarke between sips of complimentary coffee.

'So,' she said, after I'd finished, 'the last you heard was this morning's email, and you told him to eff off?'

'Yep. Fresh off the press. But then again, his contact can be like buses – nothing for days and then a batch load when he's either agitated or feeling sorry for himself. Quite honestly, there's been so much crap from him, I'm at the stage where it's pretty much like water like off a duck's back.'

'I told you he was no good the instant he started isolating you from everyone in your free time.'

I sighed. 'You did. And I was just stupidly, stupidly, blind to it at the time. And now I'm not.'

'Did you know the cafe was closed for a while?'

I told her I didn't. And from the rough timings Elena gave me, it would have coincided with our bust up. It also transpired that when he did re-open, he seemingly struggled without me, as occasionally he'd shut early or close for the day. In the end he took on an assistant manager to help run the place and cover his days off – as the cafe was now trading 7 days a week and doing pretty well for itself, by all accounts.

'Yeah, he's got some bloke called Charlie in there – does front and back of house. He's a good guy. And they've taken on a few part-time waitresses. Shame it's run by a nutter – but the food's still good, I'll give him that. Looks like trading the extra days have made it really popular, and according to Charlie, there's talk of getting a licence and opening in the evenings.'

News indeed. Which totally blew apart my image of Clarke spending his days bent over his tablet or phone, bashing out embittered emails. He really had got his shit together – albeit after a period of post bust-up meltdown – and now, he was obviously getting on with his life and driving the business forward. We'd talked ourselves, about opening 7 days a week and trading in the evening, but Clarke had always been keen for us to have some decent down time away from the business.

'So maybe he really is sorting out a new flat,' I said, thinking aloud.

'Could be. He's certainly moving on, so it just doesn't figure that he'd want to hang around when the relationship is more dead than a dodo. He probably just likes winding you up. You ended it. His ego is hurt. He's being cruel. Spiteful. He'll get bored with it. He'll get over you. He'll leave. Besides, he gains nothing by staying, and quite frankly, he's got a busy little business to run. I don't think he's got time to keep on playing silly games. He's probably targeting you when he's had a bad day.'

Everything Elena said made sense. Clarke was just trying to get a rise out of me. And as long as I responded to his messages, he was getting some form of fix. I'd be knocking that on the head, el pronto – that much was for sure. And if it wasn't for the fact I needed to know when he'd definitely be out of the flat, that bastard's number would be well and truly blocked.

With my hair washed, I smiled as I inspected the platinum blonde in the mirror. Better. Much better. And as Elena began my cut, she asked about where I was staying and what I'd been up to. Even with a heavily edited version, her eyes almost popped out when I quietly told her about nudey beach.

'Nooooo!' *Really?*' she exclaimed in a shocked, high-pitched voice, as she covered her mouth with a hand.

I laughed up at her reflection. '*Now* you sound like a hairdresser.'

'Love-leee!' she trilled.

When Elena had finished, I examined my short crop in the mirror. 'As ever, a wonderful job. Thanks for fitting me in at such short notice.'

She picked up her scissors and gently shook them towards me. 'And don't you leave it so long next time. 6 weeks *maximum* or I'll come hunting for you!'

'Well, I'll be living back in sunny Exeter by then, so hunting will not be required, if it's all the same to you. It's a good offer, mind,' I said with a smile.

Elena slid my gown off and we moved across to the reception desk. Tapping out the price into the handheld payment device, she looked at me with a grin. '*So*, have you met anyone in Brightlea to keep your mind off your Clarke woes?'

I paused for moment. I'd purposely omitted to tell her about Olive Man, not quite knowing Elena enough for *that* kind of chat. But I guessed it'd do no harm to tell her a little about Luke, if I adapted the truth and said we'd met in Flabby's.

One of the other hairdressers who'd been sweeping around her work station abruptly stopped what she was doing and piped up. 'Luke? The artist? Older guy? Good looking and Irish?'

I turned in surprise to face her. 'Yes! Do you know him?'

'Not personally – although I have seen a photo – but Jackie, a client of mine, went out with him for a while about a year or so ago. He's a bit of womaniser by all accounts.'

I raised a quizzical eyebrow and turned to Elena, who looked at me glumly with a jutting lower lip.

'Be careful, you. Out of the frying pan and all that.'

I gave a breezy wave of my hand. 'Well, nothing's really happened yet. We'll see. I'm in no rush for anyone's frying pan.'

'That's really good to hear.' Elena took my card payment and handed it back. 'Shall I book you in for six weeks or will you make an appointment closer to the time?'

'Closer to the time. And how about... when I get back from Brightlea, we hook up for a drink and chat in a non-lesbian based capacity? I was thinking, just earlier, we've never been out together and I think it's about time we did. I think it'd be good to have you properly in my new and amazing, post-Clarke life.'

Elena's broad grin gave her response.

'You're on! My sentiments exactly! Not sure how happy I am about the non-lesbian bit, but I'll live.'

'Ha! Well, I'm easy if you are!'

'So I've heard,' she joked.

We said our goodbyes and as I reached the door, I looked over my shoulder and thanked the other hairdresser. Although I wasn't entirely sure what for. Second-hand information could tend to get muddy and hold agendas. But still. I'd think about it later. As for now, I had to walk past The Grub Shack once more, but this time around, and armed with Elena's new information, I felt curious more than anything else.

I slowed my pace as I approached, ignored my

increased heartbeat and tentatively peered in. It was a bit busier than earlier and a guy, who I assumed to be Charlie, was ferrying out plates of food in the trademark small black apron I used to wear. It may even have been the same one. Catching my breath, I saw the back of Clarke for the briefest of moments as he dipped into the kitchen. I was sure there wasn't enough time for him to see me; his back must have already been turned. But at least I knew he was in there. I stood for a few moments, spotting some changes. Small specials blackboards sat on each table and strings of funky lights adorned the walls, windows and front of the counter. Yellow chilli peppers, red hearts and others that looked like they could be blue stars. Good improvements that made the place look like fun.

There were new framed posters or prints on the walls, which I only glanced over, as I briskly walked on before Clarke had the chance to re-emerge. With each step I took from The Grub Shack, I gradually began to feel anger bubble and rise. Things were definitely moving on with the business. Which was once our business. What else was he getting up to? I had no idea why I was even bothered, but knowing that the cafe wouldn't be shutting for about another hour or so, made the impulsive decision to visit the flat. The keys were in my handbag, I had time left on the parking ticket, and it was only a ten-minute walk away. It had to be done.

Reaching the end of my street, I faltered for a moment as I surveyed the blocks of purpose-built flats that lined each side. What on earth was I doing? But as I thought of Clarke taking time out of his precious (and growing) business to send me abusive messages, my resolve returned. I delved into my handbag, pulled out the flat keys and walked on.

Ridiculously, I held my breath and felt my heartbeat increase as I gently turned the key and eased the door open. I knew Clarke wasn't in there, but it suddenly occurred to me that he might have someone else in the flat. Maybe a woman, even. Like an idiot, I poked my head around the door and called out to ask if anyone was home. I was met with a still silence.

Tiptoeing into the flat, like an intruder in my own home, I looked around and was immediately struck by how tidy everything was. Aside from a few dishes in the sink and an unmade bed, there was nothing to illustrate that anyone mentally unstable could be living there. I moved from room to room, surprised that Clarke's normal tidiness and order were still evident. I think I'd been expecting – given his heartbroken/aggressive state – that chaos would be ruling, but there was certainly no sign of that.

Not wanting to risk staying in the flat for too long, I passed back through the lounge and spotted a spiral bound notebook lying open on the coffee table. I went over to examine it and felt dumbstruck to see that, amongst his trademark doodles, Clarke had written notes about various rental properties. Along with the monthly rent and some basic details were addresses, dates, times and the name of the estate agent he'd be meeting. His tablet sat neatly beside the notebook. So, he genuinely *had* been doing his homework and trying to sort out new accommodation. And according to the notebook, he even had a viewing that very evening.

The sense of relief and elation I felt was overwhelming. Through pursed lips, I heavily blew out air several times to calm myself and get over the shock. Everything was going to be okay. And Elena was right. Clarke was just vindictively letting off steam to ease his damaged ego.

I'd seen all I needed to see. It was time to go. Turning around to leave, I immediately spotted a large dent in the back of the lounge door which I'd absently closed behind me. It looked like Clarke had either smashed his fist into it, or used one of the few tools we had in the flat. The hammer, maybe.

I felt the blood drain from my face.

Without hesitation, I darted from the flat, locked its door and dashed down the stairs into the welcome sunshine and fresh air. I hurried along the street with my head spinning. Was the dent new or old? From when we'd first broke up? Or more recently? I reached the end of the street and turned to hastily make my way back to the car. And as I did, a sudden wave of paranoia made me feel that from somewhere in the shadows, I was being watched.

As I drove back to Brightlea, I tried to process the evidence. On the one hand, Clarke was very much getting on with his life. He was clearly focused on the business and looking for a flat. On the other, that dent very much disturbed me. But by the time I pulled up at my Sophia Classique, I'd convinced myself they were old; I just couldn't fathom how Clarke could be smashing up a door (or doors – were there more?) when he was going about the rest of his life in a totally normal fashion. But then there were his messages...

I went into my caravan and opened some windows to alleviate the stifling heat. My mind was soon taken off all thoughts of Clarke as I looked across to 69. With no net curtains, I could see beyond their lounge and kitchen, all along the narrow corridor – off which, ran another bedroom, the bathroom and spare toilet – and straight into the main bedroom at the end. The door was open and although I couldn't see all of the room, I had enough of a snapshot to see that the supposed, dreary looking middle-aged couple, were certainly living up to their caravan's number.

'Happy holidays!' I hooted out with a laugh. What a schoolboy and schoolgirl error! Whenever I retired to my boudoir for a solo sex session, that door was always firmly pushed shut. Otherwise, I was lying down and out of sight on the L-shaped. I dabbed a tear of laughter from my face. 'Dear, oh dear,' I said, as I watched the wife's flobby arse bounce and grind down into her husband's buried face. Who'd have thunk it? 'Go on girl, get your back into it!' I said between giggles

I turned and left them to it. The hilarity of the 69 episode made everything Clarke-related feel distant and an overreaction, as a jovial mood washed over me. I was back safe in my caravan. And he was flat hunting. That was all that mattered. Just park it, Amber. Still smiling about what I'd just witnessed, I suddenly felt like going out for some good-humoured banter with the lads at Flabby's. It was time to face the music after my pissy pants night of shame. Some dinner, a shower, a few more painkillers and a stroll to the pub seemed like the most splendid idea. I could get back to Susie the following day, when I'd be feeling a lot sharper.

When I arrived at Flabby's, Fucker Frank was the only one of the guys in attendance; his large frame unmissable as it dominated the bar. Going over to say, 'Hi,' he turned and looked me up and down. 'Well, hello, Blondie. We were wondering when you might resurface. Got over your hangover yet?'

Here we go, I thought. 'Got over your sunburn yet?'

Frank paused for second, inspected his peeling arms and roared out a laugh. 'Actually, I haven't –

now that you mention it. Here, come and have a drink with me.'

I ended up quite enjoying my time with Frank. It transpired that the rest of the lads were off for a pool match somewhere else, while Matty was still slaving over his fryers, what with the chippies closing ever later as the season unfolded. Anyway, amongst the various blokey tales of football away matches and drinking escapades, Frank did tell me one rather disturbing story about a precious family heirloom vase he'd recently broken. Due to his clumsy nature, he'd taken to keeping superglue in his van for such eventualities and had had a plucky stub at putting the vase back together. With less than satisfactory results. Undeterred, and moreover, resolute in his desire to not confess to breaking the vase, when instructed by the owners to place it on a bookcase shelf, Frank carried it over in his big hands and positioned it so all the damage was at the back, with the perfectly intact front facing outwards. That was a few weeks ago, and as things stood, the game wasn't up. Which by Frank's reckoning, would strengthen his case should he ever be challenged by the owners about damaging it.

'I'd just say, it wasn't me,' he said, downing the last of his pint. 'And say, if something was broken, then they should have said something on the day – before they paid me. And I'd tell 'em, they can see me in court if they want. As long as they've got some proof.'

'Oh! You are *such* a fucker, Frank.'

Frank shrugged. 'Can't help the way I am. Besides, I'm dyslexic – what else am I going to do? Try having a one man taxi firm like Steve One did? Can't see that working out any better for me than it did for him? Besides, I don't break *everything*.'

'You should put that on your business card,' I said.

'Cheeky cow. Fancy another?'

I did. And then another. And so on...

A while later, as Frank involved a bored-looking Jen in a heavy duty speech about the merits of frozen meals for one, I got talking to a pleasant middle-aged couple from Taunton who, after ten minutes or so, made the reveal that they were actually staying at Happy Holidays! My vodka beaker runneth over!

'So. In their clubhouse,' I began, 'is there some sort of outlandish compère on stage, whipping you into a frenzy each night by getting everyone to repeatedly hoot out, 'Happeeeeeee Holidays!'?' I could hear myself get gradually more animated as I warmed to the topic.

The couple eyed one another, unsure what to say.

'Sorry. I'm a little drunk. And have an unhealthy obsession with the name of the place. I think it's rather cheery.'

The wife put her hand to her throat and looked at me sympathetically. 'I don't believe we've seen that,' she replied, before adding in a soothing tone, 'But there's time yet, I suppose.' She was just short of patting my hand and saying, 'There, there, there.'

It was my cue to leave. I *was* more than a little squiffy and certainly didn't want to get any squiffier. The hangover from hell was still a recent and painful memory. I said my goodbyes and left, and in doing so, surreally passed the podgy couple from 69, who were sat at a table by the entrance, each contentedly munching on a packet of crisps.

'Ooh, hello!' I said in a knee jerk reaction as I swept by. I sounded like something from a Carry On film, and in the moment it took for their eyes to flicker into recognition, I was gone.

Back at the caravan, I side-stepped a nightcap, drank some water, and like a good little girl, went straight to bed.

And as I slept, Clarke sent me seven vile accusatory texts calling me every name under the sun.

10.

A Busker and the 69ers

My immediate reaction had been to delete them all; their content was horrendously disgusting and disturbing. I felt shaken to the core when I first read them; they were by far his worst – but I'd vowed to keep everything he'd sent me in case I ever needed them. I thought about the tidy flat, thriving business and signs of flat hunting, and struggled to correlate that the same person was capable of writing such abuse.

Then I thought of the dent in the lounge door.

I tried telling myself I'd antagonised him with my last message, but instantly dismissed it as nonsense – he was the aggressor. Then I knocked around the idea that given the early hour he messaged, he must have been drunk. Maybe he went out in Exeter for a few post-work beers with Charlie that got out of hand. Clarke wasn't the best of drinkers. Maybe they had an argument and he took it out on me.

After all, and as Elena suggested, I was an easy target for any bad moods. Whatever it was, the minute he was out of the flat, every aspect of my communication contact was being changed. Along with the locks.

And now I had to lock him out of my mind. I had things to do and was dedicating far too much precious time wondering what his game was. As the anger began to surface yet again, I felt steadfastly resolved to not let Clarke stand between me and my writing goal. Late night drunken abuse was one thing – but I absolutely *refused* to let him hinder my Susie progress. Absolutely nothing about Clarke made that trade-off worthwhile.

I spent the next couple of days tackling Susie in the morning and doing something different to fill my afternoon beach void. Mentally, I was feeling sharper and my stomach cramps had gone. So, all good on that front. The first day, I took a reasonably uneventful, but lovely drive up to Dartmoor. I climbed to the top of Haytor, sat on a rock and spent a good half-hour admiring the beauty of the rugged surroundings and savouring the tranquillity. In the far distance was the shimmer of the sea, which made me wonder how things were on nudey beach. I felt a real yearn for the nutty old place, and was glad it wouldn't be long before my return. After making my descent I treated myself to an ice cream from a kiosk in the car park, then took a gentle drive around before finding a stunning ye olde pub. I sat beside the tinkling stream in its beer garden, drank a couple of soft drinks and jotted down some Susie notes.

Then a bit later on, I got talking to an elderly lady, Marjie – who was on the next bench along with her border collie, Frank, who came over to say, 'hello' and ask for a pat by pressing his nuzzle into my lap.

An extraordinary woman, she gossiped about herself in the third person and in conspiring whispers, which I sometimes struggled to hear. She spoke at some length about unwashed net curtains, un-recycled food waste and cheating the self-service till at her local Tesco. She was gentle. A hoot. A tad mad. And I was sorry when we said our goodbyes and she took Frank home.

It was a good afternoon. Solitary – in the main, peaceful and surprisingly needed.

That night, I typed up my notes and relaxed on my L-shaped listening to music. I smoked a couple of cigarettes outside and wondered about Luke's "womanising" ways. I briefly thought about texting him to say, 'Hi,' but decided to leave it. There was still a bit of a lingering aftertaste with the Clarke thing, plus I hadn't really decided how I now wanted things to develop with Luke. Besides, I was feeling content in my own company and didn't particularly feel like hearing from anyone.

Unless Susie had something interesting to say.

The day after, I was up bright and early and feeling super great. I picked up my phone. 'Go on, I triple fucking dare you!' I challenged it out loud. Nothing. From Clarke. I felt up for doing a kettlebell session and as I stood on the carpeted area by the L-shaped and began my routine, I sensed eyes upon me. Slowly turning towards 69, I saw the couple sitting by the window and wearing matching dressing gowns as they each gave me a smile and small waves. Or in the husband's instance, waving a piece of toast at me.

I timidly waved back and threw them a weak smile. 'Dear God,' I murmured, 'please don't tell me they're sizing me up for a threesome.'

Susie made a real nuisance of herself that day. She wailed and flapped around, resisting my every move. But I persevered in my attack and ruthlessly assaulted her from all angles.

Biff! Bash! Boom!

And by the time I closed my laptop, I was satisfied that I'd given her a good slapping around the chops. That'll teach that pesky Susie.

I stood and stretched. All quiet in the vans. 69 looked empty (including the bedroom), as did the others. It seemed everyone was out enjoying the fabulous weather. I cursed my curse, but remembered that the long-term forecast was good; there'd be plenty of beach time left in the tank before returning to Exeter. I wondered what to do for my substitute nudey fix, and decided I felt like doing a bit of shopping. I had no desire to return to Exeter, but instead fancied somewhere a bit less High Street and a bit more independent. I wracked my brains for a while, then came up with the perfect place; Totnes – I hadn't been there for absolutely yonks. I couldn't remember when the market days were, but no matter; there were still plenty of indie shops, some really great eateries, and even though the whole place was a bit new age and alternative, it normally threw up some interesting stuff to look at. *And* it was only about an hour's drive away. Ideal. It was time to shower, sort myself out, and get on the road.

Ta ta, Susie!

Laters!

And stop your drippy sulking and behave yourself while I'm gone!

The long, narrow High Street in Totnes was bustling and full of colour. I walked along and browsed through a health food store, an interesting retro shop and an independent bookshop. I visited a cafe, where I sat outside and enjoyed a slice of organic ginger cake, drank a strong black coffee and watched the world go by. I listened to the faint strains of a busker playing a violin and smiled at the passing hippies with their braided hair and colourful, flowing clothes.

When I finished at the cafe, I wandered along to seek out the busker. I didn't recognise the exquisite music he was playing, which was both mournful and light, but I was really taken with it. Further ahead, I spotted a small crowd on the pavement and presuming they had gathered around the busker, set off to join them.

A scruffy young man in dirty cut-off jeans, an open multi-coloured shirt and layers of long beaded necklaces stood in the middle of the crowd. He had thick, matted shoulder length dreadlocks, a wispy goatee beard and a beautifully smooth chest. As he played, his eyes were closed in concentration, or perhaps, just the moment. He was achingly mesmerising and beautiful, as was his music.

As I wondered if he was a professional busker and might have some CD's for sale, I was jolted out of my thoughts by someone saying my name. I turned and looked into the faces of my parents.

'Oh, my God! Mum! Dad! What are you doing here?' I couldn't believe they were here, in front of me.

As they both enveloped me in their arms like a trippy Dracula's cape, each kissing my cheeks and hugging me, I could smell the reek of marijuana on their skin and clothes.

After our embrace, Mum held both of my hands.

'Amber, darling – it's Cassandra and Michael,' she reproached, 'not dull old Mum and Dad, alright?' Then she jiggled my hands to accentuate the point. I gawped at them, too dumbfounded to speak. They looked dreadful and had aged beyond their years. Dad's tall frame had developed a stoop and his face had adopted the characteristics of a fictional simpleton, looking seemingly clueless as to why he was standing there smiling with an open mouth. His once sharp eyes seemed to look through me.

Mum seemed a bit more with it, but her once beautiful face was ruined; ravaged by drink and drugs. Her long coarse grey hair fell halfway to her waist and her mascara was in congealed lumps. She still wore a trademark flowing skirt, but she was tiny now, having lost a lot of weight from what was, an already slender frame. She smiled at me, making her badly drawn eyebrows disappear into the heavy creases in her forehead. And as I looked into the green eyes I'd inherited from her, all old spats and hostilities were instantly forgotten.

'Seems we've got some catching up to do,' she said. 'We're just on our way home from getting some groceries,' she said, indicating to a cloth bag that hung over a shoulder. 'How about you pop back with us for a chat?'

I put my hand to my mouth and silently nodded my agreement; I was still blown away by bumping into them.

She turned to Dad and spoke to him in a slow and measured tone. 'Michael, Amber's going to come back home with us.' It sounded more like an explanation than a statement.

Dad looked vacantly into the distance and was yet to speak. I suddenly wondered if he'd merely followed Mum's lead when entering into our embrace or even knew who I was. Mum gave him a small nudge. 'Come on, Michael. Home time.'

He appeared to understand that bit, as we slowly set off, gradually distancing ourselves further and further away from the sweet sound of the violinist.

We walked the 5-minute journey there in silence. It was only interrupted by Mum occasionally coaxing Dad along with things like, 'Almost there.' I had a sudden and clear flashback of a childhood car journey to the seaside, and being told, 'Not far now,' to my repetitive, impatient and whiny question.

I never visited the basement flat in Lewes, as during my parents' time there, things were at their worst between us. But I always imagined it was a chaotic and rancid, hippy shit hole. And when Mum opened the door to a ground floor flat, I expected I was right.

The place stank of stale air and joint, and was a

nightmare version of our old home. At least back then, despite the disorder and untidiness, there had been an element of hygiene and cleanliness. The lounge reminded me of one of those programmes about hoarders. There was stuff everywhere. The floor was a sea of old newspapers, boxes and God-knows-what else, along with crusty, dirty plates and glasses and mugs containing solidified liquid.

The garishly painted walls were adorned with dusty strings of crystals and artificial floral garlands. While a wonky bookcase by the window housed more crystals, a large brown Buddha and Mum's battered collection of 'alternative lifestyle' books. I even recognised some of them from my childhood.

On a cheap pine coffee table, amongst the dirty crockery and stained, curling newspapers, lay the drug paraphernalia. And it was hot in there. Stiflingly hot. As though a window had never been opened all summer, despite the temperature outside.

My Dad lowered himself into the sagging sofa in front of the coffee table and seemed oblivious that he was sitting on a newspaper and the toe of a lone, discarded 'Jesus Creeper' sandal. He leaned forward and set about skinning up a joint. His movements were the most fluid since I'd met him – he was obviously in familiar territory – and as he set about his task with that vacant, open-mouthed smile, I noted a tendril of drool slowly swing down from the corner of his mouth. I could barely bring myself to look.

'Tea?' Mum asked brightly, as she stood in the doorway leading to the kitchen. I peered behind her at the filth and almost heaved.

'No, I'm fine, thanks.' I hastily extracted a bottle of water from my handbag. 'I'm on a detox at the moment, just drinking water.'

'Well, it *is* herbal,' she replied in a lofty voice. 'I'm sure that wouldn't do you any harm.'

I tapped the bottle. 'I'll stick to this, thanks.' The heat was oppressively overwhelming and I gratefully undid the cap and took a long drink.

'Well, sit down, then,' she said.

I looked around for the best option and spotted a hard wooden chair that had a mangle-haired toy cat on it. Using my handbag, I edged it onto the floor, causing particles of dust to explode into the air. I sat down and felt grateful my shorts were long enough to avoid any skin contact with the filth-infested chair. Mum emerged from the kitchen carrying a film-covered tumbler containing a red liquid, and with a groan of aches and pains, carefully lowered herself into an old brown corduroy armchair that had a full ashtray resting on each arm.

'So, Amber dear,' she began, raising the tumbler to her lips. My eyes darted to the encrusted remains of an amber liquid inside the base of her glass. 'Still working hard for the bastard capitalist regime?'

Then she took a large mouthful and cast me a look that was only too familiar.

I moved my gaze and watched Dad intently apply the finishing touches to a sizeable joint. The spittle had further lengthened, and suddenly, what had seemed like a good idea at the time, now seemed the very worst.

I lasted less than half an hour, then had to get out. There were two types of oppression in there and I could bear neither of them a moment longer. So I fled. There was no other word to describe it. I said I had to leave, and did just that. No goodbyes for Mum, or *Cassandra.* And although I did briefly squeeze my Dad's shoulder, he was oblivious. Stoned. And still smiling that fucking smile. His vacant eyes tracked something invisible moving along the ceiling, as his head loosely swayed from side-to-side as it rested against the back of the sofa.

As I reached for the door handle, Mum threw in her parting shot.

'You don't know who you are if you're not true to yourself, you idiot, *idiot* girl. Don't you ever dare coming back.'

I cast them a final look. Dad – on Planet Pluto. And Mum relighting the joint with a pinched expression, before heavily dragging on it. Both of their faces glistened with perspiration. She eyed me with an expression that held no love, and that's the one I'll make sure I remember.

I burst into the street, bent over and let out a gagging sob. Unsure if I was going to throw up from the stifling stale heat and heady joint fumes, I wiped the sweat from my forehead and glugged down mouthfuls of water before pouring some into a cupped hand and smearing it over my face and the back of my neck several times. I gulped in the fresh air, drank some more water and waited for my breathing to regulate. I fought back another sob.

And walked away.

I hurried back to High Street. The violinist had gone – but I wasn't looking for him; it was a pub I was after. I needed a drink, a cigarette and time to regroup. I found one on a corner that looked spot on. It looked fairly quiet – which was just what I needed. A friendly barmaid promptly served me a glass of wine and in an unsure voice, asked me if I was alright.

'Why?' I asked. 'Do I look terrible or something?'

She motioned with a hand around her eyes. 'It's just that you've got mascara all over your face.'

In reaction, I put a hand up to my face and touched the still-damp skin. 'Oh, have I?'

'Yeah, It's all over. I'd go to the Ladies, if I were you – it's over there,' she said, pointing.

I thought back to when I was outside the flat, cooling down and splashing water onto my face.

'Ah. Gotcha. Thanks.'

Despite everything that had happened in the past hour, when I entered the toilets and first saw my panda eyes in the mirror, with streaks that ran the entire length of my face, I could do nothing but let out a short burst of raucous laughter.

'Ha! I looked as fucking fucked up as my trippy parents!' I cried out, feeling slightly hysterical. I ran a bit of toilet tissue under a tap, added some soap and set about a bit of damage limitation to my face.

Christ Almighty, I thought, as I rubbed away; no wonder people were smiling at me when I walked down the street – I must have looked like the living dead.

And somehow, against all the odds, I managed another laugh.

Albeit, a bitter one.

After thanking the barmaid again, I took my patched-up face and drink outside and lit a cigarette. Exhaling heavily, I inspected the cigarette between my fingers and the glass of wine and sourly thought of my own addictions. Like mother, like daughter, I thought. Fuck it.

I didn't even get as far as finding out how they'd wound up in Totnes, although the place was obviously the perfect match for a couple of ageing hippies. The vitriol had been relentless, and upon reflection, I had no idea why she'd looked genuinely pleased to bump into me – such was the fury of her condemnation.

Naturally, I had fought back and challenged Mum about her own lifestyle choices.

'Look at how you're living!' I shouted. 'Look at Dad! He's become an empty shell because of all your stupid bloody drugs – is that what you want for me? To live in filth like this and lose my mind?'

She'd shouted back. Telling me to mind my own business. Saying that 'Michael' was fine. Just getting older. And a bit tired, sometimes. But he was happy. And had inner peace by never jumping on the capitalist gravy train and causing inequality. Like I had done. And was still doing.

'He's not even sixty-five yet – that's nothing these days! And he's not got inner peace!' I screeched. 'He's fucked on drugs! And besides all that, you both used to work!'

She lowered her voice at that point, leaned forward in the armchair and spoke to me as though a little girl again.

'Yes, Amber. And that was until we found a more *positive* way of living. Something you seem reluctant to grasp. Why can't you understand that we'll never return to lining the pockets of corporate fat cats again?'

I let out a snort. 'Trust me – they wouldn't want you!' I got up and walked across to the filthy sash windows, desperate for some fresh air and feeling trickles of sweat run down my back.

'Don't you *dare* touch those!' Mum barked.

I spun around. 'Why on earth not? It's unbearable in here! We're all roasting to death!'

She wiped her forehead with her free hand and inspected it, as if surprised to see the moisture. 'We've got used to it. Besides, this freakish weather won't last forever – even the summer of '76 ended at some point. Besides, if we open the windows, then our busybody neighbour upstairs might smell our smoke and report us to the Council.'

'Oh, *that's* rich, even from you. So let me get this straight. You despise the fact that I've worked for years, been in the so-called establishment 'system' and paid taxes. Yet, you're happy to let those self-same taxes pay for the roof over your head and your druggy lifestyle. You're a disgrace!'

'And you're not my daughter,' she replied with chilling calm.

We went around in circles, getting nowhere. Mum waved the joint in the air as she rambled on about her soul being put into a physical form to help her develop spiritually. She needed the freedom to grow and learn and couldn't do that if working or chained to a desk.

Not all of what she said made sense, but I reminded her she used to be an art teacher and hadn't been chained to anything – she was doing something she loved and was good at.

Mum hit back, telling me how she'd begun to feel emotionally 'shackled' by the demands made of her as a teacher; she'd hated imposing exams and rules on the children – so had to quit – in order to be true to herself and recapture her spiritual balance through her freedom.

With a sarcastic laugh, I gestured at all the crap on the floor. 'And *this* is your freedom?'

I couldn't remember all the details of our exchange, but at one point, Dad broke from his stupor to babble incoherently. His eyes swept about the room and passed over me without recognition. As he continued, the words grew form. 'Wassappening? Wass going on?' The length of spittle dangling from his mouth swung wildly before finally snapping and dropping to join the disgusting carpet.

'Look! You've upset Michael!' Mum spat out. 'Are you happy, now?'

But Dad had already flopped back deep into the sofa and returned to his vegetative state.

Everything began to close in on me. The heat. The smoke. Them.

'I have to leave,' I said, simply. 'I have to get out of here.'

I numbly collected my bag from the chair,

squeezed my Dad's shoulder and walked out to those final words from 'Cassandra'.

I crushed my cigarette butt into the ashtray on the wall and wandered back in. I took my drink to the bar and watched on, in sadness and anger, as a mother and daughter sat at the nearest table and excitedly discussed the purchases they'd made and what their evening plans would involve.

I downed the rest of my drink and left.

Mindful of the wine, I took a slow, careful drive back to the caravan, where I spent a quiet evening of reflection, drinking and gazing at the nearby trees from my L-shaped. I couldn't work out if I was angry, sad, or just numb. A bit of all three, I supposed. So when a cheery text arrived from Luke, asking how I was feeling and telling me about his 'nightmare' students – some of which, he suspected, painted with their knuckles, I didn't reply. His message seemed somehow intrusive, and unknown to him, his timing couldn't have been worse. I switched off my phone, poured another drink and settled back down with my thoughts and trees for company.

The next day began very positively. My bleeding was well and truly on its way out – the teeniest bit of light spotting – the standard indication it would all be over within an hour or so, and therefore, nothing worth wasting a tampon on. For possessing a womb

I had no use for, I was always grateful for at least being blessed with very short periods. Which in turn, meant only one thing – Return to Nudey Beach! Which I thought would make a rather good film title. I was just itching to get stretched out and naked again with my notebook.

A night of surprisingly good sleep had left me feeling refreshed and taken away some of the sting from the previous day's events. And any thoughts of my parents that tried to creep into my mind were swiftly brushed aside. I was determined to have a good day.

After breakfast and exercises, I firmly grabbed Susie by the blouse collar and gave her a good duffing up. Then I bagged some clothes and towels and took them to the rumbling onsite laundrette. Washing machine on the go, I made a quick visit to the local supermarket for some provisions, dashed back, put my stuff in a dryer, returned to my Sophia Classique for some lunch, then collected my laundry. Following all that, it was just a quick matter of applying some suntan oil, a light bit of make-up, throwing a dress over my head, sandals on my feet and getting my bag, yoga mat and sorry ass to the beach.

I set off at pace, eager to get back to my special world, and only managed a distracted, half-hearted murmur of 'Happy Holidays!' as I rushed past its colourful sign. It seemed odd I should be feeling so chipper when, emotionally, I should have been on my knees.

When I reached the front and found myself confronted by the inconsiderate and shocking behaviour of the tide, my only reaction was to laugh.

'Ha! Is that the best you've got?' I challenged. Oblivious to an approaching couple, I threw the sea a hearty raspberry, began my climb and made the journey over the cliff in record time. For which I was immediately rewarded by sight of some old boy, lying on his back with a pair of off-white Y-fronts covering his face. Yep. It was good to be back.

I dished out chirpy greetings and headed down towards Brokeback, managing just the twice to slide and stumble over the pebbles. As I neared, a few of the guys I recognised from the beach party gave me a wave or a muffled hello through the stiff breeze. I stopped in my tracks and waved back with my broadest smile, before deciding that where I stood was a good enough spot. As I began to organise my stuff, the towel resisted by flapping about and only succumbed to submission once I used large pebbles to weigh down each corner.

I sat down and smoothly peeled off my dress. About to quickly lie down, I suddenly changed my mind. There was something about the vitality of that strong, warm breeze blasting into my body and face that made every part of me feel alert and alive. Aware of a lone man, sitting some distance away to my left and showing an interest in me, I neatly swung my knees around to face the sea, hugged them up and closed my eyes. The breeze charged across the waves and pebbles and crashed into me head on. Memories of hot foreign holidays performed a slide show in my mind. Sun-kissed skin on a sultry summer's evening; a breathtaking view; the sweet smell of jasmine filling the air; a feeling of total freedom and wanting to freeze frame that moment forever.

I carefully extracted parts of the exchange I had with Mum the day before – namely, her repeated mention of freedom. Well, *this* was what I believed it felt like; butt naked on a beach with a warm wind against my skin, and troubles seeming a million miles away. If I had the choice, would I spend all my days doing this? Opening my eyes, I took a quick look and was pleased to see that the interested man had seemingly become disinterested, as he was lying on his front with his arse and toes pointing towards me. Turning my gaze to the sea, I realised I couldn't answer my question. Life dictated that I had to work and earn. And I dictated that I had ambition and drive, and could never be happy living on state handouts in exchange for opting out the system. Success provided choice. Choice meant freedom. My kind of freedom. I breathed in the fresh air and felt calm, as though I'd resolved something that had been troubling me.

Then I firmly parked all thoughts on the matter. I had no inclination to explore or probe further into anything Mum-related when everything was still so very raw. Reaching into my bag, I began to pull out a cigarette, but for some reason suddenly decided against it. As I pushed it back in its packet, I saw my phone and got an urge to return Luke's text, now I was feeling in a more positive frame of mind. As I took it out and re-read his message, I tried to formulate a dazzling and witty response about his students painting with their knuckles. But there was no point. I'd temporarily forgotten about the lack of reception on the beach. Feeling a brief moment of deflation, I decided I'd ping him a message later. Swapping my phone for my notebook, I lay down on my front and happily got to work.

I was keen to earn my freedom.

I worked in fits and bursts, taking breaks to relax in the beautiful weather, and before I knew it, it was time to start heading back to my caravan to take a shower, put on some sloppy clothes and start preparing some dinner. Dressed and packed up, I took a moment to stand facing the sea, soaking in every moment of the invigorating and uplifting breeze that made my mood soar. It was truly heavenly and so very good for the soul. With a deep sigh of regret, I turned and began to make my way over the pebbles.

Having passed Mister Decidedly Disinterested –

who dished out something bordering on a dirty look – I looked away, and to my amazement and shock, saw that the next sunbathers along were my 69ers from the caravan opposite. Protected from the strong breeze by a striped windbreaker, they were midway between the sea's edge and the cliff, meaning I was in direct line to walk past them on the left hand side. The shock element of my discovery was provided by the fact that the woman was tugging away at her husband's short, chunky cock as he lay on his back, propped up on his elbows and watching proceedings with eager interest. She sat sideways to him, fat legs half-curled beneath her body with her pendulous tits swinging and bobbing in time to her jerking hand. She appeared to be chatting away to her husband, as if doing no more than drying the dishes and discussing what programme to watch on the telly.

Deciding to change course and pass them on the 'blind' side of their windbreaker, I took a sharp step to the right, but was immediately foiled by pebbles sliding sharply beneath my feet. I took a comedy stagger, half-fell, half-recovered, and then promptly fell backwards and heavily onto my arse. And in doing so, further slid, causing a leg to bend in on itself at an awkward angle. Hearing the noise, they both looked in my direction. The wife used her free hand to shield the sun from her eyes for a moment, before giving me a cheery, yoo-hoo wave.

'Hello there!' she said, brightly. Her other hand didn't miss a beat.

'Hi! We meet again!' added the husband, sounding more like a neighbour over the garden fence. Literally lost for words, I looked on as his face made a short series of wincing expressions; his eyes squinted shut and I could see his irregular breathing from the movement of his large chest and rolling stomach. His mouth formed an O-shape through which he took sharp and rapid intakes of breaths.

A glance at the wife showed she was resolutely sticking to the task at hand while smiling at me expectantly for a response.

Dear Lord, I thought. No.

There was no way on earth, I wanted to be exchanging pleasantries with all *that* seemingly coming to an imminent conclusion.

I clambered to my feet, aware of curious looks from other meerkat sunbathers who'd seen that I'd fallen. Keeping my head lowered as I brushed myself down, I threw over, 'Hi! Yes, we meet again,' before scooping up my bag and yoga mat. I took a few tentative steps, grimacing at the pain in my right ankle, but pushed on, making my way around the couple on the windbreaker side: this was no time to be hanging around.

As I passed by as quickly as my ankle and safety would allow, I heard the husband let out a lengthy and undulating high-pitched whine. 'Oh, Carol......'

he breathed out in little staggers at its finale. My peripheral vision picked out the wife's head and a waving hand suddenly poking over the top of the windbreaker.

'See you soon!' she called out.

'Not if I see you first,' I muttered, jerking up the yoga mat tighter under my armpit before hobbling on.

As I walked on in pain, I *really* hoped she hadn't used her wanking hand to wave at me.

How *rude*!

Thankfully, the tide had just about receded enough for me to slowly hobble my way around the cliff, and as I limped along the main drag, I paused for a rest and drink of water outside one of the seaside tat shops. Casting an eye over a selection of brightly coloured windbreakers stacked-up outside, I suddenly thought how splendid it would be to acquire one. Whilst I'd totally adored feeling the full whack of elements on my skin earlier, sometimes, and dependent upon who was around, a bit of shelter and privacy could be just the ticket. Besides blocking any unwanted views of 69ers giving it a thrash about in the sunshine – as sadly, who wants to watch older, out of shape people at it? – I might be able to enjoy a cheeky bit of solo al fresco activity. There had already been a number times I'd been close to finishing off as a hand strayed down for a sharp twist of my lips and a frenzied brief knead of pressure. Or the quick penetration with a finger. Or two. But even down close to the relative quietness of Brokeback (and even given my shenanigans in the sea), that had seemed a step too far. Unless, I thought with a smile, I put up a crude cardboard sign saying, 'Will wank for fags'. Which might earn me a steady supply of freebie cigarettes or roll-ups for the duration of my Brightlea stay.

As I let out a small laugh at the image of a sea of old tossers (literally) hurling fags towards me as they egged on my efforts, my thoughts turned to Luke. Maybe a windbreaker would be just the thing for us. If positioned correctly, it could offer a degree of privacy for our own bit of beach time fun in this relentless heat that only served to increase my sexual appetite.

Not that a woman like me needed much encouragement.

But today was not the day to attempt carrying a windbreaker back to my caravan with a sore ankle. And with tasty thoughts of Luke and myself pressed together naked on the beach, I hobbled my way back to number 56, and felt nothing but relief when finally getting inside and offloading my stuff. I had a lengthy shower, made myself something to eat, and as I sat down at my table with my meal, I noticed the return of my 69ers, who somewhat predictively, gave me cheery waves once they'd carried in their beach bags and settled on their L-shaped to catch a bit of early evening television. The husband even added a thumbs up to his broad grin.

'I have no idea what's going here,' I mumbled, as I twisted a cupped, raised hand in stilted response.

Leaving them to it, I ate my dinner, stood on one foot to wash up my dinner stuff, then returned to the table to type up my earlier notes. As I waited for my laptop to sort itself out, I checked my phone. Nothing from Clarke. I didn't know if I was surprised or not, but clung to the hope he realised his terrible onslaught a few days earlier had been a step too far. Even by his twisted standards. I seriously hoped so.

I then re-read Luke's text and wondered about his so-called 'womanising' ways. Maybe he was a womaniser, maybe he wasn't – but ultimately, I wasn't looking to get engaged or set up home with anyone anytime soon. And if I got to know him better, I'd make my own mind up. Besides, I'd been no nun recently.

I tapped out a reply.

Knuckle-dragging students? Who are they? A bunch of have-a-go orangutans? Been doing a bit of dragging myself today– finally went arse over tit on the beach... and did in my ankle. Ouch! Safely back in my caravan, but hoping to drag myself out later for a drink. When are you back? X

I smiled at my text. Maybe I was a bit old-fashioned on that front, but I could never bring myself to use text speak with its ugly abbreviated words, and had been pleased to note Luke obviously felt the same way. Pinging off his message, I wondered if I really did fancy going out for a drink. Probably. Once I'd typed up my notes. Despite everything ugly and upsetting from the day before – this had been a good day. A healing day.

Ankle aside. And tugging 69ers.

I thought about going somewhere else for a change – but once you took Flabby's and the dreaded Captain's Table out of the equation, that only left the various clubhouses, with their family 'entertainment'. I briefly played with the idea of getting drunk and causing havoc at the apparently superior Happy Holidays' clubhouse – but soon dismissed it. I wasn't part of anyone's family. And the thought of once more sitting alone amongst a load of them held no appeal.

So – work. Then Flabby's.

Deal.

I sailed through Susie – even managing to decipher some dreadfully scrawled passages, where my imagination had worked faster than my roller pen. Satisfied with my efforts, I saved my work and closed down the laptop. I tentatively stood and stretched. It sure felt like I'd earned myself a few drinks.

Glancing over to 69, I could barely believe my eyes – they were at it *again*!

'Go on, me son!' I called out. 'Give her what she's begging for!' I descended into a fit of giggles as I watched the tangle of limbs writhing away, but after a moment, realised there were a few limbs too many. Someone else was in there!

It was like a car crash – I didn't want to watch – but couldn't stop myself. What was worse, or maybe a blessing, was that I couldn't really see a lot, such was the narrow angle I had to work with. I sank onto my L-shaped and like the world's worst Double O spy, peeped my head over the top – all the while in fits of giggles. Between which, I began to give a running commentary.

'You join us here, live at Brightlea Sands Holiday Camp, where the occupants of 69 are seemingly living up to their appropriately numbered caravan once again. But this time, kiddies, it appears they've recruited the services of one other – or maybe there's more in there, forming an orderly queue. I'll update you as soon as I have details. As things stand, it appears Mrs 69 is on all fours, giving her husband the blow job of his life, while a random male hand is alternating between massaging and slapping her fulsome arse. We can only surmise at this juncture that his other hand is employed in that age old trusty pastime of having a ruthless tug. Ooh! Hello! He's chucked a few fingers inside her!'

I collapsed onto my L-shaped and roared with tears of laughter.

Then boldly rallied.

'Update! A change of events! I now have partial sight of Mrs 69 on her back, legs akimbo – well one of them, at least – and being pounded by our mystery man. And even with my restricted view, I can reliably inform you that he has an incredibly hairy arse. Meanwhile, Mr 69 continues to enjoy oral pleasure from his enthusiastic – yet markedly, unathletic – missus.'

I felt as though I should be nibbling my way through a bag of popcorn as I watched on.

'Ah, yes... I now find myself privy to the final act, and as we all could have wagered – and I must confess, it's a personal favourite of mine – it's the time honoured male tradition of synchronised ejaculation over the female form. Which is quite an art form, really. Although not in this particular instance. And there's Mrs 69, taking turns to suck the last drops of come out of those weary cocks as though in dire need of an oxygen supply.'

It was no good. Once more I collapsed into a guffawing wreck on the L-shaped. This had been quality viewing of the highest order. I rolled onto my back and as my laughter gradually subsided, managed, 'This has been Amber Stone, aka The Bond Girl, reporting to you live – and licensed to thrill your discerning voyeuristic palate on this warm summer's evening. Thank you for listening. Have one for me. Over and out.'

I remained on my back, still smiling at what I'd seen and my own silliness. I looked at my trees and wondered if it'd been wrong of me, watching their boudoir antics – particularly as I hadn't remotely found any of it a turn on – no, it had more been the comedy value, curiosity, and yes, voyeurism. Maybe they'd wanted me to watch, having not taken the precaution (yet again) of closing the bedroom door. Either way, I wasn't overly bothered; I'm very partial to selected pornography, and have been known to visit high-end London strip clubs on occasion with a few keen boyfriends du jour.

And twice with Spencer.

Before.

I always admired the strippers and their beautiful, sexy bodies. The confidence they had, how they moved their bodies – and the power they had over men with their, 'you can look, but don't touch,' teasing. My understanding is that the girls in these kinds of top clubs are treated well and can do well, financially, and I'll readily admit to having my fair share of masturbatory sessions, imagining that I was strutting on a stage in spiked stilettos, not much else, and giving it my best shot with a pole.

I let my thoughts linger on a particularly stunning Latino-looking girl I'd taken a shine to during one of my visits with Spencer. She was truly exquisite.

And knew it. She had a smouldering sexuality about her and didn't even need to take all her clothes off to get everyone in that club wanting to be her sexual partner that night. I recalled Spencer and I looking at one another at the end of her act, which saw her comparatively modest panties kept on throughout, but giving tantalising brief exposures of her flesh as she slid them about into reveals. It culminated in pulling the front of her panties into a narrow strip between her legs, before tugging them up tight between her vaginal lips and wiggling and sliding them back and forth.

'I would if you would,' I said to Spencer, feeling flushed with arousal.

'Oh, definitely,' he replied, not taking his eyes off her. 'I think that would make for a memorable night.'

As it was, we went back to the flat and had our own memorable night.

Sigh... sometimes I still can't get my head around the Spencer Situation.

But now was no time to be dwelling on strippers or my ex-husband! It was time to get ready for Flabby's – Fucker Frank's latest breakage story was surely waiting for me!

I sat in an upright position and without thinking, peered over at 69, where to my surprise, discovered Mr Decidedly Uninterested standing dressed in the kitchen area, looking Decidedly Pleased with himself as he accepted a mug of tea from a robed Mrs 69. They carried their drinks over the L-shaped and joined Mr 69, who was also wrapped in his dressing gown.

'Please don't look at me,' I murmured. But it was too late. As if on cue, all three turned and gave me a wave. With Mr 69 raising his cuppa in silent toast.

It seemed Mr Decidedly Disinterested had been interested after all. But decidedly not in me, rather by what he'd seen of my swinging 69ers earlier on the beach.

And if I'd paid a bit more attention before, I should have recognised his hairy arse.

I gave a reactive half-grimace/half-grin and hurried my limp into the bedroom. After firmly closing the door, I changed my clothes and applied some fresh make-up. And when I came back out, wearing a short denim skirt, halterneck top and spray of perfume, my 69ers were sat with their back to me, seemingly engrossed in the television and eating snacks, with Mr Threesome Interested nowhere to be seen. As I gathered together some items for my handbag, I glanced up and saw Mrs 69 twirling her husband's sparse hair and whisper something in his ear that got them both rising to their feet and heading back to their passion den.

Happy holidays, indeed.

Having no desire to witness another middle-aged

flabby shagathon, I quickly picked up my phone, keys and bag and left them to it.

Dear Lord. That mattress...

11.

In Your Double O Dreams

When I arrived at Flabby's my ankle was having a fair old grumble at me. Nothing a couple of vodkas wouldn't sort out, I reasoned – but it was plain to see it had become quite swollen.

'Oi! What's happened to you, Blondie? Look at you! New hair – bolloxed foot! What's going on? Come over here and tell Stevie all about it.' Steve Two stood in a corner by the serving hatch and patted the bar stool beside him. Grateful of the offer, I happily limped over and joined him.

'Nurse!' he called out to Jen. 'Urgent vodka medication required! Dispense IMMEDIATELY, please!'

I laughed at his daftness, his passion for fun and total uncomplicatedness. He was the ideal drinking buddy. As Jen confirmed 'the usual' as my 'medication' and went about her dispensing duties, Steve leaned into me. 'So, Double O Blondie – secret mission, was it? Some daring feat that went tits up?'

I laughed again. 'Well, I did go tits up, actually. Right in front of some wife giving her husband a bit of gruesome hand relief on the beach.'

The words were out. Without any filtering or thought. And I couldn't take them back. A flush of colour filled my face. Stupid, stupid Amber.

An awkward silence fell between us and I was forced to look away from Steve's triumphant smirk. Jen arrived with my drink, and I gratefully took the opportunity to divert my attention as I delved about in my handbag for my purse. As I picked out the right money, I engaged in some idle chit chat with her, while Steve Two looked on in continued silence. When she was called away by another customer, I took a couple of hefty mouthfuls of my drink, raised an eyebrow and managed a half-hearted attempt at giving Steve a challenging expression.

'So where did this happen, Bondie?' he asked. I was grateful he'd lowered his voice.

I flicked a hand in the air. 'It didn't happen,' I replied as breezily as I could. 'I just made it up.'

'No, you didn't. You've been going to that nudist beach, haven't you? Ha! I knew it!'

'You don't know anything,' I replied a bit too quickly.

'So where did you see this wanking couple and fall over? On this *supposed* area you sunbathe, further along the main beach – where all the families go?'

'I told you, I made it up – for a laugh. You know, us wannabe writers have huge imaginations.' As I uttered the words, I knew how pathetic they sounded.

Steve leaned into me. 'And you must think I've got a huge imagination to believe you. I've never seen you on that main beach. And neither has Jen. No one has. Yet, look at the colour of you. It just doesn't stack up.'

About to respond with some flippant remark, I changed my mind and put the brakes on. The more I denied it, the more Steve would keep on, like a terrier nipping at my heels.

'It's not anyone's business where I go or what I do,' I said calmly, looking Steve in the eye.

'So, it's true, then?' he said with a broad grin.

It was hopeless. Steve was never going to believe any bullshit I spun him. I took another large mouthful of drink and immediately felt its soothing effect take the edge off me. Letting out a big sigh, I gave Steve a smile.

'Yes. It's true,' I conceded. 'I sunbathe on the

nudist beach. Alright? And I'd be very grateful if you kept that information to yourself.'

Steve let out booming laugh that turned a few curious heads. I put a finger to my lips and gave him a serious frown.

'I knew it!' he said, loudly.

'Keep your voice down,' I hissed. 'I told you, I don't want everyone knowing. I go there for peace and quiet and to work on my novel. And I don't want that spoiled. By *anyone*.'

Steve raised both palms in surrender. 'Look, I'm not here to spoil anyone's fun. It's just that I *knew* you were going there – but you'd never say. Trust me, Pussy Galore, I won't breathe a word. Okay? You have my word. Double agent to double agent.' He put out his hand for me to shake. And with a laugh of relief, I did.

'So. What's it like?' he asked, leaning into me. And then I knew we were getting to the crux of the matter.

In an attempt to discourage a nudey visit, I threw him a few mildly interesting crumbs – such as the old boy with the pants on his face – and painted it as though an overweight middle-aged wife giving her husband a furious tug had been the most sexual thing I'd witnessed. I was relieved at his disappointment.

'As I said,' I concluded, 'I just keep myself to

myself, crack on with my writing and have no desire to be disturbed.'

'But it still makes you a Bond girl,' he pressed. 'Coming out of the sea wearing only a knife belt.'

I quickly stopped that particular imagery in its tracks. 'No. No, it doesn't. As I don't ever swim in the sea. Sorry – but it really is surprisingly dull down there.'

Steve considered this for a moment before breaking into one of his broad grins. 'So exactly *how* grateful would you be for me to keep quiet about all this?' And then he click-clicked out the side of his mouth and threw me a wink.

I felt a wave of panic through the vodka. 'I thought we had a Double O agreement?'

Steve put his arm around me and laughed. 'That we do, Bondie. That we do. But one day, eh?'

'In your Double O dreams,' I replied, giving him a squeeze around the waist and a peck on his cheek. And although I had no way of being certain Steve would keep his promise, I somehow had a feeling he probably would. Although I couldn't discount the possibility of him one day making a visit to see what a naked Bond Girl looked like. But who cared? With his good looks and laddish charm, he wouldn't be the worst person to approach me on the beach.

I was saved from any further nudey beach discussion when Steve One, Fucker Frank and Wayne arrived en masse, with jovial talk of scratched bedside cabinets and how a cheat Wayne had projected from his arcade had landed headlong into a passing traffic warden. Steve turned his back on me to join in with the banter, and while I drank and listened out for a mention of nudey beach that never arrived, I felt myself relax. As the guys got more engrossed and moved a little further along the bar to where there was more space, I realised I had no one to talk to, so pulled out my phone.

Calling them Orangutans is an insult to extremely intelligent creatures. But I suspect you might not be too far off the mark. Bad ankle? Sorry to hear that. Guess that beach was always going to get you one day. How about I give it a good rub? Back in 2 days. Lx

A broad grin spread across my face as I read Luke's message. I caught Jen's attention, ordered another vodka and tapped out a reply.

2 days? A rub? What did you have in mind? Something with your knuckles? X

I smiled and quietly said, 'Ping!' as I pressed 'send'.

It didn't take long for Luke to respond.

That rather depends upon what you'd like rubbed and by what part of me. Why don't you show me? And tell me? Lx

Well, well, well, I thought. This was new territory between us. It had been a long time since I'd indulged in some sexting. Far too long, in fact. I felt my clitoris begin to pulsate in heady, strong throbs at the inference in Luke's text and looked up. The guys were now onto their cherished subject of football, and paying me no mind as I perched in the corner, phone in hand. I took a large swig of my drink, unsure how to respond. Feeling playful, and increasingly horny, I decided I'd be a tease and leave him for a while.

Leaning slightly forward, I jutt out my backside and grinded into the bar stool, feeling its solid pressure against my clit. In miniscule movements, I rocked side-to-side or to and fro movements, to gain some friction.

Oh fuck, it was heavenly! What *was* I like after a few drinks? Aware of the first sweet release of wet, I knew I had to be careful; I had no panties on – and if I didn't behave, I'd be having an orgasm on the bar stool – which wouldn't be the first time – that being, when watching a band with Spencer years before, in a dark, dingy basement bar in London, while everyone else was either drunk or on drugs and definitely not caring less what I was up to.

Meanwhile, I was in a reasonably well lit seaside pub in Brightlea, Devon. No, this wouldn't do at all. I decided to cool things down a bit. Cool myself down a bit. I straightened up, took a few breaths, drank more vodka, and tapped out my response.

Ooh, I don't know. You sound like a real womaniser to me. Are you?

I sent it with a small laugh.

Only with women that interest me.

I looked at the screen in thought and supposed that was a reasonable and truthful enough answer. In its own way, it also felt flattering. Before I could reply, another text came through.

Are you a maniser?

Touché, I thought. And to that one, I roared with laughter.

'You alright there, Blondie Bondie?' asked Steve Two, as a few heads swivelled my way.

'Yep, fine,' I replied, indicating to my phone. 'Just some old mates pissing about on Facebook.'

Satisfied with my explanation, they promptly returned to bemoaning the long wait until the start of the next season, and that the impending England rugby tour to South Africa was just a load of bollocks and played by guys who 'licked balls' and 'felt each other up' when scrummaging.

I was completely off their radar.

I tapped out a couple of responses to Luke, but deleted each of them. I drained my glass and ordered another large vodka. How to respond? What to say?

Enjoying the fun of exchange, I drank a few mouthfuls of vodka in quick succession and decided to go all in. What the hell?

Only with men I want to fuck.

I hesitated for a second, pinged it, and immediately felt like a naughty schoolgirl flashing her knickers behind the bicycle shed to some boy she fancied. I could feel myself get a bit breathy in anticipation of Luke's response. Whilst down below, the throbbing had picked up with a vengeance.

A couple of minutes passed. I sat staring at my phone, waiting for the blue light to start flashing in its corner. Nothing. Another mouthful of drink. Had I gone too far? Been too sluttish? After all, on our Shaldon date, he'd seemed like he wanted to take things slowly. But then we began flirting. And then my period... but then again... if it hadn't...

My thoughts were interrupted by the flashing light. I opened the text: a photo of Luke's erect cock. The picture was cropped from just above his belly button to mid-thigh. Pre-come glistened over the tip of his perfect knob. His balls, as I remembered; clean shaven. It all looked impressively magnificent. And filthy. What a delicious surprise.

With it, two words.

Any good?

I checked over my shoulder, to make sure Jen wasn't close by and getting an unexpected eyeful. But she was serving elsewhere, and as I looked about the pub, at the lads, the families, the couples and groups – I got a wicked thrill, knowing that none of them knew I was sitting on my stool, with no panties, and having some guy text me a photo of his solid and sizeable cock.

Dunno. I teasingly tapped. *Let me have a think for a*

few minutes and get back to you. Then stifling a snort, added, *I do hope you haven't been encouraging your students to paint with that thing.*

Barely containing a fit of giggles, I pinged it off to Luke. Poor sod. For all his tugging efforts, that *really* wasn't the response he'd been after. I took another mouthful of drink, slid off my bar stool and took my phone to the Ladies.

It was time to make it up to him.

Entering the second of two confined cubicles, my initial intention had been to return the favour, picture-wise. I was in desperate need of an orgasm, and reckoned I could kill two birds with one stone, as it were. And the way I was feeling, it certainly wouldn't take too long.

I used the toilet for its designed purpose, wiped and kept my skirt in its hoisted position over my hips. About to set to work with my fingers and the camera on my phone, I let out a silent groan of disappointment when two, maybe three women entered the toilets. Meaning an instant queue and every chance they'd hear what I was doing.

Tugging down my skirt, I quickly scooped my tits from the front of my halter neck top, so they were pressed tight together by the material. I put the camera onto selfie mode, flushed the toilet and fired off as many shots as I could. In the last few, I roughly squeezed one of my breasts, sandwiched its hardened nipple between my thumb and forefinger and took some close-ups. That should do the job, I thought.

Emerging from the loo, I came face-to-face with a sunburnt woman in her fifties. 'Thanks, love,' she said in a broad Brummie accent, 'I've been busting.'

'All yours!' I replied, as she half-barged past me. I went to the sink, washed my hands as I grinned at myself in the mirror, then returned to my bar stool.

I'd kept Luke waiting long enough. Checking once more for privacy, I scanned through the pictures. (What ace fucking nipples, you have, Amber.) Rushing and unable to decide, I sent two: one of my tanned tits pressed together, and the second, of a tightly squeezed nipple.

Let the jury decide! I thought with a smile.

I've had a think, I tapped, *and for something that's so very much more than good, I think you need somewhere to off load all that delicious cum. Any good?*

Moments later.

You beautiful filthy bitch.

I am. Problem?

Only that you're not here.

And what would you do to me if I were?

The phone went quiet for a minute or two. I imagined Luke wanking hard while looking at my photos. I leaned forward on my bar stool for a moment and pressed down. Stop it, Amber. Remember you're out.

Flashing light.

I'd fuck you the way you deserve to be fucked.

Which is?

As rough as fuck.

Oh fuck, indeed. Now he was talking my language. I re-read his words with a sharp intake of breath. Checking that no one was looking my way, I ground down on the bar stool and shifted and rocked in tiny movements for some more clit stimulation. Then I crossed my legs, placed my bag over my lap, slipped my free hand beneath my raised cheek from the side, and gave my aching clit a brief, firm massage with two fingers, before sliding their tips inside. I withdrew them, smeared my wet over my clit and pulled my hand away. This was too much. Too delicious. Too horny.

Imagine I'm there with you. Kneeling in front of you. Looking up at you. Tits pushed together, pulling on my nipples...

After a half a minute or so...

Then what

Maybe you'd like me to spit on your cock then suck it as you wank...

Nothing.

I tapped out another.

Would you like that?

Well, this was all rather exciting. And totally unexpected. I could barely believe what was happening – it just seemed so 'un-Luke'. Maybe he'd been drinking after a hard day with his talentless students and was feeling a bit frisky. Maybe he was shacked up in his B&B – or wherever he was staying – watching some porn, and just fancied a hand. I had no problem with either. In fact, it turned me on: the sexual arousal flowing from the texts was definitely two-way traffic.

Nothing.

Then, *yes.*

Then, nothing.

Then, nothing.

Nothing.

Then, *Have I ever told you you're a dreadful woman?*

I had to laugh at that one.

Once or twice. All better?

Ha! Very much so. For which I thank you. You?

About to turn this bar stool upside down...

You're out?

Yeah, Flabby's – for my sins.

Of which you have many, I'm sure. Listen – gotta crash. Long day/early start tomorrow and suddenly feeling a tad done in for some strange reason... make you sure you get back safely with that dodgy ankle – can anyone give you a lift?

I drank some vodka and looked at my handsome fellow double agent, as he stood holding court with the lads and cracking bad jokes that raised boisterous laughter.

I'm sure I'll be able to find someone with a functioning chariot, I pinged.

Ha! Just make sure you do! I'll text tomorrow.

Cool. Enjoy your kip x

Thanks. Enjoy your evening.

Will do...

Marvellous work, by the way... xx

Goodnight, Luke xxx

Xxx

As I took some more sips of my drink, I watched my phone a while longer, and when it became obvious Luke really had gone, put it back in my bag. With a smile, I thought of him partaking in the male, time-honoured tradition of post-come sleep. I'd never minded that, unlike some women. Nothing like your man entering a satisfying sleep after being satisfied. It what's they do. Mind you, I've been known to sleep like the dead after a good session.

Talking of which... now that Luke had had his fun, it was time for mine; I *really* needed to get back to my Classique and give myself some relief. And without delay. Or I'd be getting done for a public disorder offence, and that *seriously* wouldn't do – not with literary fame looming large on the horizon. Perhaps.

A little further along the bar, Fucker Frank was ordering a round while simultaneously dishing out jocular grief to Jen. Steve Two stood closest, with his to back me, laughing at the exchange as Jen gave back as good as she got.

I got down from my bar stool, limped over and gave the back of his t-shirt a small tug.

'You alright, there, Blondie?' he asked, turning around and smiling when he saw me.

'Yes. Well, kinda,' I replied. 'It's just...' I bit on my lip for effect, 'my ankle – it's feeling worse. And I was wondering... if you're not too much over the limit – is there any way you could quickly run me back to my caravan? It'd only take a few minutes.'

Steve looked in turn at my cleavage and enquiring face before breaking into a broad grin.

A lift had never been in doubt.

As Fat Frank loudly asked Jen if she needed casters to help her pour any faster, and she threw back – that was a great idea – she'd nick some from his wheelchair, I dipped out of Flabby's unseen. I could have left half an hour earlier for all they knew.

I found Steve's transit parked a little further up the road, with its SPS logo above the wording, 'Steve's Plastering Service' along with his mobile number and work email address. As I leaned against the van and waited, I realised I'd already made up my mind up to have sex with him. As things stood, I was no-one's girlfriend or partner. And I was in dire need of some cock action that didn't require a battery to operate it.

A few minutes later, Steve walked towards me, whistling and jangling his van keys in a hand.

'Ready for your ride, Bondie?' he asked with a smile.

'As ever as I'll O O be,' I replied, giving him the direct kind of look I hoped spelled everything out for him.

We walked around to the passenger side.

'Jump aboard,' Steve said with a wink and click-click out the side of his mouth, as he held the door open for me.

As I gingerly climbed in, wincing at the sudden pain that shot through my ankle, I heard his voice behind me.

'Need a hand?'

I knew he was getting a pretty good view up my skirt. Not all the way up. But close enough.

'Not at the moment, thanks,' I replied, sweetly.

As we turned into my row at Brightlea Sands and slowly approached my Sophia Classique, I noted the surrounding caravans had their curtains pulled shut for the night, and the only signs of life were dim flickers of TV screens behind a few of them. Steve swung the van up tight behind the battered old Golf.

'Well, then...' Steve said, as he turned off the ignition and undid his seat belt.

'Well, then,' I replied, as I slowly released mine.

We looked at each other as creases of small smiles broadened into the start of laughter. Steve leaned forward, traced a finger along my cheek, took my chin in his hand and pulled my face towards his and kissed me. Gentle, sensual and probing. He kissed as well as any self-respecting charmer should. His breathing was getting heavier. And I felt my body aching for sex.

I pulled away. 'Coming in?'

'Dunno, you'll have tempt me,' he replied.

'Tempt you?' I asked in genuine surprise.

He buried his head into my neck and kissed along its length. 'Yeah,' he breathed, huskily. 'Tempt me.'

I looked around to check on our privacy.

Lifting my backside, I tugged up my denim skirt, opened my legs and lazily began to rub myself.

'Fucking hell,' Steve whispered. I reached over with my other hand and felt the hardness of his cock pressing against his jeans. 'Fuck... ing hell,' he hoarsely repeated with his mouth against my ear.

Knowing how damn hot it looked, I continued rubbing myself, then lifted my hips and slid two fingers deep inside. I expertly finger fucked myself for a while, before slowly dragging out my fingers and spreading my wet lips in the process. Steve was plainly enjoying the ringside view of my swollen clit and opened vagina. Turning my hand into a pressed palm, I rubbed to and fro, teasingly spreading the fingers before dipping one of their tips inside, and when I withdrew, I looked Steve in the eye as I tasted it.

He watched me open-mouthed, as though a

schoolboy seeing his first porn film. And for the second time that night, I was fuelled by the power I had over a man, which only served to turn me on more. Steve grabbed the back of my head, pulled me towards him and hungrily tasted my mouth.

'Tempted?' I asked, as I pulled away.

'Nearly,' he replied, unbuckling his belt and beginning to unzip. I gave a small laugh. 'Are you playing hard to get?'

Steve released his cock and encased it in his fist. 'Not with you, Blondie – never.'

I looked down. Smaller and thinner than I'd expected. But as they say, it's what you do with it. Besides, it was the only one on offer and I was gagging for it.

I ran a finger around its tip and lifted off all the pre-come, while my other hand reached behind my neck and undid the loose knot of my halter neck top. I let it fall to fully expose my breasts, then dotted each of my erect nipples with his fluid. Bending my left leg to rest on the dashboard, I plunged the two fingers deep back inside me. Steve watched on goggle-eyed as he furiously tugged away at his cock.

Extracting my fingers, I licked off a little of my taste before smearing the rest over my breasts and cupping them. Steve needed no encouragement. His head plunged forward to suck and lick and suck so very fucking hard… I felt as though I might explode into orgasm on the spot.

I ran a hand roughly through his thick black hair. 'Come on, Steve. Let's take this inside,' I said to the top of his head.

I needed some serious fucking. And without further delay.

Steve bit down hard on a nipple, convulsed a few times, and with a series of gasps and whines began to ejaculate.

'Oh, jeez…' I murmured, as I watched him helplessly try to decide where best to direct his come. And so very much of it, too. His free hand and jeans copped a good few dollops and as I felt some land on one of my thighs, decided it was high time to help him out. I slid down in my seat and raised my arms up above my head. Steve awkwardly half-stood and leaned over me. With his final grunts, he jerked out the last of his come over my tits, with one rogue bit ending up on my chin.

Sagging back down, he reached over and smeared his come-filled hand over my chest – almost as if wiping his hand on a towel. As I slowly massaged it in, I felt nothing but disappointment at such a premature ending to proceedings.

Steve quickly pulled up is boxers, jerked up his jeans, buckled his belt, and turned to me with the expression of a puppy that had just tinkled on the new lounge carpet.

'Sorry,' he said, simply.

Oh, those big brown puppy eyes.

I edged myself up into a sitting position, retied my halterneck and tugged down my skirt. I was gutted – but what could I say?

'No need to say sorry to me,' I offered, trying to sound indifferent.

Steve reached into to the glove apartment, pulled out a couple of tissues and handed one to me.

'I mean, sorry – but I've got a girlfriend – a new one.'

I rocked back my head and laughed. 'Girlfriend? Is that why you wouldn't come in?' I asked, as I wiped my chin.

Steve nodded glumly. Well, this was a new Steve, one I hadn't seen before. It sure seemed that a few of the men in my life were full of surprises tonight.

'If you see me with her in Flabby's – you will keep quiet about this – won't you?' Steve was unrecognisable from the usual swaggering charmer of Brightlea.

'Do you really like this one?'

Steve bit his lip and nodded.

'Well,' I began, 'as I seem to recall, we have a double agent pact in place. You keep quiet about me going to the nudist beach, and I keep quiet about tonight. Double O deal?' And this time around, I was the one putting my hand out.

I was glad to see Steve wipe his hands before they

wrapped around mine for a firm shake. His relief was obvious.

'Deal,' he said, immediately looking a lot brighter and more like the Steve I knew. 'Of course, I don't normally come that quick,' he added. 'You know, normally, I'm like, going at it for hours... known for it.'

'Don't worry,' I said, picking up my bag, 'you were in the company of a *highly* qualified temptress.' I watched the false bravado on Steve's face have a slight confidence wobble and added generously. 'I mean, *come on*, just show me the man who could hang on. I seriously don't think he exists.'

'I say you're right, Blondie,' Steve said. 'I say you're right.'

'You know so.'

We smiled at each other with affection. And I hoped his ego was firmly back in place.

'Thanks for the lift.' I leaned over and gave him a peck on the cheek.

He returned the kiss. 'One day, Pussy Galore. One day.'

'In your Double O dreams,' I laughed.

I carefully climbed out the van, and like a naughty Auntie, stood waving him off. As his van conducted its 3-point turn, Steve gave me a cheery wave and pulled away, exposing number 69 and a distinct twitch of its curtains.

Whatever, I thought, as I flapped a hand their way.

Deciding to have a quick smoke before going inside, I pulled out a cigarette and settled on a caravan step. I lit up, inhaled, looked up at the sky, exhaled lengthily and chuckled to myself. What a night! What a day! What a deliciously sex-themed day!

And who'd have thought the Italian Stallion would have been so premature? Just goes to show – for all that laddish and bragging behaviour...

Mind you, little did he know, that for all his efforts, I'm quite partial to bringing myself off whilst covered in fresh come.

I finished the cigarette, said goodnight to the trees and stepped into my Sophia Classique.

Yeah. Not a bad night, at all.

And back in my bedroom, assisted by my trusty jelly dildo and wand, I got the relief I'd so craved. Twice.

Man, oh man.

With filth fuckery images of Luke and Steve and randoms.

In my kooky new world of freedom. Devoid of Clarke. But full of lads and womanisers. But sadly, no Spencer.

Spencer.

Always Spencer.

My Spencer Stone.

12.

Ugly Sandals and Having a Snoop

Back at the cottage, Susie consoles her battered ego by glumly devouring her cardamom reject in one sitting. Allowing herself a small sequence of post-scoff, bullet-fire belches, Susie decides she has what it takes to overcome TwirlGate. After all, if surviving a cheating boyfriend *and* a bastard perm has given her anything, it would be resilience. By the bucket load.

And whilst the recent battle for Doctor Roger's affections may have been lost, the war was still very much up for grabs. Bit-titted Nurse Simmons or not. Already feeling more positive, Susie pushes her swirl-laden frame up from the sofa and sets about making herself a cuppa. As she waits for the kettle to boil, Susie thinks about Doctor Webb's impending retirement party at The Old Wreck and decides this could be the final battleground to win over the man of her dreams. And as she pours hot water into her florally decorated mug, Susie concludes that this social event may well demand the purchase of a push-up bra and killer blouse.

That's the ticket, Susie.

Monday morning sees our Susie returning to work with her chin defiantly thrust out and ready to tackle any dissing quips that challenged the calibre of her swirl. But she need not have feared – the whole sorry episode is seemingly forgotten or not worthy of mention. Either way, Susie is relieved; her chin had begun to ache and she was a little fearful of it locking in its unflattering position. Which wouldn't do at all.

Susie sets about her tasks, which that morning mostly consist of audio typing the GPs referral letters. She is delighted to see that the first is from Doctor Rogers and eagerly pops in her earphones. Susie finds the intimacy of his words privately spoken into her ears rather sensual, even when, as in this instance, Doctor Rogers is referring an elderly chap with troublesome and persistent haemorrhoids for a colonoscopy.

Susie positively bristles with pleasure when, at the end of the referral, Doctor Rogers' velvety voice says, "Susie – could you give the Endoscopy Department at the hospital a quick call to find out the current non-emergency waiting time? Given the advanced age of Mr Perkins, I'd like to get him in there sooner rather than later. Thanks Susie."

Oh, Doctor Rogers, thinks Susie, as she twirls a lock of unbolloxed hair around a finger, I'll be doing *everything* to get you in sooner rather than later.

Shocked by her brazen thoughts, Susie lets an embarrassed giggle escape into a cupped hand before reaching for the phone on her desk.

Steady, Susie.

She spends the evening online in the quest for something appropriate to wear at Doctor Webb's retirement party, and is more than a little surprised when an email pops up from chinless berk, Jeremy, begging forgiveness and informing her of making a "dreadful error of judgement". He further reveals that Clara is not "a patch" on Susie and cites her total disinterest in Game of Thrones as causing a "major rift" between them. Along with a neglect in regular toenail-trimming sessions. In short, they were no longer together – Jeremy had had to "let her go" and now wanted to make a trip to Trewithiel to "talk things through" with Susie. To see if they could "get back the old magic" between them. He further had the cajones to suggest he might stay in Susie's cottage, having seen what a lovely cover photo it made on Facebook.

Facebook? Susie stops reading and loads up Jeremy's profile page for a nosey. All the gummy photos of himself and Clara looking smug have been taken down. His status has changed to 'single'. Susie switches her attention to Clara and lets out a snort of pleasure when she discovers her old foe looking gummy and smug with another chinless berk. Unsurprisingly, she is 'in a relationship'.

Returning to the email, Susie reads on. Jeremy talks of the "fun" they could have in the West Country whilst "catching up" and makes mention of having some "snazzy new shorts" he could sport – should they visit any of the countless beaches and coves in "dreamy" Cornwall. He signs off by asking Susie to have a "think about it" and offers to bring any old favourite nibbles from M&S should she answer in affirmative – which he very much hoped she would.

Susie pours herself a large glass of wine and does have a think about it. Well, well, well, she thinks as she presses the reply button and takes another large mouthful of wine. And as she types, she says the words out loud with a smile.

Fuck off.

And off the email jolly well fucked.

Bravo, Susie.

Feeling decidedly chuffed with herself, Susie gently hums as her attention returns to the shopping task at hand. Unsure whether it's the effect of the wine, or the acknowledgement that something is gradually changing in her, she picks out a black lacy wired bra and a sheer dark green blouse. If Doctor Rogers needed things spelt out to him, then some sexy plunge underwear covered by a semi-transparent top would surely make things crystal clear. And Nurse Simmons could go and do one.

That night as Susie snuggles deep beneath her duvet, she thinks of Doctor Rogers slowly unbuttoning her blouse to reveal her new bra in all its bosom-filled glory. And as he reaches his arms behind her to unleash its clasp and huskily whispers in her ear, 'I can't fight this any longer,' Susie discovers that, she too, can fight it no longer and reaches down for an overdue fiddle with herself.

Well, well, well, Susie...

The retirement party draws ever closer and Susie is buoyed by the safe delivery of her bra and blouse, which not only exceed her expectations, but make her come over a bit breathy and howsyerfather when tried on with a tight straight skirt and the highest heels she can safely walk in. As she admires herself in the bedroom mirror, Susie thinks back to Doctor Rogers' earlier enquiry in the staff kitchenette as to whether she'll be attending the party, and moreover, his subsequent look of genuine pleasure when she answered in the affirmative. The memory makes her run both hands lightly over her breasts before giving them a cheeky squeeze.

Susie wonders once more about the recent

change in herself and if she indeed possesses 'suppressed feelings' which, beneath the surface, bubble away with pent-up frustration – feelings, which in turn, make her think back with abject disappointment to Jeremy's grunting pump-pump-squirt efforts in the boudoir department. He was only her third lover. And sadly, the best.

Yes, she thinks, giving herself a final approving look in the mirror, Doctor Rogers was certainly bringing out the woman in her. Although, what kind of woman that was, Susie wasn't yet entirely sure – but it was more than time for a change of direction.

Friday night's retirement party cannot come quickly enough. Time drags by, with Susie increasingly frustrated by her minimal contact with Doctor Rogers as she counts down the days. She even has to deal with the disappointment of his no-show at the Thursday night quiz and distractedly joins in with half-hearted attempts at answers. To the rest of the team's dismay, Doctor's Orders finish an unprecedented distant fifth, with Nurse Simmons casting Susie a distinct look of disapproval as the final scores are called out.

But Susie is unconcerned. Instead, she sips on her wine and wonders what Nurse Simmons' face will be like in less than 24 hours, when both she and Doctor Rogers realise what a temptress smoulders beneath her "sheer and shimmering racing green blouse".

£16.99.

Postage and packing included.

And you can't say fairer than that, thinks Susie, as she downs the remainder of her drink and throws Nurse Simmons a smug sideways glance. Tomorrow, this will be our battleground, Susie thinks, and I will be the victor and claim the spoils. And 'she' can take her crepey, sun battered cleavage straight to the nearest ironing board for a good going over.

Such fighting talk, Susie. What a battle cry!

Friday arrives not a moment too soon, and just one week on from TwirlGate, sees our Susie eagerly carrying something altogether different to work. Her bag contains her party outfit and shoes, along with her make-up bag, hairspray and favoured perfume. Leaving nothing to chance, Susie has even popped her toothbrush and toothpaste into the mix. She is hopeful of some mouth-on-mouth action with the dishy Doctor Rogers as the night unfolds, although in highly controlled conditions.

Throughout the day, her colleagues are bubbling and babbling with excitement about such a dizzy social event. But as the time finally arrives to get changed, Susie is dismayed to find herself competing for mirror space in the ladies loo, alongside a lurex-cardiganed Maureen and worse yet, Nurse Simmons, in some form of gaudy and synthetic figure-hugging jumpsuit. A monstrosity that not only featured a zipped and plunging cleavage which struggled to contain her flobby knockers, but – and to Susie's delight and amusement – a well-rounded stomach, and fat thighs that showed clear evidence of heavily dimpled cellulite showing through the thin and s-t-r-e-t-c-h-e-d material.

Affording Nurse Simmons' reflection an insincere smile as she touched up her make-up, Susie wondered if The Old Wreck was ready for such a display of tasteless attire and vulgarity. Surely, Nurse Simmons would be the laughing stock, dressed up like an out of work drag artist in such tame surroundings. And *surely*, any efforts to procure the educated and classy Doctor Rogers would be brushed away with a dismissive hand and concealed contempt. Maybe a hefty dollop of pity.

No, thought Susie, as she eyed the hint of bra beneath her shimmering blouse that offered but a suggestion to the treasure chest that lurked beneath – and moreover, the woman beneath – *she* had the measure of what a man like Doctor Rogers was after and it certainly didn't involve having all her goods on display like some commonplace market stall. After a quick application of lipstick and some squirts of perfume, Susie gives her reflection a satisfied once over and leaves Nurse Simmons to continue her pathetic attempts to backcomb and lacquer her mousy lank hair into anything resembling a style.

'See you there!' Susie cheerily throws over her shoulder as she walks out.

'Yes – see you in the pub, Susie!' she hears in reply as the door to the Ladies slowly swings shut.

Yes. We'll all see you in the pub, Susie.

I looked up from my laptop and lazily stretched and yawned – last night had been quite a night. Movement opposite caught my attention; I looked across and found my 69ers busily emptying kitchen cupboards and getting ready to leave. It felt later than the designated 10 o'clock check out, and as I picked up my phone to see what time it was, I found an email from Clarke waiting for me.

Amber Stone. Amber Stone. Slow, slow, quick, quick, slow. No worries. Everything's coming along at last. It's all over now. Quick, quick! I'm gone. So are you.

I held the phone in the flat of my palm and re-read the message several times. My phone felt as though contaminated with Clarke's twisted mind, and when I'd finished, I gently placed it on the table and vacantly stared across to the trees. What did it mean? Had he left the flat? Did he mean 'gone' from each other's life? Or did it mean something else – something more sinister? I considered replying, to ask for clarity, but immediately decided against it. Things had been quiet on the Clarke front since his vile outburst, and if this was him leaving – as I suspected it was – then just leave him alone to crack on with it. No need to rattle him. Or do anything to make him change his mind.

Standing up, I realised how unsettled and edgy Clarke's cryptic message had made me feel. I plucked a cigarette from the packet in my handbag and went outside, into the real world, the normal world, for a rare morning smoke. I sat on a step, lit up and exhaled through moving pursed lips that made the length of smoke rise and fall. My 6-week stint at Brightlea was nearing its end, making my return to the flat ever closer. I thought about Spencer's offer to come back with me – maybe I'd take him up on it. Besides, it'd be so very good to see him. And if nothing else, it'd be an excellent excuse to spend some time together and catch up.

I was abruptly shaken out of my thoughts by the sudden and unexpected arrival of my 69ers approaching with extended hands, almost causing me to jump in shock.

'Well, we're off, now,' said Mr 69. Reactively, I offered my free hand with a weak smile. He took it in both hands. 'Bye, bye, love. Been nice seeing you.' As I numbly mumbled, 'You too,' he released my hand and let his wife take his place. 'Yes,' she said, warmly shaking my hand while stroking it with small, pressed movements of her thumb, 'it's been really lovely, hasn't it?'

I had no idea what to say. I looked into her squidgy face and couldn't decipher the broad grin or read the glint in her eyes.

'Yes. It's been really... special,' I managed, immediately regretting my choice of words.

'Perhaps we'll see you again next year!' she said, kneading her thumb deeper into my skin. 'We always come the same week every year.'

I pulled my hand away in slow increments.

'Well... I'm not sure...'

'Well, it would be *so* lovely if we bumped into you again!' She gave my hand a final squeeze and let go. 'Bye, bye, love!' And as she retreated backwards to stand alongside her husband, they both gave me small waves. 'Bye, bye, love!' Then they dipped from view and were gone.

I found myself waving to thin air.

'Happy holidays,' I said quietly.

I stubbed out the cigarette, took the butt inside and put it in the bin. Reluctant to engage any further with Mister and Missus 69, and unsure if I could carry on working without glancing their way to see a final, God-knows-what from them, I retreated to my bedroom, ensured the door was firmly shut behind me and treated myself to a very satisfactory session with my aptly named, 'thrusting' rabbit, helped along by similar images that had done me so proud the night before.

Very satisfactory, indeed.

I dropped off afterwards, and had the kind of light snooze where you're neither one thing nor another. I was aware of families walking past my caravan – maybe on their way to the clubhouse or pool – yet asleep. When I later emerged from my bedroom, rubbing my eyes and feeling a bit groggy, I looked over to 69 and felt relief at finding a sour-faced middle-aged woman lethargically going about her cleaning duties with a scowl.

I checked the time. 12.15pm. And couldn't blame her. The army of cleaners were normally all done and dusted by eleven. Half past, max.

Those naughty 69ers. I dread to think what might have delayed them. Maybe a 'goodbye campers' gangbang with Benny the Bear and Duckface Ducky in attendance. Followed up by a swift conga around the car park.

Happy holidays, indeed.

That afternoon, I did something I should have done ages ago. On the way to the beach, and from the shop where I'd checked out the windbreaker (that idea now firmly on the backburner – I was already carrying enough clobber over that cliff), I bought a pair of walking sandals. As ugly as fuck – with big clumpy Velcro straps and thick springy soles – but the instant I tried them on, I distinctly heard my sore ankle say, yes please, mistress. And that was that. I kept them on, popped my normal sandals into my beach bag and pegged it over that cliff top like a mountain goat on amphetamines. And when I reached the dreaded pebbles, I said to ankle, shall we? And ankle said, you betcha. So we did. And it was a whole new world. And such a piece of piss. Stupid Amber, for not buying some ugly sandals earlier.

Or maybe, vain Amber. Possibly.

Probably.

As I made my way towards a good spot I'd picked out before Brokeback, relishing the newfound surety and ease of movement with each step, I became aware of something going on down there. Guys were stood in a huddle and seemingly shouting at a bloke who was dressed in shorts and a baseball cap and hurrying towards me. As he further neared, he cast me an angry look and for a moment, I stood, feeling uncertain; questioning my safety, but alert to his actions. I needn't have worried. He sped past, muttering something under his breath and was soon halfway back to the cliff path, amongst the couples and oldies. As I watched him weave his way through the sunbathers, Mister Tall & Skinny from the beach party arrived at my side. He was partially dressed and out of breath.

'You okay?' I asked. 'What's going on?'

Mister T&S squinted along the beach before replying. 'Pah! He's gone! I'll never catch him.' He took a few moments to catch his breath and wipe beads of sweat from his brow. 'He's been taking photos of some of us – a *real* beach no-no – then we think he was zooming in on the photos and treating himself to a wank while looking at them. Do you know Jed? Bald? Tattoos?'

I nodded. 'From the beach party?'

'Yeah. Well, he caught him out. The bloke was trying to hide his phone behind a newspaper, and Jed was thinking, like, *who* do you *ever* see with a newspaper down here?'

'Well, I normally have a paperback *and* a notebook,' I offered.

Mister T&S gave me a grin. 'Well, unless I've missed something, I've never seen you use them as cover for bringing yourself off.'

I had to smile at that one.

'Besides, you're part of the fixtures and fittings down here,' he went on. 'Like us lot. No – none of us have seen this guy before. Oh, hang on... here comes Jed...'

I turned around to see a dressed and angry-looking Jed stomp towards us over the pebbles.

'Did he get away?' he growled.

'Yeah,' Mister T&S replied with a shrug. 'Time it took to get my shorts and trainers on – he was almost at the cliff path. I would never have caught him. And even if I did, I don't know what I would have done with him. A citizen's arrest? Not sure what the Police would have thought about that.

And I'm not sure you even get the 'Emergency calls only' down here – I don't think so. Someone had a bad fall last year, tried to call an ambulance and couldn't get through. The person had to be piggy-backed over the cliff.'

'So, how did this guy get away so quickly?' I asked.

'He kept his trainers on,' Jed replied, 'and shorts partially pulled down. But had his dick firmly in his hand. Thought he'd got away with taking photos, but I had my eye on him – I mean, it's more unusual to see someone *with* clothes on down here. And when his newspaper started jerking around – it didn't take much working out what he was up to.'

I remembered from the party that Jed was a smoker, so quickly offered him a cigarette. He gratefully accepted and once lit, added, 'You know, it really fucks me off – people think that, because you're gay, you don't get affected by this kind of shit, like we're all subhuman in a way and immune to some wanker's inappropriate behaviour.'

'Is everyone okay?' I asked quietly.

Jed let out a bitter laugh. 'Well, as much as you can be – knowing someone's going home with photos of your privates that you didn't give permission to be taken in the first place. God knows where they might end up – I mean, there's a few down there who haven't even come out yet!'

'*Anyway*,' interjected Mister T&C, 'none of us

like it when anything happens to *anybody* down here. It's normally pretty much self-policed. Yeah, bits and pieces go on – you know that...' he let the words hang for a second as he looked at me, '... but normally, it's pretty discreet, with adults making choices. Mutual consent and all that. What went on today was... well, it was just wrong.'

'I'll kill him if I ever see him again.' Jed spat out the words with unconcealed rage.

'Oh, *come on*,' began T&S. 'You're just pissed off he didn't get a decent enough shot of your knob to splash all over the internet!' Then he winked at me and let out laugh.

I had no idea how Jed was going to react, his face had been like thunder earlier, but after a moment's thought, it creased into reluctant laughter.

'Oh, piss off, you!' he said, taking a playful swipe at T&S, who looked at me and shrugged.

'What can you do?' he asked. 'The bloke's got away with it. Do you start crying? Let it affect you? Or do you carry on living? I mean, it was wrong, *very* wrong. It was highly unpleasant – but no-one's died. No-one's got cancer. We all get to come to the beach for another day.'

'You've got a point, I suppose...' I said.

Jed slowly shook his head. 'I agree – you're right. As ever. It just... it just makes me *so* angry when people get away with shit like that.' His face softened. 'But I think we'll all get over it.' He smiled at me. 'Couldn't cadge another cigarette, could I? Just need to calm down a bit more.'

'Christ, yes!' I replied, delving into my bag. 'If memory jussssst about serves, I must have smoked loads of yours that night.'

'Ooh! Which reminds me...' began T&S, placing a hand to his throat, '... have you seen your *friend* again?'

'Sadly, not,' I replied with a smile. 'It was just a one-off meeting of minds.'

They both laughed, and it appeared that all thoughts of illicit photos were already fading. I politely turned down their invitation to join them at Brokeback, so they said their ta-tas and left me with my thoughts as I quickly undressed in the sunshine and settled onto my front.

Maybe I had been a bit blasé about my safety on the beach – what with the daily greetings and recognising so many of the nudey beach 'family' – and was blind to what was really going on – what with spending most of my time writing, reading, stretched out with my eyes closed or having the occasional nap. Of course, other times I'd be having a curious look around – and as much as all the times nothing would be going on, something would, to whatever degree.

Yes – there were the blatant and not-so-blatant tugging and sex sessions. And the pestering arseholes who needed informing that their presence wasn't welcome. The naked desperados who wandered along the beach, pretending to show an interest in the cliff formation whilst copping a look at whoever took their fancy.

Now thinking about it, some of them did use a phone as a prop, in a pathetic attempt to disguise the intent behind their meanderings and supposedly surreptitious gawping sessions: the sudden halt at an 'interesting' spot to inspect and/or photograph the cliffside. Or going through the pretence of sending a text or making that vital phone call to no fucker at all – a breezy one-sided conversation into a silent mobile. And the over-the-top phone waving in a fake display of trying to get a signal we all know doesn't exist. I'd seen a lot of that. All affording the ogler a seemingly innocent right to continue their stop/start meanderings amongst us.

And *maybe* take the occasional photograph they shouldn't.

Or maybe, (just maybe) they really *were* snapping away in the name of Instagram. I didn't suppose that'd be beyond the realms of possibility. The dramatic cliffside with its bird nests dotted about sure attracted a lot of attention.

But was it the right kind?

I took a deep breath and a moment to wonder if the Brokebackers weren't the only ones being violated by surreptitious snappers. And expected not.

Should I be angry? Or just resign myself to that kind of behaviour coming with the territory when naked on a beach? I let out a sigh and looked ahead at my fellow nudies happily soaking up the sun. A bit of both, I supposed. And if I didn't like it, I knew what to do. But on balance, it was a small price to pay for the freedom and enjoyment I felt from being stretched out in the sun. Besides, if I was honest about it, I liked men admiring my body. Just a pity I couldn't choose which ones were doing it.

And Jed was right; it *was* odd when someone was mooching around or sitting on the beach with their clothes on. At least naked, we were all on a level playing field, and thinking about it, I'd always been a tad wary when someone dressed sat in a reasonably close vicinity or wandered up and down. At the time, I'd speculated whether they were new to the nudey scene and still deliberating whether to make the 'big reveal' – and how best to go about it. But maybe there were more sinister implications to their behaviour.

I supposed a lot went on that I didn't know about. Particularly during the long warm evenings when most people had left. Yeah. Plenty, by my reckoning.

I picked up a pebble and rolled it around in my hand, enjoying its heat and smoothness.

But then again, I thought, I'd fucked a random guy in the sea. And very nice, too – thanks for asking. So I guess that'll be my name added to the Nudey Beach Hall of Shame.

I twirled the pebble between two fingers and thought about my recent behaviour. My liberal views about sex. How very different they were from the female friends I'd discussed such matters with over a glass of wine or three. They'd never understood my liking for what they called "rough sex" – without the intimacy they enjoyed during their slow and gentle lovemaking sessions. Candles, soft music, maybe some seductive lingerie, and the whispered terms of endearment.

My appetite was certainly different. I always felt an overwhelming urgency to enjoy the other person in some kind of unfettered, animalistic way. Slow lovemaking turned me off. And bored me. I always just wanted to let go – and go with my sexually charged needs that had no patience for all that faffing and fannying around. Spencer and I used to joke that we never made love, but rather, fucked hard with love. No inhibitions. Just raw emotions and desire.

Maybe, if my mother knew, that would at least be one thing about me she'd be proud of. Go with the flow, Amber! Go with the flow! Listen to your heart. Listen to your body. Listen to your desires. And just do it!

Problem is, my body's a greedy bastard. *Plus* I wasn't used to going too long without sex. Hence

Olive Man. And the other randoms picked up over the years. Consenting adults sharing their bodies for an hour, a few hours, a night – or a frantic ten minutes.

Admittedly, there'd been some disaster stories along the way. Episodes of non-compatibility. Men shocked by my eagerness to skip the pleasantries and get down to business. Or my aggressive behaviour when grabbing hair to firmly press a head between my legs. The smacks. The spitting. The rimming. The biting. The blindfolds. The toys. The candles (and their sweet dripping wax). The poppers. The anal...

Etc.

Et cetera.

Or just the energy. The solid hard fucking. That's what turned me on. And made me come. Not soft stroking or sighing or a dithering and tentative build-up. That might work for a Susie type, but would have me reaching for my clothes and the exit without so much as a glance over my shoulder.

Sometimes I wondered about my insatiable and blokey outlook to sex. Was it blokey? What even counted for blokey these days with the onward march of the touchy/feely 'new man'?

Fuck it, I thought. I'm me.

I tossed away the pebble and watched it tumble a few times before coming to rest against a broken shell. I turned onto my back and closed my eyes.

With a smile, I thought back to my antics of the previous night. How sluttish and vulgar it would have appeared to some of my London girlfriends. How *appalled* they'd be. Tut tut, Amber. But I saw it differently. I was single, randy, and as things stood, didn't have to answer to anyone. Besides, I didn't hear any complaints from Luke or Steve. We were just like-minded people. Doing like-minded things. And everyone else could just go whistle.

I thought about Luke getting off on my photos and texts. It made me feel both horny and powerful. He was due back sometime later and should be pinging me a text. Maybe we'd be able to consummate our kooky relationship before too long. I wondered what he'd be like... it would be like... and felt the familiar throb of my ever-ready clit and the subtle pulse of wetness ebbing downwards. I had high hopes for Luke. And there was every indication there'd be nothing vanilla about him in the sack.

I let my mind switch to Steve. Lovely, funny, charmer, Steve. With his winks, cheesy one liners and bravado. All that front. But I bet he'd just be a pussycat in bed. An enthusiastic one – but a pussycat, nonetheless. I was pleased he had a new girlfriend and suspected, given the right one, he'd dote on her. In my experience, the loud bragging blokes weren't unknown to be hiding a more sensitive side they didn't want their mates to see.

While the quieter and markedly more Machiavellian ones slipped under the radar until it was too late. And the damage done.

Clarke…

I picked up another pebble, inspected its mottled pattern and came to a decision; I would call Spencer and get him to come down – maybe spend my last day and night here with him – if he was free. I could even bring him down to the beach – he'd love that – before going back to Exeter to kick down the flat door and storm in side-by-side, each holding a raised gun in our hands.

FREEZE! MOTHERFUCKER!!

Smiling at the image, I let the pebble drop from between my fingers and sat up for a cigarette I shouldn't have. As I lit up and exhaled, I silently congratulated myself for not feeling sad when thinking about Spencer. But as I watched the waves lazily roll and spread into wide fingers of foam, I knew I wasn't kidding anyone.

Still, I had Luke to play with before having to surgically remove myself from my beloved caravan. And hopefully, beyond. With light traffic, we could land at each other's doorstep within half an hour. If that was on the cards. Nice and slow, Amber. Nice and slow. Let's see.

Hugging up my knees, I took a last drag on my cigarette before crushing the stub on a pebble and burying it. I closed my eyes, raised my face towards the sun and let my senses fully absorb my surroundings; the kiss of heat upon my skin, the waves' gentle rhythm, shrill calls from swooping gulls and the warm combination of smooth and rough pebbles pressing against the soles of my bare feet.

God, I'd miss this place!

I opened my eyes and gave a smile to one of the old boys as he took his regular afternoon stroll. Glancing over his aged body, I threw him a small wave.

'Lovely day, isn't it?' he called out.

'Beautiful! Just beautiful!' I replied. Watching him go on his merry way, with his crinkly arse and spindly legs, I let out a sigh. This little episode of my life was coming to an end. And although I knew I'd be back, I felt a sudden injection of sadness. My daily routine – the writing, the beach – even my forays into Flabby's, had become very special to me.

Endings.

Beginnings.

I had a new life, a different kind of life waiting for me in Exeter. A happier, Clarke-free life. And who knew where Susie would take me? Somewhere? Nowhere? She'd at least be part of my journey.

My little old boy had reached Brokeback and stood chatting to a couple of the guys – doubtless discussing the lovely weather. Amongst the smattering of creeps, there sure was a nice little community of decent people down here. I'd be more than happy to see them again, hopefully over many summers to come – or as long as my body held out.

But meanwhile, and with thoughts of endings in mind, Susie was creeping along towards hers and needed my urgent attention.

I pulled out my notebook, and with a warm, fuzzy feeling of contentment, settled on my front and found where I'd last left off. As I readied my pen and tried to re-work a sentence in my mind, I glanced out to the sea to find a lone male canoeist bobbing about on the waves with a set of binoculars pressed to his eyes and pointing my way.

'Jeez,' I murmured. 'What *is* it like here, sometimes?'

I looked away, raised my middle finger in the air for enough time to relay the message, and got to work. Although not before catching sight of a couple of naked fishermen happily casting off a bit further along the shoreline.

This place...

New happy campers back at Brightlea Sands! 69 has a young family in there, and as I put my beach stuff down, I caught glimpses of a boy aged about 7 or 8, still in his trainers and using the double bed as a trampoline. His parents were plonked in front of the television, paying no mind to the little shit going at somebody else's property as though trying to crush the bed like a disused tin can.

After a visit to the bathroom, I found the boy had changed tack: presumably becoming bored with bouncing on the bed, he had instead opted to use it as a landing mat, as I caught him taking the short run-up along the corridor before throwing himself head first onto the mattress. I watched him, spread-eagled, head buried in the pillows and momentarily wondered if he was unwittingly inhaling the ghosts of a billion sperm from the previous 69ers shenanigans through the thin bedding.

I let out a short snort of laughter.

'Go on son,' I called out. 'Fill your boots!'

Once again, I pushed away any thoughts of what might lurk in my own bedroom – what you don't know can't harm you.

Or so I tried to convince myself.

And as I watched the laddo nestle his face further into a pillow, as his arms performed swimming motions, I concluded that, sometimes, ignorance can indeed be bliss.

Mind you, I was probably sunbathing each day on top of a sperm graveyard. Mental note, Amber – give that yoga mat a good sponging down.

I looked across at 70 to see who I had in there. Hmm... this looked interesting. A couple. Around about my age. Smart-looking. Too smart for this place. Silver BMW. She's helping him unload the boot. Not much stuff. Him on the top step. Her handing over the last of it – looks like a bag of groceries, some bottles – and now they're saying goodbye to one another. A light hug. A kiss on the cheek. A small wave from him as she gets in the car. Off she goes. He stands there for a moment. Senses me looking. Looks. Looks displeased. I dip from view. Then immediately wished I'd stayed put. Rather than appear to be snooping. Which I was.

Hmm. Hmm, indeed.

Is she coming back? Has she deposited him at the caravan as punishment? Is he *another* writer, here to get some peace?

I waited a few moments, stepped forward and risked a peep. Standing in the lounge with his back towards me, he was speaking to someone on his mobile. He must be from a different caste, I decided – he's not put the telly on. I watched as his free hand gradually became more animated, as though emphasising an important point to whoever was on the receiving end of his call. When his hand finally came to rest upon his forehead, as though squeezing his eyebrows tight together, he slowly began to turn my way. I beat him to it and stood back, out of sight.

Jeez. I really was getting to be a nosey parker at this place. Still, as a wannabe writer, I decided I was allowed such indulgences. After all, everything, in all its forms, could one day become material. So snooping was allowed.

Hearing the distinct ping of a text landing in my phone, I went to my bag and unearthed it. Relief it wasn't Clarke, was instantly replaced by pleasure – it was from Luke.

I'm finally back on Shaldon terra firma. How's that ankle of yours?x

I smiled at the message. I liked Luke's texts – both the decent and indecent. Taking a couple of moments to think, I tapped out a reply.

Both ankles present and correct and in good working order, thanks. I treated them to some REALLY ugly sandals, designed for cliffs and nudey beaches. You okay?x

Ping!

While I waited for Luke's reply, I put the kettle on to make myself a coffee. Standing by my kitchen window, I was able to cast an eye into 55 alongside me. Yet another elderly couple. White-haired and stooped. It looked like the husband had had the same thought as me, as he was finishing off two mugs of hot drinks and carefully carrying them over to the lounge area where his wife sat with the back of her head to me. On the small window ledge behind her sat – what I guessed to be – a couple of framed photos they'd brought along. I don't know why, but I suddenly got a sad feeling about them. The photos. The couple. Odd, I know. And I hope I'm wrong.

I turned and looked through to 57. No signs of life in there at the moment, but the scattered toys and mayhem meant another family had clearly landed. It was coming up to peak time now, and not long before the schools would close for summer. The camp would be crammed full of families. And I'd be gone.

The ping of my phone.

Just seen out the Priest who's rid me of student demons – so all good at this end. Would you like to meet up?xx

I stopped myself from replying too quickly. Instead, I poured water into my mug, swirled the coffee and carried it over to my L-shaped and sat down. As I gazed out at the trees, wondering how to word my reply, switching between a variety of smart alec responses and earnest ones, an old blue Peugeot pulled up at 70 and a woman got out. The door to the caravan opened and our man stood there with a broad grin of greeting on his face. The woman was a real looker. Dressed in tatty sweat pants and a cheap looking vest, her dyed black hair had been dragged into a tight pony tail. She wore big hooped earrings and had an indistinct tattoo running the length from her shoulder to elbow. But she was a looker, alright.

Oblivious to the top of my head poking out from my seating, they passionately embraced just inside the caravan door. I watched as he ran his hands over her back and down to her arse, which he firmly squeezed with both hands. Their kissing was frenzied, as if seeing each other after being kept apart, and when it came to an end, they briefly dipped into the caravan and out of sight, before emerging again, the man carrying a holdall, locking the door behind him and getting into the Peugeot with the woman. As they pressed their lips together for a few moments, our man's eyes suddenly opened, flicked my way, and caught me in the act of looking over. Too late to look away, we met each other's gaze for just an instant, but his eyes had spoken enough for me to understand.

It's none of your business.

I turned my head, heard the engine start up, and the car move slowly away.

What a weird shit place this is, I thought as I looked back out the window at the now empty 70. What the buggery was that all about? But it was pretty obvious. It was life. Life happening. Just in a goldfish bowl.

I picked up my phone.

Only if your head won't spin around. Otherwise, yes. xx

13.

Susie Goes Big and Goes Home

Doctor Webb's retirement party is already in full, heady swing when Susie makes her entrance at The Old Wreck. She takes a moment or two to take in her low-beamed surroundings while smoothing down her blouse and letting her fingers make the impromptu decision to surreptitiously undo an extra button. Susie easily picks out Doctor Webb amongst the throng, who is flanked by two animated biddies who cluck and fuss over him in unison, and to his obvious delight. And there's Maureen, forging a path through the masses with her lurex cardigan, a tray of nibbles and loudly alerting everyone to the presence of a buffet lurking on a back table.

Susie takes a few tentative steps into the pub, still scanning amongst the brasses and wood panelling for sight of Doctor Rogers' tall frame. She recognises patients from the surgery, colleagues, reps, suppliers – but still no sign. As she is flagged over to the bar by a couple of fellow secretaries, Susie nearly stumbles as she receives a firm nudge in the small of her back. Before she has the chance to turn and discover its source, her question is answered by the loud and brash, jumpsuit clad, yoo-hooing of Nurse Simmons.

Susie straightens and faces her, ready to give the ignorant cow a bit of what for, but is instantly aghast to find her sandwiched between two men and locked arm-in-arm with each of them.

One of the arms belongs to a smiling Doctor Rogers.

Susie feels a tidal wave of a blush cover her face. This was not how she envisaged making an entrance. At all. Collecting herself, Susie politely greets Doctor Rogers and the unknown man before throwing Nurse Simmons a strained smile and the advice, 'Mind where you're going'.

Nurse Simmons dismisses Susie straight away. She wiggles her hands from her still-locked arms. 'Couldn't have been me – I'm all tied up with these two!'

'Whatever,' Susie quietly mumbles, before throwing Doctor Rogers a brief Princess Diana doe-eyed smile.

Doctor Rogers returns it with his own dazzling broad grin. 'You look very nice this evening, Susie'.

As Susie feels both a-quiver with pleasure and the unmistakeable bristle of jealously from Nurse Simmons, the trio unlock arms and immediately get swallowed up by approaching guests. Susie is nonplussed by the sight of Doctor Rogers moving away from her; it is clear they have unfinished business and the night is still young. She is further encouraged by the sight of a dejected Nurse Simmons getting detached from the two men, as Doctor Rogers steers his companion deeper into the pub.

What a deluded fool, Susie thinks as she eyes Nurse Simmons in her Cher cast-off outfit – thinking she could dazzle someone like Doctor Rogers with that ridiculous get up.

Susie joins her colleagues at the bar and readily soaks up their compliments about her appearance. How different from the previous Friday's cardamom swirl shame! Opting for a very large glass of white wine, Susie keeps her eye on Doctor Rogers as she sips away. My, he does seem in particularly good spirits this evening! Look – there he is – laughing again as he leans in to share another joke with the group and giving his guest and Paula from Dispensing hearty squeezes on the shoulder at the punchline.

As she takes another mouthful of wine, Susie

begins to daydream that Doctor Rogers had it in mind all along to make a move on her this very evening, and how it might unfold... but she is broken from her thoughts by her colleagues, whose chatter she's only been half-listening to. They ask if anyone knows who Doctor Rogers' guest is. He apparently looks familiar. One person believes he's a drug rep. While another is adamant he works in the Cardiology Department at the Hospital. Did Susie know?

Susie shrugs. She doesn't care who he is. Nor does she care for such nosey speculation about her Doctor's guest. Feeling she has to interject, she opens her mouth to speak but is stopped in her tracks by someone tapping on her shoulder.

Turning around, Susie is greeted by the sight of a nervous-looking, bespectacled and suited young man.

'Excuse me,' he says with a slight stammer, 'but I am led to believe that you're Susie. I'd just like to introduce myself – I'm Doctor Wellard – Doctor Webb's replacement. I start on Monday.' He picks up Susie's hand and it gives it a moist, floppy shake.

Susie says she is pleased to meet him; she'd heard that the new doctor would be in attendance tonight, but had no idea that he'd be quite so young. Or goofy-looking. Or socially awkward. Susie spends some time making small talk with the Doctor, who, although seemingly eager to engage with her, is a mass of nerves, shyness, stammers, blushes and quite frankly, a bore.

It is evident to Susie that this newcomer could not hold a candle to Doctor Rogers' silky bedside manner. And further wonders how the patients might react to having such a nervy GP giving them an intimate once over. She shudders to think.

Doctor Wellard buys Susie a glass of wine and asks her a few things about herself. Susie keeps it brief and professional, and after throwing him a few snippets, decides it's high time to seek out Doctor Rogers: the wine has loosened her up, the lacy bra was letting off steam, and the new Doctor was beginning to get on her knockers. Besides all that, and despite hating to admit it, she was now curious as to who Doctor Rogers' companion was; they'd been glued together like Tweedledum and Tweedledee since their arrival. And from her vantage position, Susie could make out the dreaded jumpsuit weaving its way through the crowd to get to them.

But Doctor Wellard is not easy to shake off – he sticks to Susie like a fly on a freshly squeezed Mister Whippy dog turd as he staggers his way through various tedious anecdotes, releases unattractive wheezes of laughter at the end of each, and makes the reveal of his Christian name.

Christian.

Susie eyes him over the rim of her near-depleted

wine glass with a fixed grin. Pity he's not Christian Grey, she thinks with a silent sigh.

Salvation comes in the form of the ever-clucking Maureen. Her lurex breezes over and whisks Christian away to be introduced to other colleagues. Susie watches as he clumsily knocks into people with stammered apologies, and cringes at the awkwardness of his greetings.

Fifty Shades of Twerpdom, she thinks with a little giggle.

Susie secures her third glass of wine and glances over once more to the smiling, handsome head of Doctor Rogers which pokes out above all others. He does seem to be enjoying himself. Susie has a large mouthful of wine. It may be too late to head off Nurse Simmons at the pass, but now was the time to get over there, before she tried to get her false nails into him.

Susie nudges her way through with series of 'excuse me's', but annoyingly gets delayed by brief 'hellos' and exchanges, and as she finally closes in on the trio is dismayed to find Nurse Simmons half-draped over Doctor Rogers like some floozie in a wild west saloon. The three of them are rocking their heads back in laughter, with Nurse Simmons' bright red lipsticked mouth open obscenely w-i-d-e.

You could get a double-decker bus in there, Susie thinks dismissively.

Doctor Rogers espies the approaching Susie and

flags her over to join them. Susie beams with delight, gives her tits a bit of a thrust and completes her journey. She is further sent into seventh heaven when the evidently, slightly squiffy Doctor Rogers wraps an arm around her, clinks glasses with his free hand and gives her a few deliciously tight squeezes.

'Here she is!' he exclaims. 'The wonder woman of the surgery!'

Her heart bursting with pride and passion, Susie presses herself into Doctor Rogers and somehow finds the temerity to encircle an arm around his waist. She casts Nurse Simmons a look of the cat who's got the cream, but finds it a wasted gesture; Nurse Simmons has the vacant idiot grin of someone who's already quaffed a Prosecco too many.

'Ah! So you're Susie!' says the mystery man. 'I've heard plenty of good things about you. Sorry – we didn't get introduced earlier. I'm Adam – pleased to meet you.'

Susie is irritated that she has to release Doctor Rogers in order to change wine hands and accept the handshake on offer.

Doctor Rogers looks down at Susie like a proud parent.

'Yes, it's Susie who keeps us all organised and on track in the surgery. I don't know what I'd do without her – but I never tell her that or she might go and get a better paid job elsewhere.'

Susie looks up into Doctor Rogers' hazel eyes that glitter with affection and feels a prickle of anticipation run down her spine. And with one final heavenly squeeze, Doctor Rogers releases his hold on Susie. But she doesn't care one jot. Tonight was going to unfold *exactly* the way she had dreamed. Back in the arms of her Doctor Rogers.

Susie gladly stands talking and drinking with both men, while Nurse Simmons – who has seemingly thrown in the towel – staggers off to doubtless latch herself onto some other poor sod. Or maybe home, for an outfit rethink. Susie discovers some more about Doctor Rogers' guest; his surname is Bassett, making his nickname Bertie. He knew Doctor Rogers from their University days together and more recently, at medical school, from where Adam/Bertie did indeed go on to become a cardiologist, and having secured a job at the local hospital, recently moved down to Cornwall, therefore reigniting their friendship.

Susie finds all this most satisfactory. She envisages becoming Doctor Rogers' wife and moving in a select circle of medical professionals. Hosting intimate soirees where she could further display her cooking skills – whilst taking *great* care to ensure no nuts found their way into the ingredients – she wouldn't want her darling husband keeling over and choking to death over one of her famed stir-fries.

Adam turns out to be delightful company. A wholly fitting friend for her Doctor. She approves. With his own boyish good looks, Susie can see that this eligible bachelor may well need her assistance for securing some suitable female company along the line. Although, Nurse Simmons and her crisp packet décolletage would be firmly scratched off the list.

As others come over to mingle and chat, Susie takes it as her cue to excuse herself and give Doctor Rogers some space to spend time with them. She feels it's important for him to realise early on that she's a gracious lady and not some clingy bunny boiler.

'Catch you later, Susie!' Doctor Rogers calls out with a grin.

'Will do!' She replies cheerily.

By now, Susie is in need of something to soak up the wine that is already making her feel a bit heady. As she makes her way over to the buffet, she thinks about this new, more relaxed side she's seeing in her Doctor. Maybe she was bringing out the best in him, Susie decides. Feeling a twitch of anticipation rustle her black lacy panties, she further concludes; and him the best in me.

Susie makes her selection from the buffet table and curls a fist around a jumbo sausage roll, which she readily devours in hungry mouthfuls.

Heady stuff, indeed...

The evening rumbles on. An emotional speech from Doctor Webb culminates in one of his biddies dramatically stepping forward to present him with some well-timed tissues for a blow of his hooter and dab at his eyes. He is given a rousing three cheers! With a smile, Susie watches on as Doctor Rogers and Adam both raise an arm in the air for each hip-hip-hooray. She very much approves of Doctor Rogers' loosened mood this evening. It'll certainly be coming in handy later, Susie decides, as she licks a sausage roll crumb from the corner of her mouth.

Maureen makes the rounds with the remains of the buffet on a tray.

Doctor Webb retires to a chair, looking drained and emotional.

The background music gets turned up.

And Doctor Wellard is back. Pushing his glasses further up his nose and asking a reasonably drunk Susie if hospital test results are filed manually or scanned onto electronic records. But our Susie has no time to indulge such boring nonsense; the injection of louder tunes has already got some of the squiffy brigade dancing or hopelessly flailing their limbs about.

Or in some instances, both.

And there amongst them, is the unmistakeable jumpsuit, busting grinding horror moves to the obvious delight of Doctor Rogers and Adam, as they egg her on with boozy cheers.

There is no time to lose. Susie brushes aside the hapless Doctor Wellard, citing a sudden need to relay something urgent and work-related to Doctor Rogers and forges her way forward. If things were going to come down to a dance-off between her and Nurse Simmons, then let battle commence.

As Susie steps into the arena she finds Doctor Rogers and Adam swaying and clapping along to the music as they continue to watch the gyrating and perspiring form of Nurse Simmons, who seems lost in the moment and without a care in the world. Susie takes a moment to eye her challenger with distaste, then acknowledges the grinning nod from Doctor Rogers' that encourages her to join in with the other dancers. Our Susie needs no second invite. She twirls and moves and shakes and raises an arm above her head, then shakes some more. And delights in seeing Doctor Rogers' attention, hand clapping and occasional cries of, 'Woo hoo!' are now directed at her. As Susie moves, she feels her racing green semi-transparent blouse (£16.99 p&p included) shift and slide over her frame until finally sliding from one shoulder entirely.

A sober Susie would have scooped it up immediately and secured her modesty. And done up that last button she'd hastily decided to unfasten at her entrance. But our Susie is a bit wankered by now. And Doctor Rogers is showing no signs of dismay. If anything, he is whooping louder as Adam cheers at his side. Clapping harder. Smiling wider. His eyes, sparklier.

The song changes to Madonna's 'Like A Prayer'. One of Susie's all time party favourites.

And that is that.

For tonight, Our Susie *is* Madonna...

The blouse is down from both shoulders. A shimmy here. A shimmy there. A forwards cleavage-revealing wiggle here. And there. In fact, everywhere. The claps increase in intensity. Susie finds herself the sole dancer within a circle of colleagues and guests. As she moves and pouts, swishes and throws her non-bolloxed hair about, she soaks up their approval and dares to throw Doctor Rogers a finger-wriggling seductive smile. Even Nurse Simmons looks on in bewildered and reluctant admiration. Susie feels sexy and vibrant. Irresistible. The Temptress of Trewithiel. What man could possibly resist?

Just one, it appears.

As Susie outstretches both palms in front of her and bends and wiggles backwards, she is slap in front of Doctor Rogers and Adam. Her cleavage and lacy bra are on full view, but she doesn't care. This was her finale. Her sealing of the deal. But as she flips away some hair that has fallen over her eyes, she is mortified to see Doctor Rogers briefly run his hand over Adam-cum-Bertie's arse and give it a quick squeeze. With his mouth almost touching his ear, Doctor Rogers whispers something to Adam before pulling away. They look at one another with broad, knowing smiles. Adam throws him a wink and the kind of look Susie has only dreamed of.

Susie twirls away.

She can't think straight.

She can't think.

She feels so drunk.

The claps get louder.

The circle seems to enclose around her.

Faces seemingly loom in and out.

Contorted cruel smiles.

Or is it laughter?

Susie stops abruptly.

Puts a hand to forehead.

She's hot.

She's clammy.

She's struggling to breathe.

Susie needs to vomit.

She puts a hand to her mouth.

She bends over.

She is aware of someone cupping her elbow and steering her outside with coaxing words.

Oh, the *shame* of it all, Susie!

As Susie chucks up her sausage roll over a selection of potted geraniums, she is vaguely aware of someone holding her hair out of puke's harm.

When finished, a glass of water of is held in front of her face.

'Here, drink this,' is the instruction. 'It'll make you feel better'.

Still on her haunches, Susie takes the glass and slowly drinks her way through the water before handing it up for collection. Glass taken away, she tries to stand, but needs assistance. Hands around her waist hoof her up into an unsteady standing position. Her saviour stands in front her, his arms outstretched should she wobble or begin to fall.

Christian.

'Do you live close by?' he asks.

Susie manages a nod.

'Right, I'll walk you home. Make sure you get back alright. Have you got anything left inside?'

'Handbag. By the bar,' Susie mumbles. 'Maureen knows it.'

Christian creases his brow. 'Maureen… Maureen… ah! Gotcha! Right, let's sit you on this wall. I won't be long.'

Susie is assisted to a low wall and gently sat down.

As Christian goes back inside the pub, a figure steps out. Susie has her head in her hands, but can see through the gaps in her fingers. She lets out a groan. As if things couldn't get any worse…

Nurse Simmons lights a cigarette before sauntering her jumpsuit over and joining Susie on the low wall.

'I saw what happened,' she says, blowing smoke up into the night. 'These ears and eyes don't miss a trick.'

Susie manages to rotate her head sideways to Nurse Simmons, but doesn't possess the energy to tell her to fuck off.

'I'm afraid you've rather made a fool of yourself, my dear. Jonathon and me go back years. He tries to be discreet. Village life. Village busy bodies and all that. But the people who know him well, *know*. I guess the alcohol made him a little off-guard this evening, but by my reckoning, I think he got away with it. After all,' she said, inspecting a painted false fingernail, '*all* eyes were on you.'

Nurse Simmons flicks her cigarette away and unsteadily rises to her feet.

'Bertie only moved in with Jonathon last week – that's why he's not been around so much – so I very much doubt he'll be wanting to change tack anytime soon. Do you?'

Susie has no words. But Nurse Simmons has a few more to spit out before leaving.

'You know, Susie, I thought you had a bit more class about you. I mean, your outfit tonight. Your dancing. And before you question my get up, this clobber was at the request of Jonathon, I'll have you know. The last time I wore this was when we both went with some friends to watch an Abba tribute band in Plymouth. Had a brilliant night. Totally brilliant. Pity you couldn't have been there. Anyway. Enjoy the rest of your evening. You stuck up cow.'

Susie despondently walks home bare-footed alongside Christian. She hugs her handbag to her chest. He talks. But she isn't listening. She feels like she never wants to listen to anyone again. He sees her indoors, makes her a black coffee, pours her a large glass of water to drink before bed and puts some headache tablets on the kitchen table for her impending hangover.

Susie mumbles her thanks. She's grateful. He's been a real trooper. But now she just wants to be on her own.

Doctor Wellard bids her a good night's sleep.

And our Susie is alone.

So very alone.

Poor, poor Susie.

I sat back in my seat and looked at the screen. Truth be known, I didn't entirely know what I was doing with Susie. But if it was shitty chick lit I was after, then that was certainly what I was getting. Hey ho. I checked the time on my phone; I was meeting Luke on the beach later and wanted to make sure I could fit in a little tidy-up of the nether regions before hitting the pebbles. *And* I'd already made a pact with myself – strictly no pre-beach masturbating – I wanted to keep myself primed for orgasm, as I had high hopes for whatever was going to pan out between us. Luke had suggested meeting at the dreaded Captain's Table for a quick drink before joining the nudey masses, but I'd soon put the kibosh on that. Two reasons. Firstly, I didn't fancy a repeat of WeeGate by necking drinks in the pub beforehand. And secondly, going to beach on my own was *my* thing, *my* little adventure, and had been since that very first day I went over the cliff top and into the unknown. It had signalled my new independence, my new freedom and the new me. Or rather, reinstating the old me. And I simply wasn't ready for that feeling of attachment to anyone. Coming off the beach was different. The time had already been spent there. The journey made. I'd happily walk off the beach with Luke, but not onto it. For now.

We made the arrangements last night, through a series of witty but *very* civilised texts. I guess neither of us wanted to build up something into what might amount to nothing. Plus, he *had* let me down once before. Although this time it felt different. As if we'd moved on a bit since then.

It was obvious both of us wanted sex. And we would be sunbathing naked next to one another. But by not teasing or suggesting or mentioning sex, somehow made last night's exchanges between us more exciting. I guess the unspoken word can have such power.

I was having a tame one in Flabby's when our texts picked up again. They came as a welcome distraction, as I'd earlier been outside and having a cigarette when I put in the call to Spencer, asking if the offer still stood for him to come to the flat with me. It came as no surprise when he responded: 'Just tell me where I need to be, and when.' And he'd laughed his delicious and familiar laugh when I told him he'd be staying in a Sophia Classique. Number 56.

'I'll be there,' he said at the end of the call.

Spencer didn't have time for a chat, he had to dash off to a client's launch party – but as he was coming down for a night, we'd have plenty of time to catch up. I knew I could rely on Spencer. I supposed I wouldn't really be needing him, all was still wonderfully quiet on the Clarke front – and in real terms, he'd already told me he'd left – so wondered, if deep down, I was just using the flat thing as an excuse to spend some time with Spencer.

Probably.

Yes.

I'd gone back into the pub, deep in thought and attempting my usual regrouping after a Spencer phone call. Most of the lads were in there. Steve One and Fucker Frank, the latter brandishing a cupboard handle and loudly wondering if, "that snotty and patronising tight-arsed bitch" would be missing it later. Seems like someone didn't get a tip for their efforts.

And Matty was out, enjoying an increasingly rare night off. He stood cradling his pint, looking like always, as if he didn't approve of Fucker Frank, didn't want to laugh at his foul-mouthed offerings, but never won the battle. Matty never laughed whole-heartedly, preferring to let it out in begrudged blurted increments.

I was happy to be close to their company, but not amongst it. I settled on a bar stool in the corner, pulled out my phone and smiled at Luke's latest text. Apparently he'd just managed to make his latest commission of Exmoor look like the contents of a madman's drugged and hallucinating brain. I doubted that very much.

As I tried to shrug off thoughts of Spencer and think up a witty retort for Luke, Steve Two walked into Flabby's with his new girlfriend. I was immediately grateful for being tucked away in a corner. I had no desire to spoil anything for Steve, and furthermore, didn't want him to break our Double O agreement.

The guys had obviously been introduced before, as she was readily greeted by her name – Freya. And she was a beauty, alright. Tanned, tall and slender, she wore a cropped top which revealed a perfectly toned stomach, while her short skirt showed off athletic legs. It was clear that Freya, when she wasn't working out with Steve in the bedroom, was very much doing so in the gym.

I felt the usual attraction when seeing a beautiful woman. And briefly wondered how good she'd look naked. Or taste. I guess I was just thinking the same as some of the lads. Sadly, I was yet to have a lesbian encounter, but it was something firmly on my bucket list and always rated highly on the fantasy fodder scale for masturbatory purposes.

The only time I'd come anywhere close, was in my mid-to-late twenties, when holidaying in Ibiza. On a boozy night out, I suddenly found myself and another similarly aged woman as the sole dancers in a busy music bar. She was blonde, *very* attractive and as drunk as me. We laughed as we danced, trying to out-sexy the other and to the obvious delight of the male onlookers. To add to their pleasure, we embarked on a smooch of sorts and lightly trailed our hands over each other's bodies as we giggled and nestled our mouths into the other's neck.

We stopped when the music changed for the worse and she left the dance floor to seek out to the toilet. After a minute or two, I followed, catching her as she emerged from a cubicle. Without a word, I gently nudged her backwards with a smile and closed the door behind us. I ran a hand through her long hair, grabbed the back of her head and passionately kissed her. She kissed me back with equal intensity. And when I slipped my hand under and up her top and began to massage her breasts, she returned the compliment.

I'd been more than eager to get her back to my apartment. Or go to hers. As my hand reached to tug up the hem of her skirt, I suggested it to her – but with a jolt – she wanted to stop. Her bi-curious episode had run its course. She smoothed down her skirt, shook her hair into a wild mess, drunkenly apologised and left me in there.

I've often wondered, what might have been...

Steve and Freya made for a good-looking couple. She was around his age and as I studied her some more, I suddenly remembered who she reminded me of – what with that sleek bob haircut – none other than Elena, my gorgeous hairdresser. Who I *really* needed to call, to fix up my, 'Exeter – I'm back!' hair appointment. And of course, make arrangements for our first night out on the town together.

As I tapped a reminder into my phone, I heard the familiar, 'How's Bondie Blondie this evening?'

I smiled and looked up at Steve Two. Glancing over his shoulder, I saw his girlfriend had her back to us and was laughingly examining the cupboard handle.

'I'm good, thanks. Saving the planet from the bad guys and nuclear devastation – you know, the usual stuff.' I gave a nod of my head towards Freya. 'She looks like a lovely girl.'

Steve looked awkward for a second, before breaking into a beamed smile.

'She is. She really is.' He leaned in, lowering his voice. 'I... just... I just don't want anything to spoil it. I think this one's the real deal.'

I threw Steve another smile.

'Agent Steve Double O Two, you disappoint me. We shook hands. Or at least you shook something, from memory. But we made a pact. And for my part, that still stands. Besides,' I added, as Steve opened his mouth to speak, 'not only will I be leaving here in a few days and returning to sunny Exeter, but I too, have someone of interest who's just popped into my life.'

'So we're good, then?' Steve asked with obvious relief.

'We're Double O good,' I assured him.

Steve looked at me with genuine fondness. 'Sorry Amber, but I've got to get back. We had some fun though, didn't we?'

'That we sure did.'

'Will you be in before you go?'

'Oh, I very much expect so.'

'I'll see you later, then.'

He threw me a wink, a couple of clicks from the side of his mouth and returned to the others. Leaving me to return to my texts. And the task of pushing any Spencer-related thoughts to the back of my mind.

14.

A Hot Date

I hit the pebbles earlier than the arranged time with Luke. I'd wanted to arrive first, to pick our spot down towards Brokeback, get undressed and settled. For some reason, I just didn't want to be faffing about, undressing and sorting out my yoga mat and towel with Luke already naked and watching. Let him do all that. And I'll watch instead.

It was yet another glorious scorcher with just a few bonny puffs of cloud dotted about the sky. On discovering the tide out, both my ankle and I sighed with relief; I'd be sweaty enough by the time Luke arrived, and didn't fancy being half-exhausted before our date got underway.

As I picked my way along the beach, it struck me – now that my time at Brightlea was coming to an end – just how many familiar faces (and bodies) I now exchanged my, 'Lovely day, isn't it?' with. It *really* was like being part of a big and friendly, naked community.

Weirdos and perverts aside.

What did everyone do in the winter? I wondered, as I eyed an old boy swatting at a persistent fly that seemed overly interested in his shrivelled bits – put their knobs into hibernation? Smiling at the thought and the sight of the old fella increasing his efforts by batting his penis with a sun hat, I continued on my way.

After a few steps, I looked up from the pebbles and was surprised to see Luke in the distance. He was dressed, sitting with his back resting against the cliff, sunglasses on and giving me a small wave. He'd beaten me to it. The crafty bugger.

I let out a small laugh as I smiled and waved back. My cunning plan had been foiled. Although it did appear that great minds thought alike.

'Thought I'd get here early,' he called out as I neared. 'I didn't want to keep a lady waiting. Not after my no-show the last time.' He climbed to his feet, brushed his salt and pepper hair off his forehead and stepped forward to relieve me of my yoga mat and bag.

'Here, let me take those,' he said.

With the heat bearing down, I put up no argument and gratefully handed them over.

'What a gentleman,' I told him.

'Oh, I wouldn't count your chickens on that

front,' Luke replied. And although I couldn't see those blue and grey eyes behind the sunglasses, I strongly suspected they were having an Irish twinkle.

'I wondered if you were up for heading down the far end? Past your mates in Brokeback Bay,' Luke asked. 'Ever been down there?'

I squinted through my sunglasses into the distance, to the recesses in the cliff where some of the guys had disappeared to during the beach party.

'What? Down there?' I asked, pointing.

Luke followed my finger. 'No, further than that. See the far tip of the cliff? You can walk around in low tide and there's some private space down there. I've checked the tide times and we're good for about 3 hours or so.'

'And you know about this place *how*?' I asked, with a smile.

Luke leaned forward and whispered in my ear. 'My friend has a fishing boat. I've seen it.'

'Hmm... the kind of answer only a Mother would believe. Okay. Let's do it.'

'Good decision. After all, it'd be a shame not to put those beasts on your feet to good use.'

'Very funny,' I replied with a smile.

Luke picked up his backpack from the pebbles.

'Ready?'

That was one hell of a loaded question.

'Ready,' I replied. 'Both myself and the beasts.'

However Luke knew about it, it was a fantastic spot. We trudged past Brokeback where I said my 'hellos' and 'lovely days' to the guys I knew or recognised. Penguin Man called out, 'Have fun you two!' and I couldn't bring myself to look at Luke, who I sensed was smiling.

The walk turned out to be deceptively longer than it originally looked, taking another ten minutes or so from Brokeback. And beasts or not, my ugly sandals came up trumps – with only the slightest squeak of complaint from my ankle. When we finally rounded the edge of the cliff, there was a recess about 6 or 7 metres in length and about half of that in depth. The left side was the height of the cliff, while to the right it had a more sweeping shape to its base, creating a mini wall that meant, when standing, you could look over and along the deserted and stunning coastline

'Thank God for that,' said Luke, putting the bags and mat down, 'we've got it to ourselves.'

Also relieved that our long walk in the heat hadn't been in vain, I lifted my sunglasses, stood with my hands on my hips and took in the view as I got my breath back.

'It's beautiful, Luke. Truly beautiful.'

He walked over and stood behind me. Resting his head on my shoulder, he looped his arms around my waist and quietly said, 'It is beautiful. A painter's dream. Just crying out to be put on canvas. Like you.'

It's funny. I'd run through so many scenarios as to how the afternoon might unfold. All of them based upon being way back on the beach and with no real privacy to speak of. I'd imagined there'd be touching and kissing. And I would have asked Luke to put some oil on me. I had hoped there'd be the opportunity for some mutual and surreptitious body exploration beneath the cover of well placed towel – just a tame taster of what might be on offer later, back at the caravan or Luke's cottage. The main event, as it were. And with no holds barred. Hopefully.

So what happened in that recess, all came as a delicious and unexpected surprise as I'd had no time to formulate any real expectation, what with the sudden change of beach venue and its added bonus of total privacy.

With his head still on my shoulder, Luke buried his head into my neck, nuzzled and kissed it softly, before I felt the sudden sharp nip of a bite. Holding my flesh between his teeth, Luke gave it a playful wiggle and tug with exactly the right amount of pain; pain – but not too much. Like a horny vampire. He took my hands off my waist, placed them on the wall in front of me and roughly pushed my legs apart with a foot. I felt a hand run up the inside of a thigh, kneading the flesh along the way, then the yank of my dress being pulled up above my waist before the tip of his finger ran expertly over my lips and clit, briefly teasing, before one finger became two and he plunged them deep into me.

I let out a sharp intake of breath as I felt a powerful release of wetness cover his probing fingers. I spread my legs further apart. He withdrew his fingers and ran his hand over my cunt, massaging my clit until I groaned aloud. I could feel my wetness. Hear it, even. And as my groans increased, he plunged his fingers back inside. Deep. So fucking deep. It was driving me crazy. His other hand reached around my front, tugging down the top of my strappy dress and freeing my breasts so they rested over the neckline. He grabbed one roughly, squeezing it and pulling hard on the nipple.

'Is this how you like it, Amber?' he huskily breathed in my ear.

I squeezed my eyes shut for a moment. 'Fuck yeah.'

'I fucking thought so.'

He slowly dragged out his fingers and leant up tight against me. I could feel his hard cock pushing into me through his jeans. He pressed a hand over one of mine, while the other, the one he'd used on me, was placed inches from my face.

'Taste yourself,' Luke ordered.

I didn't need to be told twice. But as I put my face forward, Luke smeared the two wet fingers around my mouth before crooking them just inside. I sucked on the fingers, bit down on them and sucked again. The fingers explored my mouth, probing deeply, retreating a bit, then probing again. A mouth fuck. Luke slowly withdrew the fingers, trailing their wetness along my chin, neck and chest. He took his other hand off mine, and still pressing into me, gave the most exquisitely rough tit massage of my life. My breath was shortening into irregular gasps. I looked up and along the empty beach and felt even filthier that this should be happening out in the open, where we might even get caught. Luke's palms were now flat and rubbing with a mixture of circular and back and forth motions over my deliciously sore and hardened nipples. The friction was causing sensations that made me tremble and my clit feel engorged to bursting point. With a sharp intake of breath, I felt a mini-climax rush over me. It offered little relief and caused some wetness to trickle out and onto the inside of my thigh.

I urgently needed Luke's cock inside me.

I tried to reach behind to feel him, but he grabbed my hand and put it back on the wall.

'You're staying right there,' he said, gruffly.

I could hear him unzipping and getting out of his clothes. I stood staring at the coastline and waves, wondering what he had in store for me.

'Bend over and open your legs,' came the next instruction.

As I walked my hands down the wall and onto the beach, and opened my legs further, I heard the crunch of pebbles behind me as Luke lowered himself to his knees. Luke plunged his fingers back in my sopping cunt, withdrew them and pulled my cheeks apart. After smearing my juice around my ass, he let a teasing finger momentarily enter, before spreading my cheeks further and burying his face. In a frenzy, he licked and sucked my asshole, while two fingers went back to work in my cunt as his thumb stimulated my clit.

I felt like I was going to explode. Luke, you dirty, dirty, filthy bastard.

He took his fingers away and moved his mouth to my begging cunt. He went at it as though he'd wanted to do so his entire life; as if he couldn't bury his mouth deep enough. Both his hands dug sharply into my thighs – but that only added to the pleasure.

'Oh fuck,' I groaned, as one mini-climax was swiftly followed by another.

Luke kept on. It was almost too much to bear. He took a hand away from my thigh, and as he sucked on my clit, pressed his thumb into my ass. My senses were almost dizzy. Between breaths I managed to talk.

'Luke... please... get your cock in me.'

He carried on sucking for a few moments more before pulling his face away. He took his hand from my thigh, and again massaged my clit with a flat palm before giving it a series of heady sharp slaps that nearly had me climaxing again. Removing his thumb from my ass, Luke stood and teasingly ran his cock between and around both of my holes, smearing my wet further, before suddenly ramming deep into my cunt.

Our loud gasps were synchronised.

'Oh fuck, you're beautiful,' Luke half-groaned as he pounded me roughly.

I could feel an orgasm begin to build and swell. Luke had my arse cheeks roughly in his hands and sporadically took turns to slap them. My breaths shortened, I looked at the pebbles and shut my eyes – I was close.

So close.

Luke abruptly pulled out, causing my orgasm build-up to stall and float, then a second later, I gasped once more as he pushed his cock into my ass.

Luke groaned loudly. He began his movements slowly, taking his time to pick up the tempo. Both hands were firmly clamped to my cheeks. I lifted my right hand from the pebbles and manipulated my clit with rapid movements.

'Oh, you filthy bitch.'

Luke's increased groans indicated he wasn't far away. As his cock moved from my ass to my cunt, the velocity and strength of his thrusts intensified. And as he sank a thumb into my ass, I finally felt the sweet release of powerful orgasm make a series of small contractions pulse along my cunt, as I loudly whimpered and groaned and felt my legs quiver.

As the waves of my orgasm began to fade, I felt a final deep thrust from Luke, before he dug into my hips and pulled me deeper onto his cock. As he held me there I felt the distinct pulsating as his come began to ejaculate into me.

'Fuck. Fuck. Fuck,' he breathed.

He pulled out, rushed his cock back into my ass, released some come, withdrew and shook the last throes over my ass hole and cheeks.

As he lengthily groaned, I reached behind and rubbed his come into both holes and my cheeks.

'Oh, God. Oh, God,' Luke said, as he squeezed my hips. He folded forward, kissed my back, and after a several moments of trying to regain his breath, straightened. 'Oh, God,' he said again. 'Amazing. Fucking amazing.'

He wasn't wrong.

Acutely aware of being upside down in the heat for a while, and with my legs still feeling shaky, I reached for the wall and slowly straightened into a standing position. I scanned the empty beach, and was momentarily unsure if I wasn't disappointed to see a crowd of voyeurs politely applauding the show we'd just put on. Taking a few seconds to ensure I felt okay, I turned to face Luke.

Standing with his hands on hips, he blew out air through pursed lips while his chest rose and fell from his exertions. I looked at his spent cock, the sheen of sweat on him and then down at myself; dress up over my waist, tits sticking out and also covered in sweat. We both burst out laughing.

'I think you can take that off now,' said Luke.

'You think?' I replied, smiling.

Luke stretched a hand towards me. 'Come on. Get that sweaty ol' dress off you and let's go for a swim to clean up and cool down.'

We cuddled and kissed in the sea and joked around. I told Luke I'd decided to just use him for his body. He told me if that was the case, he'd die a very happy man. Without his sunglasses, I could admire the glinting flecks of blues in his eyes that turned to grey. Or maybe it was the other way around. His wet hair was swept off his forehead and when I playfully wrapped my legs around him, strong, tanned arms engulfed me.

When we returned to our recess, Luke towelled me down and rubbed in my sun oil, paying more attention than necessary to some areas. He cock was twitching into life again.

'I don't think anyone could accuse you of being a selfish lover,' I said over my shoulder as he massaged oil into my calves. 'I didn't have to do a thing. Except enjoy it.'

'It's simple,' Luke said. 'Giving pleasure gives me pleasure.'

'Oh, I hear you loud and clear on that front.'

'I thought you might.' Luke straightened, stood before me and took one of my hands and placed it around his stiff cock. 'Maybe you'd like to prove it?'

Feeling too hot for anything more energetic, I gave him a leisurely blow job, massaging his balls as he come in my mouth. We embraced afterwards, before sitting up for a cigarette.

'Ah, the post-sex cigarette,' Luke said, inspecting it between his fingers. 'The one to be savoured the most.'

'Amen to that.'

We spent the rest of our time sunbathing and talking. I spoke about trying to find a job when I got back to Exeter. Luke said he'd ask around; he knew plenty of gallery owners in the West Country. He'd try his best. I kissed his hand and thanked him. I said I was leaving in a few days' time. Luke frowned. He'd be unable to see me again before I left. He was off back home to his beloved West Cork to judge an art competition and teach at a 3-day residential course. We agreed to keep in contact and meet in a couple of weeks. I told him about Spencer coming down. Luke told me, he'd have happily seen me back safely into the flat, had I asked. But you won't be around, I replied. Ah, he said.

Was the sex all you dreamed it would be, I asked, placing a pebble on his chest. You need to ask? You? Oh, let's just say, you've totally got the measure of what presses my buttons. And what fine buttons to press, if you don't mind my saying. Say on.

I'd like to take you to Ireland one day – show you around some of the stunning scenery. I'd really love that.

Regrettably, it feels like time to be making a move – packing waits for no man.

As we sat up, we were greeted by the sight of a naked, middle-aged male paddleboarder crossing our line of vision. He gave us a cheery wave. We returned the compliment with murmurs of, 'Just what *is it* like, here?'

'That's nothing,' I said. 'The other day I had a naked canoeist with binoculars.'

'Dear Lord, where will it all end?'

We had a quick drink at The Captain's Table – having polished off my water supply long before – and were both thirsty after the walk back. As I toyed with my glass, I realised I was going to miss Luke, but said nothing. He looked at me thoughtfully over his pint. Maybe he was thinking the same.

I walked with him as far as the car park, but not to his car. He was parked at the far end and feared my jumbo sandals might explode after all they'd been through. Oblivious to any onlookers, we put down our stuff, tightly hugged and enjoyed a lengthy and sensual kiss. I could feel him getting hard again.

'Feel what you've done to me, you dreadful woman,'

'Well, we'll simply have to do something about it in a few weeks' time.'

'That's a date. You look after yourself, Amber.'

'And you look after you. And him,' I laughed, as Luke and his erection broke from our embrace.

'Oops!' he said, picking up his backpack and holding it in front of him.

I let out a laugh. 'And let's text in the meantime!'

'Try and stop me.'

A final soft kiss. Then he strode away. Backpack first.

Bye bye, lover, I thought as I watched him. It'll be very interesting to see what happens next.

I stayed in that night. Writing time with Susie was quickly running out, but I still felt optimistic of finishing the first draft before leaving Brightlea. I enjoyed a long shower and dreamily thought back to the afternoon's events. There was no doubt that the jelly dildo or rabbit would be coming into play come bedtime. Post-shower, and settled at my table with my laptop and music, I looked over and saw that 70 still showed no signs of life. The curtains remained open, and from what I could see of the kitchen area, it was completely bare. I supposed 70 was still away with his beautiful bit of rough.

'Dear Lord, where will it all end?' I said out loud with a bad Irish accent and smile.

Indeed, Amber. Where *will* it all end?

15.

A Naked Twirl

I was up bright and early the next morning, happily swinging my kettlebells towards the smug face of Piers Morgan. I was feeling really invigorated and positive about life. My writing was nearly finished. Clarke was mute. And hopefully gone. Probably gone. No, *definitely* gone. Spencer would be arriving tomorrow. And with Luke now away, I finally felt, and for the first time, ready to finally leave my Sophia Classique and go back to Exeter.

Yeah, all good.

Mind you, I thought, getting a right royal seeing-to had been known to put a spring in my step. I grinned like a Cheshire cat as I once more thought about Luke using me so *ruthlessly* on the beach, and swung those kettlebells a bit harder towards Piers.

Exercises done, I flopped on my L-shaped and put in a call to Elena.

'You must be a mind reader!' she said after picking up. 'I was going to give you a call later.'

'What? To bully me into my next appointment?' I laughed. 'No need – that's why I'm calling – to get all Exeter shipshape after my impending return from static writing paradise.'

'Actually, it wasn't,' Elena replied. 'It was to tell you – if you didn't already know – that The Grub Shack's all closed up. It's been like it for a few days. No signs of life. No Clarke. No staff. No sign in the window to say when or if they're reopening. Just a load of chairs upside down on the tables and all the lights off. And us having to go somewhere else for our takeaway lunches. Did you know anything about this?'

It took a few moments to absorb Elena's news.

'No. No I didn't,' I mumbled as my mind raced. 'He did send me a weird message a while ago. Some mumbo jumbo about 'it's all over now', and since then, nothing. Not a peep. I just thought he was finally getting on with his life. I even visited the flat for a snoop, straight after you last cut my hair, and found it tidy with signs of his flat-hunting efforts.'

'Hmm. Perhaps he's decided to sell up and start afresh somewhere else?' Elena said.

'Now *that* would be music to my ears. Do you really think he has?'

'Well,' Elena began, 'it's got to be a strong possibility, hasn't it?'

I took a few moments to think it through. 'I guess it has.'

'Well, in that case, when we go for our night out together, we can toast Clarke's good riddance and your new beginnings!'

'I'll certainly drink to that!' I said. 'So let's get me booked in for my next appointment, and when I come in, we'll arrange our night on the town, when I'll be able to fill you in on how things are going with the Irish womaniser.'

'Oh! I'd forgotten all about him!' Elena exclaimed. 'Going well, I trust?'

'Early days,' I began, as the memory of Luke's tanned and smiling face suddenly loomed large in my mind. 'But yeah, despite not wanting to get involved with anyone else so soon, we're doing okay. Slow and steady and all that.'

'Good girl. You deserve some luck on that front.'

'Ha! Don't I just?'

'Right. Let's get you booked in. You're lucky to have caught me here this early, I'm only halfway through the delights of doing a stocktake, so when you rang, answering the phone seemed a more attractive option than counting spatulas and rolls of tin foil.'

'Nice to know I'm so high up in the pecking order!'

'Don't get too bigheaded!' Elena replied. 'Cutting my toenails ranks pretty high compared to this monthly dirge.'

We fixed an appointment, which by my reckoning would fall before next seeing Luke. We exchanged goodbyes and finished the call. Which left me gazing at my trees with some new thoughts in my head.

Careful, Amber, was my first. You're taking Luke into consideration when making a hair appointment? Slow and steady, remember? I glanced over the still-empty 70 and thought about Luke. And my emerging feelings for him. Was it just the surprisingly excellent sex? No. No it wasn't. I was definite about that. He was brilliant company; interesting, intelligent and witty. We shared similar tastes in things and had plenty in common. And it didn't harm matters, that for someone just over ten years older than myself, he also happened to be a fine specimen of a man. In all aspects.

Yet he supposedly had a track record for being a womaniser.

And I was only recently out of an abusive relationship...

I wondered, could it be true? Had Clarke finally sorted himself out a new place to stay? In a new area, even? Would he be putting The Grub Shack's lease up for sale and starting afresh somewhere else? It certainly seemed that way. He was finally shipping out and moving on by the looks of it. I was glad. And relieved. I hadn't really believed he'd still be in the flat when I returned; one phone call to the Police citing a squatting, violent ex-boyfriend would have resolved that pretty quickly. Plus he'd probably guess I'd be keeping all his vile, threatening messages – so it served no purpose for him to be hanging around.

But I was still glad Spencer would be seeing me back to the flat. To have his dependable familiarity around me, in what would initially seem like alien surroundings. Plus, we could have a giggle about being *so* dramatic in thinking Clarke might be lurking behind the sofa with a French stick as a weapon.

I could almost picture it, and let out a small laugh.

So. All good. And as for Luke, maybe I was getting a little soft on him, but I wasn't in deep. So be careful, Amber. Use him for his body. And his mind. Take up his delicious offer to be shown West Cork. Enjoy each other. And just see where it goes with him. The deliciously filthy Shagmeister.

Team talk over, I briefly toyed with sliding down my shorts and L-shaped, and having a crafty wank or two over Luke's intention to paint me one day. There was *plenty* of mileage in that particular scenario. But, (and with regret) common sense prevailed – Susie's countdown clock was ticking – I had to get to work. As our Susie waits for no man. Woman. Or Shagmeister.

The pesky taskmaster.

Susie has taken to having post-work strolls along the nearby beach with Doctor Wellard. Or

Christian. As he insists. After Susie's walk of shame to work the following Monday, she endures the onslaught of cupped whispers and sniggers, and finds her only ally is the new Doctor, who is seemingly oblivious to her fall from grace with colleagues. Even Doctor Rogers gives her a wide berth, limiting any brief exchanges to purely work-related matters.

The awkward and clumsy Christian offers Susie iced buns at work and a listening ear during their early evening walks. Our Susie spills her guts out to him, as she is truly past caring. And it transpires that Christian does indeed possess the good bedside manner any self-respecting Doctor should have, as he listens intently while Susie regales him with her woes about a cheating boyfriend and her foolish crush on the gay Doctor Rogers.

'It could happen to the best of us,' Christian suggests with a weak smile as he offers her a wine gum.

Susie looks out to sea while she considers this, then turns to Christian. 'But it keeps on happening to me,' she whines, with a mouthful of masticated gelatine-based sweet.

As Christian contemplates Susie's response with a deep frown, he removes his spectacles, breathes heavily over each lens and gives them an efficient polish with a crumpled tissue he has plucked from his pocket.

Despite her feelings of despair, Susie is surprised to note a distinct improvement in Doctor Wellard's appearance sans heavy bins. In fact, a complete transformation for the better.

Who knew?

Susie and Christian quickly slide into their roles as surgery misfits. Susie knows she won't be bouncing back any time soon following her Madonna/pot plant projectile vomiting displays. She has become a figure of mockery and the butt of a whole selection of Like a Prayer/Virgin-themed jokes. And even has to endure Nurse Simmons' exaggerated shimmy impersonations at each Friday cakefest when, without fail, she produces an empty wastepaper bin "just in case" of a chunder emergency. On one horror occasion, Susie even espies Doctor Rogers' feeble attempt to conceal a smile, as he watches on with a twinkle of amusement in his eyes and a slice of Maureen's lemon drizzle held to his mouth.

Susie takes to burying herself in work to avoid these staff gatherings and gradually feels the disconnect between her and colleagues deepen. And as for returning to the scene of the crime for the weekly quiz night... she *really* doesn't think so.

Doctor Wellard fares better. He quickly gains the respect of his peers and patients. He is a good Doctor. Attentive, knowledgeable and thorough. But it is as though he is two people. The confident calm manner shown in a professional capacity quickly dissolves into a virtual lack of social skills once Christian safely tucks away his stethoscope for the day, or takes a rare break. In the tea room, when he's not knocking over mugs or spilling milk, his stammer reappears, his chit chat is tedious or he simply fails to get heard or make his point.

Yet Susie takes solace in his quiet company as they pick their way over the beach's rock pools or simply sit side-by-side watching the sunset in silence.

At night, as Susie buries herself oh-so-deep under her duvet, she relives the dreadful exhibition she made of herself at Doctor Webb's retirement party. Oh, the shame of it all! Will she ever get over it? She thinks not. And what a fool for believing she was some kind of sex siren. What a joke she is! Susie further believes that it'll be a good while yet before she can even contemplate a fiddle about in her lady garden again. And as for getting her leg over...

Yet part of her knows an urgent knee trembler could be just the ticket for how she's feeling. It has, after all, been a terribly long time...

Keep in there, Susie – we're all behind you!

A text from Luke.

Greetings from sunny West Cork! I managed to drag my abused old body across the water and am now steadying myself for judging duties with the wax crayon brigade. May the Lord take mercy on me! x

I laughed aloud. Another of Luke's winners.

Less of the abused, Sir. One is quite sore from what you dished out yesterday, so I rightfully claim today's title of 'abused' – let's not do anything like that again. X

I pinged it off and waited.

Oh, is one? Madam, I wholeheartedly apologise for my ungentlemanly behaviour and concur that there must never be a repeat performance... x

Cross your heart?x

I cross my Irish heart x

So. Rough sex again in a few weeks' time? X

I think it's best. Just to keep up one's morale, you understand. Right, have to dash. My presence is required. If you're going, enjoy the beach – but not too much... xx

Ha! Will do. And be gentle with the wax crayon brigade. Laters! xxx

Xxx

I looked at my phone a few moments more, wondering if – no, make that, hoping – another text might pop up.

'What are you like, you dozy mare?' I asked aloud – I didn't have time to waste staring at a blank screen on my phone – this was my last day on my own at Brightlea; I had a book to finish writing; packing to begin and a tan to top-up.

Busy, busy, busy!

Step away from the phone, Amber! There's nothing for you to see.

That afternoon, when I rounded the base of the cliff, I stood for a moment and scanned the length of the beach. Smiling as my eyes swept over the familiar sight of the old boy sunbathing with his Y-fronts over his face, I felt oddly nostalgic for what was still my present.

As the beasts marched me over the pebbles, I gave any open-eyed sunbathers a cheery, 'Lovely day, isn't it?' and soaked up their good natured responses. And I took it all in my stride, when further along, I passed a 'part of the fixtures' middle-aged couple, who threw me a thumbs up in response, as the wife tackled the complexities of giving her old fella a blow job while a sloping windbreaker balanced precariously over her jerking head.

I fleetingly toyed with assisting with their privacy-related issues by re-erecting their windbreaker. It obviously hadn't been properly wedged between the pebbles in the first instance – but I dismissed the thought – it certainly wasn't for me to be fiddling with anyone's erection at such a time. So I crunched on and left them to it.

Delighted to see that my favourite spot was free, I made my way over, dumped my stuff, and stood with stretched arms over my head as I looked into the distance. I could see it was pretty quiet down at Brokeback, but still managed to pick out Penguin Man and a few others I recognised, and returned their waves of greeting. It certainly seemed like the whole world was in a good mood today.

I lowered my arms and looked beyond Brokeback, to the jutting point Luke and I had walked around (was it only yesterday?) to our mini cove. I thought of our time spent there; the sex; the talking; the laughter, and realised I was missing him. Yet couldn't fathom if I should feel concerned or excited by that fact.

But now was not the time to think about Luke. I got myself sorted, rolled onto my front and got to work. That Susie clock was still ticking.

Come on, Amber. One last push.

I was blessed with an uninterrupted afternoon. No idiots. No chatter-uppers. No wankers. No parade of blokes wandering up and down auditioning for the world's worst meat raffle. With hugged knees, I took a few cigarette breaks, keeping my mind firmly focused on Susie as I took regular puffs. No time for a spell lying on my back, reading or relaxing. Instead, I pushed on. I pushed on.

And from seemingly being so far from the end, I suddenly reached it.

The End. Ta-dah!

I stared at my notebook, almost in disbelief. And as I stared some more, the gradual realisation of what I'd achieved dawned on me.

I'd done it! I'd only gone and bloody well written a book! And it felt fucking marvellous! In celebration, I lit a cigarette and got to my feet, did a little victory jig, punched my hands in the air and completed an unsteady twirl on the pebbles. I didn't give a single fuckerooney what I looked like. I'd done it!

A few faint cheers filtered through from Brokeback and a voice called out, 'What's happening, Amber?' I turned and saw Mister Tall and Skinny getting to his feet, as he began to shout again, one hand cupped to his mouth. 'You okay?'

I stood naked as the day I was born and yelled over, 'I'm celebrating! I've just finished writing my book!'

As a few sets of hands shot up to silently applaud, and a faint cheers travelled over the pebbles. Mister T&S shouted back, 'That's brilliant! Well done you! Don't forget us all when you're rich and famous!'

I had to laugh at that. 'Thank you! And NEVER!!'

I waved, twirled, took a few bows and sat back down. I was buzzing. Totally buzzing. I picked up my notebook, flicked through its pages and put it down again. I picked up my lighter, needlessly sparked the flame into life several times, then threw it into my bag. I fidgeted about, curling up the end of my yoga mat, before smoothing it out again, feeling at a complete loss what to do now Susie had limped over the finishing line. I raised my head to the sky, closed my eyes, took deep breaths and composed my thoughts: I needed to get back to my Sophia Classique Number 56, *el pronto*, get the notes typed up *then* begin my packing.

Yes. That sounded like a plan.

But I couldn't resist one final naked twirl in the sunshine. I climbed to my feet, ignored the moustachioed guy wandering by with his cock in his hand, and twirled away. I felt great – just great.

It was all going to plan. Everything was going to plan.

I'd achieved everything I'd set out to do in Brightlea.

Except one thing.

I looked around. All quiet behind me. And ahead, the moustachioed man was approaching Brokeback. I'd have to miss how that'd pan out – but he was certainly getting their attention.

With no time to lose, I lay down and treated myself to a celebratory speed wank. When I shuddered into an orgasm that released some of my excess energy, I let out a breathy laugh; it felt like I'd just marked my territory. I let my legs flop down, and turned to reach into my bag for a cigarette I was sure Luke would approve of. The bag had fallen on its side, and Martin Amis's latest novel looked up at me from the pebbles.

I let out a howl of laughter.

'Oops! Sorry Martin!' I said with a broad grin.

'You weren't meant to see that. I *do* hope I didn't offend or cause embarrassment.'

Poor Martin.

I hope he gets over it.

Back at the caravan, I had a bit of a hyperactive hoot as I typed up the notes. I talked to myself, made loud announcements and said things like, 'This *really* is such shit,' and, '*Whatever* were you thinking, Amber?' or, 'This has *gotta be* The Mother of all Bollocks.'

Then I'd have to stop for a fit of giggles. And another fidget.

I looked over at my elderly couple next door, who sat gloomily watching the TV. Feeling the urge to hoot out, 'Happy Holidays!' I glanced at the back of those photo frames and had an abrupt change of heart. Instead, I looked to the still-empty 70 for my sport factor.

'And look at you, you dirty stop-out. I hope she's given your arse a love bite the size of Scotland *and* dipped your wallet!'

I giggled again, returned my attention to my laptop, and continued my running commentary as I tapped away.

'Are you fucking *sure?*' 'Oh, that's just total wank.'

'*Really?* I mean, *really? Come on!*"

Some 40-minutes later, I switched to two-finger

typing. 'The End,' I said, as I tapped the keys. I sat back, hands behind my head and stared at the screen.

'It's shite – but it's my shite,' I announced proudly. 'Let's see how it does.'

I saved the work, and for the final time at Brightlea, closed down my laptop.

'Ta-dah!' I said, as I lowered its lid.

I didn't quite know what to do next. I wanted to run through the camp doing jazz hands and screaming 'I've finished!' And maybe give Benny the Bear and Duckface Ducky a big smacker on each of their flea-bitten conks.

I wanted to dash down to Flabby's and bore everyone within a ten-yard radius totally shitless about my achievement. And then tell them all over again. With lots of animated hand gestures.

I wanted to boing! boing! boing! on my bed – like the little shit in 69 – until I could boing no more.

But in the end, I settled for smoking a cigarette on my steps and sending a text to Luke.

Someone (and I'm not naming names, here) – but someone, has just finished their shitty novel. And that very same someone is very slightly overexcited. Xx

I pinged it off with a smile and stayed on my step for a while, enjoying the evening sunshine and the warm breeze that gently rustled the leaves on my trees. I noticed that the elderly couple in 55 had gone out, as I couldn't see any car tyres beneath their caravan. I sincerely hoped they were having a nice meal somewhere. All quiet in 69 – probably soaking up the laughs and japes of the 'entertainment' in the clubhouse. And 70 was the same old, same old. Collecting dust.

I thought about taking a stroll down to Flabby's; it felt tempting to spend some time chilling out with a drink and listening to Fucker Frank's latest escapades. Apart from Matty, I doubted any of the troops down there would really appreciate my feeling of achievement – and that was fine – it just felt like an attractive option, to quietly sit, listen, think my own thoughts and get a bit tipsy.

'But that won't do, at all!' I said aloud. 'You have a guest arriving tomorrow. It's your last day. You need to start your packing. *And* you can't get pissed,' I added, counting them off on my fingers. 'Plus,' I announced, waving a finger in the air, 'you can't have a hangover driving to the train station to pick up Spencer. So. Go pack. Feed yourself. And for God's sake, stop talking to yourself out loud.'

'Yes, ma'am!' I cried, saluting as I got to my feet.

I packed as much as I could. Clean clothes and towels. The laptop and lead. The wireless speaker. My notebook and paperbacks. Sex toys. Some toiletries and dry food goods. And footwear I knew I wouldn't wear again in Brightlea. I did contemplate reverting to my original beach sandals for Spencer's visit – but decided to give him the pleasure of feasting his eyes on the magnificence of the beasts for our beach visit. That would give him a good laugh, I thought, and could almost picture him shrieking at the sight of them.

It was going to be so very excellent to see Spencer again.

I thought about putting the packed bags in the Golf's boot, but decided against it – it seemed pointless to be driving them to and fro the next day. Instead, I placed them next to the door, all ready for the off, along with my kettlebells. Satisfied I'd done as much as I could, I made myself a bite to eat, washed up, showered and spent a tame evening, listening to music and feeling in a contemplative mood as I gazed at my trees.

The past six weeks had certainly been a rollercoaster. I pushed away the sudden and intrusive image of my parents sitting in that insufferable heat and suffocating dope fumes. No, tonight was a night of celebration and no-one was going to dampen my spirits. I raised my wine glass towards 70.

'Cheers,' I said. 'Whilst you've been getting up to all sorts, I've been finishing my novel. So stick that in your tattooed lady and suck on it!'

I drained my glass and as I stood up to get a refill, saw the flashing light on my phone.

Someone is an extraordinary woman. Huge

congratulations, Amber! My wax crayons. Your quill pen. We could be going places!xx

I stared at the message with a warm feeling I couldn't quite determine. Or didn't dare explore. As I tried to formulate a response in my mind, another text popped up.

Have I ever told you, you're a dreadful woman?x

I threw my head back and roared with laughter. What *was* he like?

When Spencer emerged from the ticket barrier at Exeter Central, I rushed forward like an eager child. Spotting me, he dropped his holdall and gathered me up in his arms as I reached him. We held one another tightly and pressed our lips to each other's cheeks. It felt like I'd come home.

We broke free from our embrace and checked the other over.

'Just look at the colour of you! You look so well!'

'As handsome as ever, Spencer – but what's with the grey?'

'Ah, the stresses and strains of listening to arsehole clients and dealing with idiots. I don't mind it, actually.'

The greying hair suited him. But then again, you could put Spencer in a bin bag and he'd still look stylish.

'It's so lovely to see you,' I said, squeezing his hand.

'Likewise, Amber. It's been far too long.' Spencer replied, as he stroked my hand with his thumb. For the briefest moment, I saw a flicker of sadness behind his eyes before he blinked it away.

'Right! Point me towards your chariot! I believe there's a beach somewhere with my name on it!' Spencer picked up his holdall. 'Let's go, wench!'

Of course, the instant Spencer clapped eyes on my Sophia Classique (No. 56) sign, it was love at first sight.

'I'm having a photo of that beauty before I go, if it's the last thing I do,' he announced.

And when I later made the (ta-dah!) reveal of my beach sandals, Spencer roared and howled with laughter, referring to them as "huge flappers" as he dabbed away some tears in an effort to regain an element of composure.

Which took some time...

On the car journey to Brightlea we'd gabbed away like the long lost soul mates we were. Spencer was beyond thrilled I'd finished my novel and wished me every success. I explained that I had a whole heap of editing to do first – but yeah, Susie, was well on her way to shit lit stardom. And I thanked him for his wishes. He, of all people, knew how important my writing was to me.

He spoke about his work, and how well he was doing – even getting some of his photos into a recent, and very prestigious, exhibition in Mayfair. All toffee-nosed twonks and posh nibbles on a tray – but his stuff had sold at stupidly high prices, and he'd picked up some lucrative commissions in the process.

I gave him the low-down on Elena's phone call.

'So hopefully,' I said at the end, 'this is all a bit of a big Jessie drama over nothing – it really does look like he's moved on to pastures new.'

'Well, let's not take anything for granted,' Spencer said, 'that bloke isn't right in the head. So as a precaution, I picked up a defence spray thing – the legal version of pepper spray or something like that. Anyway, we'll have it in the unlikely case we need it.'

I thought back to the image I'd rustled up before; us busting into the flat armed, dangerous and shouting, 'Motherfucker!'

'Oh, God,' I said, beginning to get a fit of the giggles, 'we're going to look like a right couple of berks going in there. Don't worry, I'll have your back – I'll score some hairspray and be right behind you.'

'Oh, *could you* imagine? We'd probably spook ourselves and start spraying all over the place and at each other!'

When we stopped laughing, Spencer patted my leg. 'It'll all be okay, Amber. Trust me.'

I took my eyes off the road for a beat to look at him.

'I know it will,' I said, feeling the familiar melt of my heart.

After a freshen up for Spencer, a quick bite to eat and some quality piss-taking about my flappers, we were ready to head to the beach. As I went over to pick up my bag from the L-shaped, I glanced out the window.

'Oh, here we go,' I said, flagging Spencer to join me. 'Come and have a look at this.'

As he stood at my side, I gave Spencer the condensed version of 70's shenanigans.

'So, *she* is now dropping off *him*,' I said, as we watched them both climb out of the old Peugot, 'and by my reckoning, the wife of *him* will be scooping him up tomorrow morning to check out the same time as us.'

We watched as 70 opened the door to his caravan, place his bag inside and turn to speak to his tattooed mistress before they hugged one another tightly and enjoyed a lengthy and passionate goodbye kiss.

'God, it all goes on here,' murmured Spencer.

I let out a laugh. 'You don't know the half of it!'

When they broke from their kiss, Mister 70, perhaps sensing our presence, looked directly over at us. Immediately, his smile turned to a menacing scowl. As he tapped the side of his nose, in a clear message to mind our own business, he said something to the young woman, who turned to stare as we stood in the window like a couple of middle-aged peeping Toms. In reaction, we stepped back and out of sight and began giggling like naughty children in a playground.

'That's gone and done it,' sniggered Spencer. 'Perhaps we should threaten to tell his wife and blackmail him.'

'Yeah, right,' I laughed. 'I don't think that'd go down too well. Do you?'

'Well, he only slightly looked like he wanted to knock seven bells of shit out of us.'

'And then some,' I added. 'Come on, let's leave them to it. Nudey beach beckons!'

16.

Selfies with Sophia

We talked incessantly on the way there. I had to make a herculean effort to break from our conversation to point out this place or that. For some reason, I wanted Spencer to get a real feel for Brightlea and the time I'd spent there. The clubhouse featured on the list, along with a mention about my one-off visit.

'Perhaps we can put our heads in there later?' suggested Spencer. 'Sounds so awful, I'd probably love it.'

'Don't bank on it,' I replied with a smile.

Happy Holidays came next. And I fessed up to my unhealthy obsession of hooting it out willy nilly.

'You really have been on your own for too long.'

Along with its glorious hanging sign depicting a hair-combing Fat Mermaid, the nickname of Flabby's was met with enthusiastic approval. Whilst further along, the shop where I bought my flappers was promptly christened, 'the scene of the crime'. Cod Almighty and The Captain's Table also got a mention in despatches, and as we reached the front, it seemed fitting, that the tide was in and I'd be hoofing it over the cliff one last time.

Or just for now. Hopefully.

When we reached the top and took a few moments to rest, Spencer took in the view and breathed out a single word; 'Wow'.

We made our descent slowly in the searing heat and when finally getting his first proper sighting of nudey beach, Spencer predictably took it all in his stride.

'Naked humans. My kind of place,' he said, hoisting my yoga mat tighter into his armpit. 'Right. Where do we go?'

We passed the little old boy I saw on my first day. It now seemed such a long time ago.

'Lovely day, isn't it?' he asked. 'Brought a friend with you?'

I smiled down as his crinkly body. 'Yes, it is lovely,' I replied. 'And yes,' I said, gesturing towards Spencer with my hand, 'this is my very dear friend, Spencer. It's his first time here, today.'

'Hi there,' said Spencer, with a small wave of his hand.

'Well, you enjoy yourself, Spencer,' the old boy said. 'We're all a pretty friendly bunch down here.'

'Thank you! And will do!'

I smiled to myself; it was just like having déjà vu.

When I offered it up, Spencer wasn't interested in getting introduced or joining the guys at Brokeback Bay, preferring to spend the time solely in my company. I almost wished he hadn't; it just made me love him all the more for it.

'Maybe next time,' he said with a smile as he shielded his eyes to look in their direction.

Without any fuss, he stripped off his t-shirt, shorts and pants like an old nudey pro, sat on his towel and took in his surroundings as I whisked off my dress and joined him.

'For a pebbly beach, it sure is beautiful down here,' he said.

There was no need to say anything. We sat side-by-side, comfortable in our nudity, each other's company and deep in our own thoughts. I leaned my head onto his shoulder, and after a minute or so, broke the silence.

'So. Are you happy?'

I felt Spencer's body rise and fall as he let out a sigh. 'Happy that I broke your heart? Never. Happy that I'm settling into my new life?' He paused for a few moments, put an arm around me and squeezed tightly, 'Then, yes. I'm happy.'

I lifted my head, looked at his beautiful face and kissed him lightly on the lips.

'Good. Then I'm happy.'

The afternoon was everything I'd hoped it'd be. Full of talking, laughing, tenderness and respect. I hadn't been sure how I'd feel – being naked again with Spencer – if I'd find it sexually arousing in any way. After all, Spencer had an excellent body and took care of every aspect of his appearance – but the truth was; it was just like sitting next to my dearest friend. I think I was a bit surprised by that, and wondered if Luke wasn't on the scene, I'd feel differently, and have a stab at making a round one fit into a square one.

Probably not.

As very sadly, that particular ship had long since sailed.

Spencer talked about his love life. Exciting. Confusing. A brave new world. No one special. Tarting around. Having fun.

'Christ,' I said, as I rolled onto my back, 'you should hear what I've been up to since we last spoke.'

And hear he did.

'Well, you've certainly kept yourself busy,' Spencer said with a laugh. 'You always did have a strong sexual appetite.'

'From memory,' I began, turning my head to look at Spencer, 'we both did.'

'Very happy days,' he said. We both fell silent. Temporarily lost in memories of different times, I suppose.

'Anyway,' Spencer said, as he shifted into a sitting position and looked down at me, 'this Luke. Are you falling for him?'

I squinted up at Spencer in the dazzling sunshine. 'I'm trying not to,' was my simple reply.

'Well, he sounds a million times better than that nutter, Clarke.'

I pushed myself up and took a cigarette from my bag.

'He *is* a million times better than Clarke,' I said, delving about for my lighter. 'Actually, he looks a bit like an older version of you. If you do the squinty-eye thing.'

'Oh, a handsome bugger, then!' laughed Spencer.

'You know it!' I replied, lighting my cigarette.

'So you're still sneaking the odd crafty fag,' Spencer remarked.

'Afraid so,' I said, taking care to blow my smoke away from Spencer. 'According to Luke, I'm a dreadful woman.'

Spencer let out a laugh. 'This Luke's certainly got the measure of you, alright. Sounds like a good guy.'

'He is,' I replied, looking out at the sea thoughtfully.

'Still wanking like a lifer in a Thai prison?' Spencer unexpectedly asked, looking at me with a crooked grin and one eye squinted shut against the glare of the sun.

I repressed the laugh that had welled up inside

and kept my gaze on the sea. 'Might be keeping my hand in from time to time,' I replied, trying to sound enigmatic and non-committal.

'Uh huh.'

I turned to look at him. One eyebrow was raised quizzically and a smug grin stretched across his face.

It was no good. I laughed and took a playful swipe at him. 'Oh, don't you know me so well, Mister Smarty Pants! Besides,' I added, 'and *as* you will recall, it's the best thing for de-stressing me.'

Spencer roared with laughter. 'Oh, perleeeeeese! This is me you're talking to, Amber. You've never needed any excuse *or* encouragement to go at it like the clappers.'

'How *rude!*' I exclaimed in mock indignation, pressing a hand to my chest.

'Ha! Rude maybe,' said Spencer, wagging a finger at me, 'but technically correct.'

Spencer suggested a boat ride in one of my flappers, but we went for a swim instead. We swam out quite far and floated on our backs as the sun beat down on our bodies. It was a new nudey experience, which served to crank up the feeling of freedom by several notches. When we got back to shallow waters, Spencer stood with the sea lapping at his thighs and swept the hair off his face before lazily stretching both arms above his head. I looked at his toned body as droplets of seawater streamed down it in kinking lines. Spencer was still one beautifully crafted man.

I looked beyond him and suddenly realised why he was posing in the water; a number of Brokeback meerkats were also taking the opportunity to admire his body. And Spencer knew it.

'Tart,' I said, giving his backside a small slap.

We spent the rest of the afternoon stretched out in the sun. Spencer spoke some more about his work; assignments he was proud of; things that had gone wrong and clients or models who drove him halfway around the twist.

And he listened intently as I regaled him with my recent family experience.

'When the time's right,' he said, wiggling one of my fingers, 'and only you will know when that is, try again with them. Regret is a dreadful thing and can come and back and bite you on the arse.'

'I'll see,' I replied, returning Spencer's warm smile.

To change the subject, I told Spencer some of nicknames I'd conjured up on knob-spotting duties as naked men literally wandered the beach willy nilly. I tapped them off on my fingers as I spoke.

'What have we got? The Unconscious Turtle – a particular favourite of mine. Then there's Terrapin Todger – enough said. The Slug Pellet – ditto. Hamster Balls – self explanatory.'

'That's an awful lot of animal-themed cocks – if

you don't mind the pun,' Spencer said when he'd finished laughing.

'I know,' I agreed. 'There's some bloke who's got a real odd bendy one, and I can't think beyond Toucan Beak.'

'How about The Coat Hanger?' suggested Spencer. 'Or Piss round Corners?' he added, warming to the topic.

'Ha! Sounds like something from Dances with Wolves,' I laughed. '*Then*, there's a very peculiar-looking fellow whose knob is disproportionately large. I'm thinking it has to be something elephant related, but can't quite think of it.'

'Nuclear warhead,' said Spencer. 'Gotta be.'

'Ha! Or Horror Helmet from Hell.'

'Ooh, just the thought,' laughed Spencer. 'And just listen to us, passing comment on people's privates.'

'Well, I guess that's just the thing,' I replied, 'that your privates aren't private down here.'

Spencer thought about it for a moment. 'I guess so,' he said. 'Ever get any women wandering around butt naked – or is it just the guys?'

'From what I've seen, it's just the guys. No idea why. But for me, being stretched out naked on a towel and walking the length of the bench without any clothes on are two different ball games all together. If you don't mind the pun.'

'I don't mind. Perhaps the women save their

nudey walking for one of those naturist camps. Naked chats around the camp fire and a game of mixed doubles ping pong.'

'That could be a lot of lost balls...'

'Boom! Boom!'

I gave him the run down on some of my neighbours at Brightlea Sands, including the antics of my 69ers.

'You should write a book about that place,' Spencer said.

'Don't tempt me,' I replied. 'Mind you, I can't imagine a Susie sequel featuring her clamped to a Sophia Classique. Number 56, 69 or otherwise.'

'Just love that name,' laughed Spencer.

When the time came to set off, I sat up and took a long look around me. I didn't want to leave the place that had become so important to me. Where so much had happened. As if reading my mind, Spencer put an arm around my shoulder, 'It's not going anywhere, Amber,' he said gently. 'You'll be back. And when I get the chance, so will I.'

'Thank you,' I said, before sighing with gratitude at Spencer's understanding and handsome face.

'Don't think it'll have anything to do with you, mind,' he said with a twinkle in his eye. 'Next time, I'll be hot-footing it down to Brokeback to see what's on offer and leaving you on your own!'

'You!' I said, giving him a firm nudge in his ribs.

'Now, wrestle those god forsaken flappers onto your feet and let's get going – I could murder some fish and chips.'

Spencer got his fish and chips. We returned to the caravan, had showers, sneaked peeps at 70 – who sat seemingly bored on his L-shaped, with his back towards us and flicking channels – then the hyperactive boy in 69, who was running around the lounge, arms outstretched like an aeroplane and visibly howling while his parents sat on their L-shaped, each staring at their phone. The family to my right were out. And my elderly couple were helping one another prepare their evening meal.

'It's like living in a soap opera,' Spencer said, towelling his hair dry.

'Isn't it just?' I replied.

Spencer looked good enough to eat in white shorts and a black and white geometric design t-shirt.

'God, you're going to outshine me. As ever,' I teased.

I went to the bedroom and emerged a few minutes later with a tight, orange cross-backed, strappy vest and short black skirt. And non-flapper sandals.

'Who's outshining who?' asked Spencer, letting out a soft whistle. 'You look beautiful, Amber. Just look at you. Your blonde hair. Those green eyes.

Tanned skin. And orange bringing everything out. You always did know how to dress.'

'Likewise, handsome.'

We walked hand-in-hand along the main drag, larking around and occasionally, wildly swinging our arms like idiots, and when we reached Cod Almighty, found ourselves an empty booth in a corner. The waitress who'd served me before had been replaced by a vague-looking lad with an interesting selection of spots. But the food was just as good, and just as enormous.

'Cod Almighty, indeed,' Spencer said, patting his stomach and blowing out air through puffed cheeks. 'At least that lot will be able to soak up some booze.'

'If you're able to waddle as far as the pub,' I laughed.

As I reached into my bag for my purse, I saw the flashing light on my phone.

'Excuse me,' I said, as I took it out and read the message.

I'm done in. I've had a hiccupping student all day. Now basking in the presence of an inattentive barman inspecting the contents of his nose. There is no hope etc. I trust you're faring better at your end? Is your bodyguard with you? xx

I grinned and tapped out my response.

Poor you! Yes – Spencer is here and we're all geared up

for a dawn raid on the flat tomorrow. We're just off to find a non-nose-picking barman to tend to our every desire xx

I pinged it off with a smile and showed Luke's text to Spencer along with my reply.

'That's a good sign,' he said. 'He's concerned for your safety. I do hope you're not going to show me all of the messages between the two of you,' he added with a smile.

'Ha! *Very* definitely not! Only the tame ones,' I replied as I looked down at my phone again.

Don't talk to me about desires... I've got plenty in mind (aside from getting served). Enjoy your evening. Stay safe tomorrow. And maybe I'll treat myself later, thinking about that wet tight hole of yours. Xxx

'Ah,' I said, 'speak of the Devil.'

'Oh, the smut's started, has it?'

I pinged off, *Enjoy!!! Laters! Xxx* put my phone away and looked at Spencer. 'You know how it is,' I said breezily, flicking a wrist in the air, 'he's just joined the appreciation society for women who've had no children.'

'Oh *yes*, I well remember. No pelvic floor exercises for you.'

'Well, that *is* one of the trade offs for being childless.'

Spencer tilted his head and eyed me seriously. 'Still feel the same way about them?'

I felt stumped by his question. I hadn't thought about it in anger for a long time. 'I don't know, to be honest. It's not something I visit very often. Besides, I'm getting a bit old for that now and still strongly suspect I'm barren. You?'

'Well, you've never actually had that confirmed,' Spencer said, looking at me intently. 'But to answer your question,' he continued, looking past me and out of the window, 'it's the strangest thing, but since coming out – or *maybe,* it's just getting older – I've gradually developed a real desire to become a parent.'

We sat staring at one another in silence. Deep in thought. Possibilities. Opportunities. Lost opportunities. On the edge of an abyss I didn't want to dive into.

'Am I crazy?' Spencer quietly asked.

I shook my head. I didn't know how to respond. 'Who isn't?' I offered with a small shrug. 'But I know you'd make an excellent father,' I added with a warm smile. A sudden confusion of loss and regret and sadness flooded through me. Things that had always seemed so clear cut now seemed muddled in my mind. Spencer must have picked up on it, as he slapped both hands on the table and announced, 'Right then. You can put your scrawny pauper's purse away – your money's no good tonight, you struggling out-of-work writer. I say, let's waddle out of here and find someone behind the bar who doesn't have a finger firmly wedged up their nostril. Sound good?'

'Sounds bang on,' I laughed.

Perfect Spencer. In every way but one.

He pulled rank and insisted on trying The Captain's Table, leaving me in the beer garden to smoke while he fought his way through the colourfully vocal crowd who were in for the twice weekly offering of Karaoke Nite.

'It's not for the faint-hearted in there,' Spencer said when he emerged carrying two garish-looking cocktails, complete with swizzle sticks, straws, foil tassels and a multi-coloured liquid. 'Frank Sinatra and Little Mix are almost coming to blows over who's next.'

'Where will it all end?' I asked with a laugh. 'And *what* are those?' I said, indicating the drinks with my cigarette.

'*These*,' said Spencer, placing the glasses down, 'have come *highly* recommended by the terrifying barmaid and bear the legend that is, 'Sex in the car park'.'

I took a drag on my cigarette and doubtfully eyed the drinks. 'Christ. What's in them?' I asked.

Spencer took his first sip. 'No idea,' he replied brightly, 'but I'm on a one night holiday to the seaside, so we might as well go for it. Cheers.'

'Cheers,' I replied, and we clinked glasses.

Later, as we walked back to the caravan, arm-in-arm and giggling, we relived some of the night's highlights. The conveyor belt of toxic cocktails; the ill-judged decision to go inside and watch the karaoke, and furthermore, take part. We concurred that our rousing rendition of 'Don't Go Breaking My Heart' by Elton John and Kiki Dee would be carved deeply in Brightlea folklore for time immemorial, and our total failure to reach any of the high notes could only be likened to a couple of cats having a red hot poker slowly inserted into their arseholes. Widthways.

We joined in with a rousing group effort of, 'wella-wella-wella-ooh-tell-me-more-tell-me-more' and even had a smoochy dance to a thuggish-looking bloke's surprisingly good rendition of Robbie Williams' 'She's the One'. We twirled one another around, sang along and smiled at each other. And when I went to the loo, I sent Luke a text of soppy *xxxxx*'s, before tagging on, *Miss you xxxx*

Flabby's was a brief pit stop. I reverted back to vodka, drunkenly introduced Spencer to Fucker Frank and Steve Two. We gargled our drinks. I asked where Matty was. Talked about God knows what. And gargled some goodbyes. Steve said he'd O O catch me later. I winked and said, you betcha, then pointed my Bond finger gun at him and click-clicked out the side of my mouth.

We both bellowed out, 'Happy Holidays!' when we wobbled past, and enjoyed it so much, we followed it up with a drunken cheer and punched our fists in the air.

Then we put our noses into the clubhouse, but decided that doing the time warp again might be beyond us. As it was indeed proving to be for the out-of-sync and sweating 'entertainers'.

We reached the caravan and stood needlessly shushing one another's giggles as I delved for my keys. I fished them out along with my phone, noting the absence of a flashing light.

'Look,' I whispered to Spencer, holding it up inches from his face. 'Nothing'.

'Nothing,' he confirmed, trying to focus his eyes on the screen.

I opened up the phone's camera. 'Photo time,' I announced. 'You. Me. And Sophia Classique.'

'Yes! Yes! Yes!' Spencer exclaimed. 'I'd forgotten all about that. Yes! Photos. Lots of them. And *right* now!'

Spencer put his arm around me and we pulled faces and pouted and laughed and pointed as I took a heap of photos of us with my Sophia Classique (no.56) plaque in the background. When we finished, we gave each other a big puckering smacker on the lips.

'Me love you long time,' I said.

'Me love you long time, too,' he replied.

17.

The End

It took me a few moments to work out what was happening. I'd stepped into the caravan with Spencer following right behind; there was a sudden thud of approaching footsteps, a grunt of effort, the loud crack of metal as it connected to bone and I was pushed to the floor as Spencer's body slumped over me. Instinctively, I tried to push myself up with my hands, but was abruptly knocked back by a crunching and head-turning kick to the face.

As I lay prone with the weight of Spencer across my back, looking into his open and lifeless eyes beside me, and his greying hair matted with fragments of skull and fresh blood, I became aware of someone standing over me.

I knew who it was before he spoke.

'You thought you were so clever, you fucking dumb ass bitch,' Clarke said, pushing what felt like an iron bar deep into my rib cage.

I tried to comprehend what was happening or say something, but the side of my face raged like hell, with the taste of blood and feel of broken teeth in my mouth. I looked again at Spencer and let out a sob of utter heartbreak.

'And don't go crying for that bastard,' Clarke growled. 'Seems like your days of fucking him are well and truly over.'

I slowly lifted a hand and gingerly felt my jaw; the pain and disjointedness told me it was either dislocated or broken.

'They already were,' I managed to whisper through short snatched breaths.

The following kick to my ribs was so powerful it knocked the air out of me for a few seconds, while its accompanying hollow cracking noise confirmed what the tearing pain already told me.

'Don't lie, you fucking bitch,' said Clarke, spitting out the words. Unable to speak or move, I tried to steady my breathing as Clarke ranted on, despite the weight of Spencer making the pain in my ribs almost unbearable.

'You must have thought I was some kind of fucking idiot,' he began. I could see the iron bar he was holding swing inches from my face. Spencer's blood and hair were on it along with something I couldn't bear to think about.

'Six weeks, Clarke!' he said, in an exaggerated mimic of my voice. 'And you walked out of *our*

home thinking that would be that! That I'd just sit there and let you walk out on me! I mean, how *really* fucking stupid are you!' He raised the bar and brought it smashing down inches from my face. I felt the warm urine spread beneath me as my bladder emptied.

Clarke was going to kill me. I was sure of it.

'I mean,' he continued, seemingly oblivious to his surroundings, 'how *hard* was it to track you to here? You dumb slut. Even as you were going out the door, I was on your email account, checking out your confirmation booking for this place. Tut, tut, tut, Amber – leaving your passwords around in the back of that note book.'

As Clarke began to pace around, I numbly thought back to his smug expression as he sat, looking at his tablet, while I was taking my bags out of the flat.

'I tried to warn you,' he hissed from somewhere behind me. 'I put that message on the boot of your car. Then there was the doll. But – no. You just wanted to carry on slutting around, like you'd probably been doing all the time we were together.'

'And as for that cunt...' Clarke's voice was closer now. 'Oh, what's this?' He let out a cackle of laughter. 'Pissed yourself Amber? Lying there in a pool of your own piss with your new lover dead on your back?'

I forced my jaw to work, despite feeling the sharp

crumble of broken teeth mix with the blood that ran freely from my mouth. I weakly spat out some of both and tried to speak.

'It's Spencer,' I groaned.

Clarke was silent for a moment, before letting out a cruel laugh.

'What? The faggot ex-husband? Your lies are pathetic, Amber. Are you *seriously* trying to tell me this isn't the bloke you were snogging and giving a hard-on after you'd come off that nudist beach the other day looking *very* pleased with yourselves? Not the same guy you had a smoochy meal with in Shaldon? No, no...' Clarke began to pace again, I could hear him tapping the iron bar against his leg and his voice sounding more crazed, '... *maybe* this is the *other* guy you came off the beach with and kissed a few weeks ago. I don't know – it's just *so* fucking hard to keep up with all of your men. I expect you've been having a bit of a free-for-all down on that beach. Open to all-comers. That's more your mark, isn't it Amber? And as for some of your displays in that Flabby Mermaid pub...'

As he ranted on, tears rolled down my face in the realisation of Spencer's mistaken identity. For which I was to blame. The weight of his body, my injuries and the wretched sorrow I felt made it difficult to breathe. I was only half-listening to Clarke as he droned on, calling me every conceivably vile name and accusing me of crimes both committed and invented.

I somehow remembered Spencer's defence spray, still in his holdall on the L-shaped, where he had dumped it only that very morning. Was there a way? My brain was too foggy from my injuries and the alcohol to think clearly.

Clarke's voice suddenly adopted a chilling calmness as he prodded me in the face with the bar, causing a fresh wave of unspeakable pain to sweep over me.

'Don't cry, Amber,' he said, softly. 'It doesn't matter that you're no longer God's gift to anyone.' He bent down and inspected my face. 'My, my, the once glamorous Amber Stone. Well, not anymore. You *do* know that you've brought all this upon yourself?'

He paused, as though in thought.

'Stay where you are,' he said with a light laugh, before straightening and walking out of sight. I couldn't distinguish the faint noise behind me, and when Clarke returned, he crouched beside me and roughly yanked my forehead back. To my immediate horror, I saw that he'd taken my small make-up mirror from my dropped handbag and now held it in front of me.

I whimpered and trembled in shock as I took in my ruined face. My jaw was already grotesquely swollen and deformed, and 4 or 5 teeth were jaggedly broken. At least one was missing entirely. A gaping split in my top lip caused blood to trickle and join the red dripping rivulets that poured from my mouth. A deep gash on my forehead had already swollen into a bloody golf ball shape, an injury I assumed I sustained after my initial fall.

I pressed my eyes shut.

'Look at yourself!' Clarke hissed as he roughly poked his fingers into my damaged ribs. I winced sharply at the pain and did as he instructed, dazedly taking in the unrecognisable person who looked back at me with such empty eyes. Dead eyes.

'See how ugly you are,' sneered Clarke. 'Both inside and out.'

Wincing and yelping in pain, I turned my head and looked at him properly for the first time. His fringe was swept off his face with the same sweat that covered his face. His eyes glittered with the madness I'd been too stupid to spot a long time ago, and his lips were twisted into a thin smile.

'Seems the kindest thing to do,' he said, as his eyes swept over me with clear distaste, 'would be to put you out of your misery.'

As he pushed on the iron bar to get to his feet, I closed my eyes and let out a sob of fear as I sensed him raising it above his head.

A charge of footsteps into the caravan.

A strange booming voice.

'Put that down and leave her alone! I've called the Police – they're on their way!'

A guttural roar from Clarke as he charged the owner of the voice.

As the commotion raged behind me, I used the last of my strength to work myself free from beneath Spencer's body. I couldn't stifle the cries of pain as I slowly dragged myself forward to the L-shaped, but the ferocity of the struggle meant they went unheard. Pulling myself up onto my elbows, I grunted myself into a sitting position and faced my would-be saviour, who was wrestling hard to free the bar from Clarke's grip. Blood ran down his face from a gash on his cheek, but he was still easily recognisable as the man from 70.

With my ribs and face in burning agony, I reached behind and felt for Spencer's holdall, pulling it towards me and onto the floor. As I frantically fumbled inside, my eyes fleetingly rested on Spencer's prone body. And the back of his head.

With sobs and growing panic, I delved deeper and felt my fingers wrap around the cylindrical canister. As I pulled it out and fumbled with the catch, a howl of pain made me look up; 70 was on his knees by the door, and Clarke stood over him, bar raised and about to strike again.

With a surge of adrenalin, I pushed myself into a standing position and lunged forwards, with the still-locked canister as my only weapon. As I brought it down as hard as I could on the back of Clarke's head, he turned and looked at me with an expression of complete surprise and amusement. And in the instant it took for him to swipe at me with the bar, causing me to reel over and crack my head squarely on the edge of the table where I'd spent so many hours writing, I saw 70 clamber back to his feet and pick up one of my kettlebells in the process.

I lay immobile on my side and felt fresh blood pool beneath me. I was aware of my right foot resting across one of Spencer's ankles. I was aware of Clarke and 70 grunting and yelling as they went at one another. A bar versus a kettlebell.

Vision dipped in and out.

The brawling figures became hazy and distant as though behind a frosted screen. All noises became indistinct and then muted.

I wanted to crawl to Spencer, to be with him, to comfort his body, to say sorry, to say goodbye and to tell him I loved him – but was unable to move any part of myself.

I wanted to cry. But could not.

I began to drift away.

There I was, a little girl again, making pebble art on the beach with my parents. Mum with a big floppy hat, helping me sort out pebbles into colours, shapes and sizes. And there was Dad, shirtless, with two strings of beads around his neck and laughing in the sunshine. He pulls out his camera and tells us to pose for a photo. Mum's arm is around me as we squint towards the lens. Before us, a big outline of a heart made from pebbles, with the word, 'LOVE' inside it.

The image froze and flickered like a faulty television, before becoming a blank screen.

I don't feel much anymore.

I roll my eyes towards the kitchen area by the door. I am aware of the two figures moving as if in slow motion. Something on the floor catches my attention. It is my phone. Spun from my hand when Clarke launched his attack on Spencer and I fell.

It is under the fridge freezer.

Its blue light is flashing.

Flash

Flash

Flash

I cannot move my eyes. I cannot close them. They are locked on the phone forever more.

I cannot move.

I cannot breathe.

I no longer feel pain.

There is another blue light. It pulses in time to my phone, flooding the caravan with snatches of blue glow.

I cannot breathe.

I cannot

Flash

Flash

Flash

Flash

Fl..............................

18.

Where Will it All End?

Susie puts up no resistance when Christian Wellard tentatively takes her hand one evening to assist in the complexities of cocking her leg over a coastal path fence. Furthermore, there is no complaint when he hangs onto it once leg-cocking activities have been successfully completed. Hand-in-hand, they enjoy their stroll, before selecting a favourably shaped rock to sit upon, throw pebbles and have a little natter.

Christian's shyness around Susie is gradually fading – along with his nervous and occasional stammer. As he throws pebbles, Christian makes the reveal of an Irish background; he hails from West Cork, but left with his parents at the age of eight, when his father took up a senior role at a London hospital. But now they have returned, to enjoy early retirement in the beautiful surroundings that the West coast has to offer.

He gives Susie a quick sideways glance, clears his throat and boldly informs her of his desire to take her there one day. To show her the breathtaking sights. To photograph her against stunning backdrops. And to meet his parents.

Susie thinks; he won't be meeting hers – their ashes were still floating somewhere along the Jurua river – but says nothing. Instead, she gives one of Christian's hands a light squeeze and says she'd love for that to happen. She also suggests that he might find some mileage in giving contact lenses a whack.

Christian gives her a small confirming nod and smile, before handing over a broad selection of pebbles for Susie to lob into the sea. Susie takes great satisfaction from lobbing pebbles; she imagines they are landing smack on the bonce of all the people who have wronged her, starting with chinless berk Jeremy, ending with crepe-chested Nurse Simmons, via hockeytart temptress Clara, saggy-titted Maureen *and* her dumbass cakefest, and the one-time object of all her desires, Doctor Rogers. And not forgetting his dear "friend" Adam-forward-slash-Bertie-bloody-Bassett.

Susie lobs her entire pebble supply with escalating vigour, getting breathier with each lob, and as the last one smashes against a large rock and cleanly splits into two, Susie finds it oddly arousing in way she never thought possible – and feels a rabbit-nosed twitch in her downstairs department.

Susie turns to face Christian in flushed-face wonder. He, in turn, lobs her a tight-lipped smile and one of his knowing nods.

Well, well, well. What *do* we have here, Susie?

Back at the surgery, Susie finds she is easily adapting to her self-imposed isolation from colleagues and enjoys the insular world she has carved out with Doctor Wellard. She remains polite and professional with her peers and surgery patients, and even affords them gracious smiles; no one knows about their secret post-work world of erotic pebble-lobbing sessions. Susie bites down on her Bic biro as she recalls the previous evening's deliciousness as they sat side-by-side, hurling with perfect synchronicity as they tightly squeezed each other's free hand.

Ooh! Such pressure!

And so much pent-up frustration...

When their pebbles are spent – when they are spent – Christian removes his glasses for a bit of hot breath and polish action before offering Susie a Murray Mint.

That night, and deeper yet beneath her duvet, Susie shocks herself by rubbing her nipples, likening them to pebbles, and feels her lady parts slowly rumble into red alert. As a hand mooches down for a delve and a fiddle, she wonders what it would feel like for

Doctor Wellard to use her arse as target practice for his lobbing sessions.

Susie sleeps well that night.

The next day at the surgery, Doctor Wellard causes a furore when his new contact lenses are given their first airing. The tea room is awash with oohs and aahs and general clucking of approval. Even Doctor Rogers casts an approving eye over the transformation and offers up a sincere-sounding compliment. But Christian feels awkward receiving such attention and scurries away with his cuppa, slopping most of it onto the floor. With obvious relief, his eyes meet the sanctuary of Susie's, as she lurks in the corridor, waiting for the others to fuck off out of it so she can have Doctor Wellard to herself.

'Usual place for tonight?' he whispers in enquiry.

Susie gives his new appearance the once over. 'You betcha,' she replies, before click-clicking out the side of her mouth and throwing him a wink.

That evening, as they lay exhausted on the beach, their pile of pebbles depleted and small fingernail indents still visible on their hands, Susie sucks on her Murray Mint and listens as Christian talks about their planned trip to Ireland. He wants to take lots of photos of the beautiful land and seascapes. Feeling heady and reckless, Susie twirls a lock of non-bolloxed hair and asks, 'And what kind of photos would you like to take of me?'

Christian doesn't get her meaning and twitters on about how they could take it in turns to take pictures of one another, take selfies, or maybe recruit the assistance of a passing tourist to take a photo of the both of them.

But Susie is still in an immediate post-lobbing flush and having none of it. She briskly releases her love muffins from the confines of her bra and post-work strappy vest, gives them a shake and a squeeze, and spells it out for Doctor Wellard.

'Not *those* kind of photos,' she says, hardly believing her words or actions. But the truth of the matter is, our Susie is wet around the gills and in dire need of some Wellard action.

Christian is visibly shocked. He glances around, in fear of anyone else witnessing Susie's sluttish behaviour. But their favoured stretch of beach is favoured neither by locals nor tourists. Nor is it easily accessible. Satisfied no-one else is within range, Christian looks down at Susie's exposed bosom and without warning, takes each nipple between his fingers and gives them a rough twist.

Susie lets out a squeal of pleasure. She has never known such a delicious sensation. And wants more. And when she glances down at Christian's unfashionable knee length shorts that depict sailing boats, she can easily see he's at full mast.

'Get up,' Christian commands in an unfamiliar

and authoritative voice that only serves to give her a fanny tremble. 'Put them away. Let's go.'

Susie's immediate feelings of disappointment and fear that she's made a fool of herself are soon replaced by excitement. Reluctantly tucking herself back in, they get to their feet, and in doing so, Christian gives each of Susie's arse cheeks a sharp slap. He grabs one of her hands and assertively marches ahead, pulling her in his wake.

'Come on,' he says gruffly.

Susie doesn't recognise this new Doctor Wellard. As he yanks her along the beach, she checks out the firm-jawed look of steely determination on his face and decides she likes this version very much. Not to mention the throbbing sting emanating across her arse cheek, which surely, still bore the imprint of Christian's hand.

Who knew?

They reach a mini cove and Christian releases Susie's hand as he flings her without mercy to the sand. And before she knows what's what, who's who or if it's wash day for her duvet cover, he orders her to take off her shorts and panties and stand spread-eagled up against the rocks.

Our Susie is more than ready to oblige. She has the pent-up frustration of someone who's been slave to a prim blouse selection for *far* too long, and endured a lifetime of unsatisfactory pump-pump-squirt sex. She does as ordered, and relishes the risqué possibility of being caught.

Doctor Wellard stands pressed up behind Susie with his wellardness more than evident. His teeth nip her neck as he releases her pert pebbles by roughly pulling down her bra and top.

Then he goes to town on her.

'Oh, Doctor,' Susie murmurs through cascades of pleasure.

Afterwards, when Christian leads Susie into the sea for a naked swim, she doesn't care if they are caught. In fact, she doesn't care much about the rest of the world – apart from her kooky relationship with Christian. And says so.

He tells her he feels the same.

'Let's go and live in Ireland,' he says, putting his hands around her waist.

Susie has nothing left in Trewithiel. Only sour memories of wasting her time pursuing a man who is gay. And all that that entailed. The lease on the cottage was almost up. And she is ready. Ready for a new adventure. A different kind of adventure. With lashings of rough sex. And with someone who might make her happy.

She looks into Christian's new eyes. 'Yes, please Doctor Wellard.' They kiss and laugh and twirl about in the sea like a couple of love-struck muppets. Susie feels free. Free of all the heavy clouds that had cloaked her shoulders.

Dressed and about to leave, our Susie can't resist a last hurl of a pebble. She picks one up and throws it with all her might into the sea with a squeal of pleasure.

'That's a dirty habit you've got there,' Doctor Wellard says with a twinkly smile and outreached hand to escort her off the beach.

Deciding to celebrate and cement their newfound feelings of 'fuckit', they decide upon dinner at The Old Wreck. Jaws drop and heads turn when both colleagues and locals see them walk in hand-in-hand. Why, there's Susie's old sparring partner, Nurse Simmons, with her mouth wide open, as though catching flies. And what's this? Doctor Rogers tucked away on a corner table with Bertie Bassett, looking like he's just seen one of his dead patients bowl in.

Christian and Susie throw everyone polite nods and small smiles before settling at a table and deciding to take advantage of the Steak Night deal on offer. Christian orders with the calm authority normally reserved for the confines of his consultation room.

'He must have needed a large dose of filth,' Susie thinks with a silent titter as she eyes her Doctor, whose newfound confidence blossoms by the second. 'Well, there'll be plenty more where that came from.'

Doctor Wellard has obviously been harbouring the same thought.

'You're good for me, Susie,' he says, clinking glasses with her.

'Likewise,' she replies, savouring the sweet soreness throbbing from her pleasure holes like a badge of honour.

'And I'm thinking you might be a dreadful woman...' Christian adds, letting the words hang as he eyes Susie over his wine glass.

'I'm praying I am,' she replies, holding his gaze.

Oblivious to the gawpers, the earwiggers and whisperers, they enjoy their food and wine and start to plan their new life in Ireland. It all sounds so gloriously simple. Susie looks longingly at her Doctor and wonders.

But when Christian leans over the table to kiss her and silences the pub, our Susie wonders no more.

That night, as Susie buries herself under her duvet, she re-runs some of the day's highlights through her mind, with a dreamy smile on her face and a hand on her pummelled lady garden.

Double-dipped *and* a steak supper?

Where *will* it all end?

Our Susie isn't sure, but as she gets to work with that hand, while the other roughly massages those greedy love muffins, she knows she's very much looking forward to finding out.

'Oh, Doctor Wellard...', she sighs, in small breathy snatches, 'are *you* my happy ever after?'

Our Susie thinks he is.

Well done, Susie! Bravo!

We knew you'd get there in the end!

The End.

Ta-dah!!

HAPPEEE HOLIDAYS!!

If you've enjoyed reading NUDEY BEACH, then please nip over to Amazon and/or Goodreads and leave a review.

Thank you!

Angie x

Printed in Great Britain
by Amazon

62170859R00210